The Lazarus Vaccine

D. L. Gould

ISBN: 9781723884719

D. L. Gould
Follow me on Twitter: @DLGould

DEDICATION

First novel for my first born. We love you, Kyle.

INTRODUCTION

Why I Wrote The Lazarus Vaccine

I was angry...

On a cold January night in the early 2000s, I watched my father die. I remember crying so hard it burned. I wasn't heaving or snorting or sobbing uncontrollably, but the tears felt like acid spilling down the cracked skin of my face, skin that had been dried and damaged by a fierce winter and dehydration (I had drank nothing but black coffee for a week). He had been in a coma for seven days. Seven days of driving back and forth between my life in Chicago and a hospital in Indianapolis. Seven days of eating shitty hospital food and sleeping in shitty motels. Seven days of confusion, pain, and anger. Finally over.

Flanked by my older brothers on either side, none of us were able to speak as our dad's chest rose and fell for the last time. The nurses had turned off all the monitors and machines, so the room was quiet. None of those stupid beeps and hums that are so familiar in hospital rooms. *Lonesome Dove* played from my oldest brother's laptop on low volume, but no one was paying attention to the movie except maybe dad. Even though his eyes were closed and the doctors told us he had almost no brain function, I like to think he was still absorbing it in some way.

The plug had been pulled and Bruce C. Gould left our world in the company of his three sons and favorite movie.

There were so many things I wanted to say to the dead man who lay before me turning cold (for those of you who are uninitiated, body heat fades very quickly after death). But a life of hard drinking had finally caught up with him, and we would never speak again.

I seemed to go through all the stages of grief at once. There was the immediate sadness, then the guilt, mix in some denial (*this had to be a dream*), and definitely anger. Oh God, there was anger (acceptance wouldn't come until several years later).

I wanted to break something. Put my fist through the window. Smash my brother's laptop against the wall. Basically, go ape-shit and tear the whole goddamn hospital to the ground with my bare hands, and I might have tried this if it wasn't for the little, white pill a doctor had given me earlier in the night.

I kept hearing a phantom sound in my head, a metallic *snap-crack-fizz*—the noise a cold can of Miller Lite makes when it's popped open. As my brothers and I sat there frozen in our own private pain, I kept hearing decades of Miller Lites opened. One after another, after another... *snap-crack-fizz*.

To this day, I can't stand the sound of an aluminum can being opened. Even a can of Coke sends me back to that hospital room with my father's cold, dead body.

My dad was an alcoholic, but his killer wasn't the beer or the vodka or the cigarettes.

It was addiction.

It's an awful thing, to feel anger in your bones. A lot of people experience this depth of rage, and all of mine was pointed at the rotten disease (yes, addiction is a disease) that had just killed my father. Before me, on the hospital bed, turning colder with every passing second, was a man I had not spoken to in a long time. A man who spent the later years of his life battling a terrible addiction, alienating his family and turning his adult sons into crying children who wanted nothing more than to bring back the man they once knew when they were little boys, before the booze.

My dad taught me how to shoot a gun, gut a deer, and throw a football (none of which I'm particularly good at, but the effort was there). And the man was always reading a book, too (usually Louis L'Amour or Larry McMurtry). This is undoubtedly one of the reasons I picked up adult fiction at a young age and became a lifelong reader (something I am good at).

Bruce Gould made a lot of mistakes in his life that pushed his family away, and there was certainly enough blame to go around for everyone. But in the end, it was no one's fault. I tried. My brothers tried. His brothers and parents tried.

He tried.

But addiction is a powerful agent, and it beats a lot of people. This acceptance would eventually arrive; however, I would never forget the rage. Rage tends to linger a lot longer than other emotions, chiseling a special place in your memories that can only be sandblasted away.

And this is where *The Lazarus Vaccine* came from.

Lazarus is a story about anger and rage. After reading this introduction, it should come as no surprise that it features a character with an alcoholic father. But all of our characters, the heroes and villains, have a lot more to be angry about. Men and women and teenage kids who feel betrayed by everyone and everything around them; they are consumed by madness and motivated by revenge. Their rage drags them forward and downward like an anchor into a black depth that is as icy and cold as death in January.

INTRODUCTION

Lazarus is certainly about a lot more than one kid's struggle with his father's alcoholism; this is actually a small, although very significant, element of his character development and the broader story arc. There is plenty of rage though, enough for everyone to pass the bottle, have a swig, and lose control.

The Lazarus Vaccine helped me deal with some of the anger that had been hanging around since my father's death. I don't know if it will ever fully go away (*snap-crack-fizz*—I still hear it in my sleep sometimes).

I sincerely hope you enjoy my book. Writing it, and this introduction, forced me to revisit some interesting memories regarding my father and his passing. There were emotions I'd been ignoring for a long time, but this experience has taught me ignoring them doesn't help. I've also learned that alcoholism and addiction cannot be ignored. They are diseases, and in real life, there is no such thing as the Lazarus Vaccine, a miracle cure for all sickness and disease. In real life, we must rely on the people who love us to help lift us out of our darkest pits.

If you are dealing with addiction yourself or know someone who is, there is help.

National Council on Alcoholism and Drug Abuse
NCADA-stl.org
(314) 962-3456

Alcoholics Anonymous
www.aa.org
(212) 870-3400

Don't wait. Don't ignore it.

D. L. Gould
29 September 2018

"The LORD has established His throne in the heavens, and His kingdom rules over all."

   -Psalm 103:19

"Reason and logic should rule over all."

   -Adam Gregory Evans

CHAPTER 1

The man that would become known as Joseph Dayspring appeared out of thin air on July 17, 2018.

There were violent electrical storms the night before. Javier Estes watched the dark clouds roll over the mountains from the quiet peace of his front porch. He sipped cool tequila from a chipped glass, listening to the ice clink and chime, relieved that his crops would finally get some rain. Lightning exploded in the black sky, brilliant, strobe flashes followed by thunder so intense it rattled his old bones. In 73 years of life, he had never witnessed a storm like this. It looked angry, almost vengeful, and Javier remembered thinking only God could make something so beautiful yet so destructive at the same time.

He drank and waited for the rain to come. His land could use the water, but the storm seemed tethered to the mountains like a junkyard dog on a leash, growling and snarling, lashing its deadly teeth.

There was a final crash of thunder and lightning, a blast so vicious it sounded like the universe itself cracked open, and for a fraction of a second, night became noon. After this, the storm lifted and disappeared like the smoky tendrils of a blown-out birthday candle.

In the morning, just as the sun was cresting the horizon, Javier walked his north pasture to survey for damage. The sky was empty, a warm void of blue peace, not a trace of last night's celestial violence. He followed the fence line, and about a kilometer from his home, near the base of the mountains where the storm had hung fixed and unmoving in the sky, the air began to smell like ozone, thick with a sulfuric sting. He came upon an area where the fence suddenly ended in a twisted line of metal, smoldering red-orange at the ends. In front of him was a jagged, concave crater of rock and sand about thirty meters across that resembled a meteorite impact. The area was burned black and covered in what appeared to be bits of charred, shattered glass.

At the center of it was a naked man in the fetal position, unconscious and shaking in the cool, morning air.

The strange man was brought back to Javier's home. Maria, Javier's daughter, went into the village for help. There were no doctors, but some of the nuns at St. Joseph's were certified Red Cross nurses. She brought back Sister Christina, an elderly, white haired Dominican Nun, who helped care for the man.

The stranger slept for two days, at times thrashing through vicious nightmares, then settling down and whispering indistinct, cryptic phrases before becoming quiet again.

He was white, probably American, his body strong and rigid, packed with lean muscle. There was a tattoo on the inside of his left forearm, a short string of letters and numbers above a chaotic grid of small, black and white boxes similar to a QR code:

SLX – 1 6

He was on the near edge of being middle-aged, perhaps early forties, with sandy-gray hair and despite his coma state, appeared to be in okay health. His body, however, Sister Christina described as *destrozado*—damaged. It was covered in scars. There were long, pink slashes crisscrossing his back and chest like giant, irregular hashtags, and several pale circles dotted his left shoulder and arm, which Javier recognized as old bullet wounds. From waist to neck, the strange man was a torn and stitched-together road map of scar tissue. He had a handsome face, though, square features and tight, tan skin, unblemished except for a jagged and ugly scar that ran vertically over his left eye from scalp to jaw.

Destrozado.

Damaged.

Sister Christina sat by his bed and prayed for the man's recovery and for his soul.

CHAPTER 2

2,500 miles away from where Sister Christina prayed at the bedside of the strange man with the scars, something dangerous was about to happen.

In the back of Jason Orchard's mind, he knew it was a stupid decision. There was a deep and buried voice desperately pleading and begging for him to stop. What he was about to do was stupid and reckless. Unfortunately, for the seventeen-year-old, this part of his consciousness—the part that contributed to wise decision making—was a tad underdeveloped (he was a teenager, after all), so the voice only registered as a faint whisper, like someone screaming underwater.

Easy to ignore.

"Okay, let's do it," Jason said giving himself a few exaggerated slaps on the face for encouragement. He stared at the basket of hot wings in front him. Twelve greasy, orange drums smothered in a fire-colored sauce called PFI Sauce—Pure Fucking Insanity.

Shake's Lake Side Wing Shack (just *the Shack* to locals) was a popular lakeside bar in Crooked Lake, Michigan that served fatty pub food and was owned by a man named Michael Shake. The walls were clapboard wood and stained by decades of ancient cigarette smoke. Split peanut shells littered the floor and crackled beneath every step like little, dry bones. Customers joked that the tables and bar top were never actually cleaned, instead Mike Shake would just add a fresh coat of polyurethane each night; every flat surface had little prizes preserved forever in the amber-clear substance—coins, toothpicks, matchsticks, peanut shells. The atmosphere was always bright and lively, but the lighting was poor, and even though smoking indoors had been banned in Michigan for nearly ten years, there seemed to be a subtle haze floating near the ceiling like a ghost that refused to be exorcised.

Everyone loved the Shack. It was home of the hottest buffalo wings in America, and people knew this was official because there was a dirty yellow sign hanging behind the bar that said so.

Mike Shake, owner, proprietor, and cook, also made killer milkshakes appropriately called *Mike Shake's Milkshakes*. He used only homemade ice cream with ingredients locally sourced from a dairy farm outside of Ann Arbor. These two staples—wings and shakes—even got the Shack featured on an episode of Food Channel's *Diners, Drive-ins, and Dives*, and of the three, it was definitely the last. Summer tourists loved it, but the local clientele loved it even more; they came for the wings, stayed for the shakes, and only got drunk and rowdy when the Detroit Redwings lost.

Jason and his friends weren't old enough to sit at the bar, but Mike Shake was ignoring that little state statute while the young man completed the PFI Challenge: consume twelve PFI wings in two minutes without drinking, and win a free dinner and milkshake for you and a guest, plus get your photograph on the Shack Wall of Fame. Big Mike (people called him Big Mike because he was a big man with a big beard, big gut, and big personality) had given everyone a free Coke because that was the kind of man he was (big hearted, too).

"You ready?" Mike Shake asked as he held up a stopwatch. He wore his standard white apron with faded orange stains on the breast, a damp brown rag slung over his shoulder.

Jason nodded, then took a breath and looked at his friends. "This is for you, Emma," he said with fake severity toward a cute, blond girl.

"You just make it home safe." Emma Landon spoke like a hometown sweetheart seeing her beau off to war, eyes fluttering and full of exaggerated sentiment.

"I love you guys," Jason said to his friends. He looked directly at a girl named Haley Hill. "I need you to take care of Adam for me if I don't make it back." He pinched the cheek of a short, shaggy haired kid next to him. "He's my best friend."

"You're an idiot," Haley replied through a wide grin. "But I will." She lifted her hand and stroked Adam's hair.

Adam Evans smiled and nuzzled against her like a happy puppy and in his best Scooby Doo impression said, "Rye-ruv-voo."

Jason took one final breath before diving hands and face first into the basket.

Witnesses said he looked like the Tasmanian Devil; food and spittle flew from a tornado of savage consumption. He tore into the wings like a starving animal, a hungry pig fighting over its share of slop. But by wing number eight, his aggressive chewing slowed. He continued making his way around the drum like a corncob, but something was wrong. He gripped the bar top and exhaled (more like vented), a steady stream of forced wind whistling out of his burning lips.

"He's gonna blow," Adam, whispered through the unquiet air.

Everyone held their breath.

And right when they thought all was lost—Jason rallied. Perhaps propelled by a second wind or inspired by divine intervention, he tore apart the remaining wings like some cryptic beast feasting on a fresh kill, letting the bones fall dramatically back into the basket one after another with a greasy splat.

"Time!" Big Mike hollered and slapped the top of the bar with an open palm.

In the basket was a pile of twelve chicken wing bones, stripped completely clean except for a few traces of gummy tendons and twisted cartilage.

Hands went up; people shouted and screamed adulations. And Mike—God bless Big Mike—slammed a vanilla shake down in front of Jason, who promptly threw back his head and poured it into his open mouth, letting it overflow onto his face, throat, and chest. Sweet, merciful relief.

Jason grabbed Emma and planted a, sloppy, milkshake-and-wing sauce kiss on her cheek. He and Adam embraced in a classic bro-hug, the kind that begins as a sideways high-five and ends with both dudes pulling each other in for two hearty slaps on the back.

Mike Shake, like a proud father on graduation day, held up his phone and said, "Smile."

Through the pure-fucking-insane burning that covered his lips and cheeks (the sauce was aptly named), Jason pushed out a desperate grin and held forward a thumbs-up.

Everything between his nose and throat hurt like hell, but his smiling face, covered in PFI sauce and vanilla milkshake, would forever be immortalized on the Shack Wall of Fame.

And he stole a kiss from Emma.

Totally worth it.

CHAPTER 3

Sister Christina Alvarez entered the nunnery because she believed she could speak to God. Not in a literal, conversational way, but in the form of an intuition and sensitivity to the pain and plight of others so heightened and precise she attributed it to divine intervention. It wasn't so much that God was speaking to her, but rather *through* her. Sister Christina possessed the ability to read the sadness within a man's soul, and where some might have said it was nothing more than a tender and loving ability to empathize, she saw it as a special gift granted by her savior and His virgin mother.

The strange man who laid before her on the bed was still. His nightmares came in short waves. They began as whispers and almost sounded like prayer. His body would twitch as if receiving soft jolts of electricity. But soon, these tiny spasms would become larger convulsions, the whispers replaced by violent, terrified screams, his entire body thrashing beneath a thin cotton sheet that snapped like a kite soaring in the wind. It was as if the poor man was possessed by a vengeful demon, something Javier even suggested, but the old nun, despite her Catholic pedigree, would hear nothing of such riotous superstition. The man was sick and needed medical help, not an exorcism. Eventually, the nightmare-wave would pass, and the man would be quietly sleeping again, his scarred, muscular chest rising and falling beneath dampened sheets.

With a small, pewter medallion held tightly in her hands, Sister Christina would pray, her fingers caressing the dull contours of the cheap metal. It was an alpha and omega medallion, bearing just the two Greek letters, representing Jesus Christ as the beginning and the end of everything—His eternal nature. It had been a gift from her mother, passed down amongst the women in her family for generations, but with her having entered the convent, there would be no more daughters or anyone to pass it onto. The medallion ended its journey with her.

With the precious heirloom flattened between her palms, she could feel the man's pain like the heat of a hot oven. There was a sadness that haunted the air around him, hovering over his sleeping body like the thunderheads from the night of his arrival. She prayed for God to release him from whatever internal agony gripped his body and tortured his soul.

God finally listened.

On the third day, he woke up.

Sister Christina had been praying, eyes closed, hands clasped around the medallion. She sat in a wooden rocking chair near the foot of the bed. It was early in the morning; yellow shafts of dusty sunlight poked through the open blinds. The small bedroom was pleasantly cool with open windows on either side, and without many furnishings, except for the bed, the rocker, and a chest of drawers, it gave off an air of spacious comfort.

When Christina finished praying, she opened her eyes and the man was sitting up in bed looking at her. It gave her a small startle, but oddly, she felt no apprehension, even as he poured a confused and fearful look upon her like a wounded animal that might lash out suddenly and violently. His eyes were gray, at least his good eye was, the one with the scar was pupil-less and creamy yellow but seemed to stare at her just the same.

"Where am I?" the man asked with a simple and calm voice.

Christina had studied English at her convent and knew the language fluently. "You are in El Rito, Mexico," she said, then added without knowing why, "you are safe."

The man craned his head around the room. For several moments, there was only the sound of his deep, nasal breathing as his gaze circled back and landed on the nun again.

"How did I get here?"

Christina leaned forward. "We were hoping you could tell that to us," she said delicately.

The man widened his eyes and blinked, stretching his face and forehead. "I don't know," he said.

"What is your name, señor?" she asked.

The man thought for a moment, turning his head toward the window as if the answer was somewhere outside. "I…"

Christina could almost see the gears in his brain turning, rusty, dry cogs that creaked and groaned as they came to life. He bit his bottom lip, gray good-eye and yellow bad-eye shooting left and right, searching the space around him for an answer that was lost in his own, empty mind.

"I don't know," he finally said with an exasperated breath. "I don't' know my name." There was a pang of fear in his voice.

Sister Christina gave the man a warm smile. "It is okay, señor. I am here to help you." She reached out and touched the back of his hand. He did not flinch or pull away, and immediately she could feel God's presence in the room.

The strange man relaxed, his anxiety dissolving. He took a few more nasally breaths and pinched the space between his eyes like a person fighting off a bad headache.

"You must be hungry," Christina said.

"Yes." The man nodded. He looked toward the nun, but his eyes went past her. Javier Estes and his daughter were standing at the threshold, just outside the room.

"¿Quieres algo de comer?" Javier said.

The man did not understand.

"Come," Christina said standing. "Come have some food. There are clothes in the dresser that should fit you."

They sat together at a small, wooden table in the kitchen. Maria made rice and beans and cut up avocado from Javier's crops. She was in her early twenties, but her deep-set eyes showed several more years of experience than time gave away; they were dull and dark, like a pair of antique buffalo nickels, and like the man who mysteriously appeared during a violent electric storm, she had her own storm clouds floating above her.

The stranger ate like a starving man after waking, shoveling forkfuls into his mouth as fast as he could, nearly choking at times, stopping only to catch his breath or take long, loud swallows from a glass of iced tea.

Javier and Maria did not speak English, so Sister Christina translated their conversation. The stranger had no personal memory whatsoever but possessed knowledge of common things like math, science, and general history. They spoke to him for hours, Maria refilling his plate several times. He seemed intelligent, even formally educated, and was equally confused and frightened about his sudden appearance and loss of memory. He had stared at his own reflection in the bathroom mirror, fingers tracing over the scar on his face with a ghostly familiarity, like a man looking at an old photograph of a dead grandfather he met only once. And the strange tattoo meant nothing to him, yet he turned away from it as if repulsed.

He was grateful for their care and hospitality but asked about being taken to a hospital. This was not a good idea, Javier explained. The cartel men patrolled the only road out of the village; they might mistake the gringo for an American agent, DEA or Border Patrol. The Texas border was ninety miles to the north. The cartel men would take him and certainly kill him.

"Cartel men?" the stranger asked with a mouthful of food, digging his way through a third plate.

"Bad men," Maria said in broken English.

Christina explained, "Drug dealers who smuggle into America." The old nun spoke with iron in her voice. "These men act like our protectors. They say they guard us from trouble; they pretend to be like police, and they charge us money for their protection. But all they really want is our loyalty, so they can continue their drug operation."

"Do they hurt you?"

Christina glanced at Javier and Maria. She said something in Spanish. Javier looked toward a framed photograph of a young man in a university blazer hanging on the wall. His eyes welled with angry tears as the man with the scars realized whose clothes he was wearing.

"They scare us," Christina finally said.

The stranger understood. "Your son?" he asked Javier. Christina translated.

Javier nodded.

"They killed him?"

"Sí," Maria said and began to cry. "Mi hermano."

The stranger swallowed and pushed his plate away. He gently placed his hand on top of Maria's. "I'm sorry," he said, and even though she did not understand his words, she knew his meaning.

CHAPTER 4

Jason Orchard was making another bad decision.

He and Adam were about to hack into Crooked Lake High School's grading record system. They were in Adam's bedroom. It was a messy teenager's room filled with dirty clothes, crumbled snack wrappers, and used dishes. And don't expect the bed to be made. Ever.

The main difference between the average teenager's room and Adam's was the fully functioning chemical and robotics laboratory.

Adam's bedroom was actually the family home's entire basement, spanning the full length of the two story ranch. In one corner, Adam had constructed his laboratory. There were beakers filled with colorful liquids softly bubbling over orange flames, test tubes and glass slides lay scattered around a large, electron microscope connected to a flat screen TV, and two live mice named Kirk and Spock nibbled around in a small cage. Circuit boards of various sizes took up the rest of the black counter space, all in different stages of construction—or deconstruction. And above everything, hung a silly poster of Albert Einstein— the brilliant scientist sticking his tongue out at the world and laughing at some secret joke only a mad genius could understand.

The room—the basement—was Adam's man cave, or geek cave. It was a messy, cluttered affair that drove Adam's mom bonkers, but she stopped trying to get him to clean his room (or even make his bed) when *Scientific American* called him the next Elon Musk (though, Adam would have preferred Tony Stark). This was after he won the White House Science Fair for building a go-kart that ran on water. A device he called *The Adamizer*, an electrolysis cell he designed and constructed himself, separated the hydrogen from the oxygen, then redirected the H1 into the combustion chamber of a 20HP four-cylinder engine. Top speed: 30mph. During the demonstration he had poured water into the tank of the Adamizer with a Brita pitcher, then offered the President's Chief of Staff a cold drink. He was twelve-years-old at the time.

Adam Evans was a special kid.

He could have graduated high school at fourteen with guaranteed scholarship offers to any university in the world. His mother, however, Dr. Maryanne Evans, a revered child psychologist, had concerns over his social and emotional development. She had made an arrangement with the Crooked Lake Public School District that Adam could still attend a few classes at the high school through his senior year merely for the *growing-up* experience. Half his day would be spent roaming the halls of Crooked Lake High School (go Catfish!), learning how to navigate the social complexities of adolescent human interaction, and the other half at the University of Michigan in Ann Arbor, studying advanced molecular biology, robotics, and computer science. In the fall, it was off to a doctoral program in theoretical physics at Caltech.

The two friends were sitting at Adam's desk, a colossal L-shaped monstrosity bursting out of a dark corner. It was a disorderly mess of papers, folders, and reports. The young prodigy hammered away at a wireless keyboard with three flat screen monitors in front of him, the two on the ends carefully angled as to create a half-hexagon configuration. It was Adam's mission control center. On the right wall was a shelf filled with tipped over text books and scientific journals, and to the left was a bulletin board with a random collage of posed and candid photographs— Adam's family and friends, the people he loved being happy and loving him right back.

Jason didn't understand much about computers except that they allowed unrestricted access to the world's greatest amateur and professional pornography. He quietly rolled a joint as Adam committed computer fraud. Jason had little interest in technology. He had no social media accounts and his cell phone flipped open—something Adam described as "*the most ridiculous fucking thing in the world.*" But Jason just didn't care about the newest apps or trends in tech and actually boasted that he lived as unplugged as possible, preferring to spend his time reading a good book, kayaking, or working on his truck (the ol' girl was close to running). But unfortunately, his keen interest in water sports, auto mechanics, and quality literature didn't help his GPA, which usually floated between a 1.5 and 2.0—all due to sheer indifference, not ability. Adam's extraordinary intelligence and Jason's laissez-faire approach to school had created a joyful balance for the two boys to build a strong and dynamic friendship.

"Right now," Adam was saying as he pounded away at the keyboard with all the drama of a concert pianist, "I'm creating a false IP address, so even if they detect the hack, they'll only be able to trace it to a nice little coffee house in Seattle."

The two had been best friends since the ninth grade when Adam and his mother moved to Crooked Lake. There were a lot of knuckle-dragging mouth breathers at school who didn't like the new kid who was *a lot* smarter than they were. This resentment led to some classic bullying, and it would have been worse if it wasn't for

Jason.

Jason Orchard knew what it was like to be bullied. His mom ran off when he was in the first grade, so he was raised by a single father—a joyless, depressed man and heavy drinker who was always between jobs. Jason grew up eating free school lunch and wearing clothes donated from community collections—faded shirts that were originally purchased by happier people on vacations: *Hard Rock Café, Las Vegas; Planet Hollywood, California; Magic Kingdom, Disney World.* But this entire wardrobe had been a lie because he had never left the state of Michigan. He was teased in elementary school for being the poor kid whose clothes didn't fit and subsequently developed a pretty solid chip on his shoulder. In high school, this chip evolved into a deep love for smacking the smug off *any* bully's face. He had naturally gravitated toward Adam and started whuppin' bully ass. Thus, a friendship was born.

Jason and Adam were like brothers. And like most brothers, they did a lot of stupid shit together.

"Okay, I'm in," Adam said cracking his knuckles.

Jason had just finished rolling the joint and set it aside. "Just change everything to a B average," he paused, "I don't want to be greedy."

Adam navigated through the school's databases, eyes quickly pouring over documents and pages until he found what he wanted. "Our school has pathetic cyber security," he said as he clicked through a few more pages. "You want me to cancel school on Monday? I can put it in the district calendar. We'll call it *National Get Stoned Day.*"

Jason laughed. "Nahh, they'll definitely trace that back to me. Now get this done so we can celebrate my slightly-above-average grades." He held up the joint as if offering Adam a pencil in class.

"B average, right?"

"Right."

Adam proceeded through various webpages, but then a door opened, and both friends looked at each other with a slight note of alarm as they heard the familiar creak of feet descending basement stairs.

"Hey boys," Adam's mom called out.

Jason shoved the joint into his pocket, and Adam pushed a small red button mounted underneath his desk like a bank alarm. All three computer monitors suddenly changed—the left went into screensaver mode and showed a litter of puppies crawling around in a basket of laundry, on the right was a CNN news article, and in the middle was an essay about nanotechnology Adam was writing for *Popular Science*.

"Panic button," Adam whispered

"Nice," Jason whispered back.

"What are you two hooligans up to?" Dr. Evans asked as she came into view at the bottom of the steps.

"Downloading porn," Jason said.

Maryanne Evans laughed and dismissed his vulgar humor with a hand wave. Adam's mom knew how to interact with young people. Dr. Evans was the chief psychologist at her own mental health clinic; she understood the inner psychology of a young person's mind. Her theories on human growth and development were widely respected, and her name was behind several therapies considered some of the best treatments in the world for teenage depression. She was also a guest professor at the University of Michigan, where her male graduate students called her *"Hot Doc Evans"* behind her back. She practiced yoga daily and played tennis in a women's competitive league every weekend at the Ann Arbor Country Club—and proudly made several enemies from her powerful serve and superior play (plus those long tan legs, frequently admired by old husbands as they smoked cigars and drank scotch on the veranda overlooking the courts). Hot Doc Evans was the total package. And she was perpetually single.

Adam never had a father. Well, in the biological sense, he did; however, this man only existed as a file at a hospital sperm bank in Detroit. Maryanne Evans was a career minded woman who had always chosen adding to her curriculum vitae over romantic relationships. But eighteen years ago, she developed an incredible and ineffable urge to bear and raise children. She wanted—*needed*—kids. At least one, a child to point all her stored up love at, love that had been shoved aside to make way for her education and career. Having a child via sperm donor was the most logical solution for the lifestyle Dr. Evans had created for herself.

With Adam only having a mom and Jason a dad, there had often been jokes about their parents dating, eventually marrying, and the best friends becoming *real* brothers. The joke, however, was that Maryanne Evans was *waaaaaaaaay* out of Marcus Orchard's league, and both boys knew it.

"Why do I let you hang out with my son?"

"Because you love me and know that deep down, beyond my rough exterior, I am a child screaming for help, forced to repress his own tumultuous history, desperately in need of maternal guidance so that someday I may self-actualize and achieve my full potential." Jason was only half-joking.

"No, you're more like a court jester that amuses me. But thanks for reading my book. Did you put all that together from the chapter on Behavioral Repression?"

Jason winked at her.

"What do you want, mom?" Adam whined.

"Thought you boys could use a snack." Dr. Evans put down a tray on Adam's desk. Whereas some moms make grilled cheese or microwave pizza rolls, Adam's mom had prepared smoked salmon and cucumber tea sandwiches next to prosciutto-wrapped, fresh mozzarella and tomato bites with a balsamic vinegar sauce.

Hot Doc Evans really was the total package.

"Wow. Thanks Dr. E," Jason said.

"Yeah, thanks mom. Now get out."

Jason smacked his friend upside the head.

"Thank you court jester," Dr. Evans said.

"My lady," Jason replied with a small curtsy.

Maryanne Evans kissed both her son and Jason on the cheek, then ruffled their hair like puppies and walked away.

Jason watched her leave, paying extra attention to her sculpted butt and the way her hips swayed as she walked. Dr. E was definitely the hottest mom on the lake. She paused halfway up the creaky stairs and took a deep breath. For a split second, it seemed as though she were about to lose her balance and fall backward. One of her hands held the rail with a loose grip, the other rested softly on her temple as if willing away an oncoming migraine. She took another breath, hesitated, then continued up the steps. They heard the door close with a soft click.

"Dude," Adam said, "don't flirt with my mom."

"She was flirting with me."

"Shut up." Adam pushed the red panic button again and the screens changed back to what they had been. He continued with the hack. Jason dove into the snack tray and watched as his D's became C's and C's became B's. No A's, though, he insisted with a mouth full of smoked salmon; it wouldn't be believable. People might notice if Crooked Lake's favorite slacker suddenly became an A student.

"Looks like you're already doing fine in Spanish." Adam indicated the screen.

"B plus," Jason said with an edge of disappointment.

"Want an A?"

"No."

Adam made a confused face and continued striking keys.

"Hey what's that thingy?" Jason asked indicating a bulky electronic device next to Adam's desk. It was cube shaped with rounded corners, smooth and black, about the size of a beach cooler. There was a red indicator light and a single USB port on the front; it was hooked up to a network of cables that disappeared behind the back edge of the desk.

"That," Adam said with a sense of haughtiness, "is one of the world's largest private servers ever created, capable of processing speeds faster than the military networks our government uses."

"What's a server?"

Jason's computer ignorance always annoyed Adam, but it was also cute and amusing, like watching a puppy explore a new environment. Adam laughed. "It's kind of like a massive hard-drive but for an entire network of computers. The Internet—cyberspace—exists on servers all across the world, constantly moving and transferring data, allowing access ways and entry ports to websites and cloud storage programs." It was clear Jason had lost interest but Adam persisted. "The digital world of these servers are essentially what you are *surfing* when you're on the web."

Jason's curiosity was suddenly piqued. "You built your own Internet?"

Adam snorted. "Well kind of, but it's more like my own access point, my own entryway and highway system off and onto the Internet. Think of it like my own piece of Internet real estate."

"And what do you need it for?"

Adam hesitated, swallowed. It felt like the scene in a courtroom movie where the defendant on the stand doesn't want to answer the smoking-gun-question. "Computer stuff," he finally said. "Storing files, programs, stuff like that."

"What's on it?" Jason asked and reached to touch the futuristic-looking box, but Adam quickly snatched his hand out of the air, gripping his wrist with long, thin fingers.

"Sorry," Adam said, letting go. "I have some super important files on this thing."

Jason nodded, rubbing his wrist. Adam had a much stronger grip than he would have guessed. "No problem,

Einstein."

A black window box with green font appeared in the corner of the middle screen. It was a message from someone named Lazarus and read, *"What are you up to this evening?"*

"And what's that?" Jason asked.

"It's a message from a hacker-chick I know named Lazarus."

"Hacker-chick? Is she hot?"

Adam laughed. "We've never met in person, but all hacker-chicks are hot."

"What's her real name?"

"Never told me."

"She's probably some fat, creepy guy who will eventually ask you to meet in person. Have you told her you're a healthy, spry teenage boy?" He lightly punched Adam on the arm as both boys laughed. "How do you know each other?"

"From the dark web," Adam said. "This is a program called Black Forest that a lot of hackers use to communicate. That's what you're looking at now." He indicated the message box. "Watch." He clicked in the box and his username appeared on the next line.

"Your hacker name is *Purple Turtle*?" Jason asked.

"Donatello was my favorite ninja turtle."

"Of course he was. Nerd. I liked Raphael."

"Big surprise. The angry, tough-guy."

"So does Lazarus know your alter ego, Purple Turtle?"

"No. True-to-form hackers don't give out their real names."

"What's this Lazarus like anyway?"

"Hang on." Adam typed into the message box: *"Just saving the world one hack at a time."* He sat forward in his chair. "Like every other self-proclaimed, rebel hacker. She usually comes on late at night and makes a few comments about fighting the power or taking down the man, then flirts with me a little bit and goes away."

Lazarus replied: *"FUCK THE ESTABLISHMENT. KEEP FIGHTING THE GOOD FIGHT."*

"I think she's one of those Anonymous hackers who wants to take down corporate America and overthrow the government." Adam was typing as he spoke. "There!" he burst out triumphantly, then leaned back in his chair so Jason could get a full view of the screen. "You are now a 3.0 student, B average, just shy of the honor roll. With your SAT scores you might even be able to get into Michigan."

"Sure," Jason said absently. He thought about his father, who was probably passed out at home in the living room recliner, a stack of bills tipped over next to him on the floor with red stamped warnings on the front of each envelope: *Second Notice... Third Notice... FINAL NOTICE... FINAL NOTICE... FINAL NOTICE...*

College was never going to happen.

"Thanks brother," Jason said and pulled the joint from his pocket. "Now see if Lazarus wants to come party with us."

CHAPTER 5

They decided to call the strange man *Joseph* because Sister Christina was serving the congregation of St. Joseph's, and *Dayspring* because Javier found him in the dawn light of the early morning.

Joseph Dayspring was a tremendous help around Javier's farm. He was strong, tough, and a fast learner. He dug two kilometers of irrigation ditches that sliced between the tree rows in parallel and perpendicular lines and rebuilt the well pump out of spare parts harvested from an antique tractor that had been left to waste in the sun and weeds. Javier and his crops would no longer be at the mercy of Mother Nature. Joseph Dayspring was good with his hands and seemed to have a keen understanding of tools and engines, design and engineering. His strength and stamina impressed Javier, who had served in the army and grown up around some of the toughest farmers and day laborers in Mexico. The strange man had all the markings of an old soldier himself—his resolute ability to take direction and follow orders, his mechanical method of figuring out a problem or challenge, and the hardline respect and gratitude he showed his hosts. Javier recognized all these attributes from his days with the infantry. Dayspring seemed naturally accustomed to harsh work and able endure exhaustion and pain without comment or complaint. He worked sunup until sundown on the farm, only taking breaks to eat and drink in the shade of the avocado trees. At night, he read the English schoolbooks Sister Christina brought him from the village. He found something familiar and comfortable in these books. *Lonesome Dove* was his favorite. *Dracula* was pretty good (although he thought Jonathan Harker was a bit of a sissy). *In our Time* was decent, but most of Hemingway's characters were assholes and depressed him.

Throughout the week, there was never a shortage of chores and tasks to be completed. It could be exhausting work for such a small plot of land that used to be five times as large, but Javier had sold most of his acreage to the larger, corporate farms many years ago. This land, however, was never used for growth and production. Through a series of political, back-scratching maneuvers, the corporate farms were essentially state controlled, and farmland this close to the American border was left bare so the cartels could move drugs around with complete impunity from government agencies. Money exchanged hands and all parties involved were satisfied.

Except for Javier Estes and the other members of the village.

Although Javier was old and nearly retired (true farmers never retire, the old man would insist), many young and able men were forced to sell their land for pathetic sums of money, nothing near what it was worth. But the cartel men were very convincing. They came into the village with guns and contracts. Sign the contract or face the gun. One stubborn, idealistic, young fool refused and was executed. The cartel men forced him onto his knees, then shot him in the back of the head. His body was tied to the back of a truck and dragged through the village streets. It was Javier's son. This was all it took. Everyone in the village and the surrounding farms signed over their land to the control of the cartel men, who in effect, had been granted state sanctioned power. And they wielded it mercilessly.

Ever since Javier's son was murdered, the Estes family had kept their heads low and minded their own business. Once a month, the cartel men would arrive at Javier's home with their guns. They came for protection money and cold drinks, claiming the local villagers and farmers were lucky because without their help, the corporate farms would have surely driven everyone out of business. The men usually never stayed long; once they got their money, and a long, leering look at Maria, they would leave.

Javier feared for his daughter; he knew that one day the men would want more than money...

Sister Christina promised not to speak of Dayspring's presence, as she knew it would only endanger him and Javier's family. She continued visiting the Estes home, praying with Dayspring, checking on his health. She brought him more books to read and taught him mental exercises that might help with his memory.

"I want you to take ten slow and very deep breaths," Sister Christina was saying. "Try to empty your head. Imagine a calm ocean in all directions, nothing but endless, shimmering water."

They were in the bedroom, sitting cross-legged on the floor, facing one another. It was early afternoon; warm sunlight poured through the open windows, making the wooden floorboards look dry and orange. Dayspring had spent the morning replacing the fuel pump on Javier's truck; his face and hands were coated with oil and small scratches. He wanted a siesta like Javier, but Christina said afternoon naps were for old men.

"Sit upright," she insisted. "It will open up your breathing." There was something pleasant yet firm in her voice, like a Spanish-speaking version of Mother Shipton from "The Outcasts of Poker Flat." He had read the short story last night in a beaten-up textbook the nun had given him but was fairly certain she would not appreciate being compared to an old—albeit wise—whore.

Dayspring did as he was told. "Do you know what you're doing?" he asked.

"Yes," Christina replied with confidence. "I Googled it."

Dayspring raised an eyebrow. "Googled?"

Christina nearly burst out laughing. It was incredible to meet someone who had never heard of Google. Even in these far out regions of Mexico, everyone understood or at least recognized Google. "The Internet," she said. "I found a lot of good information online."

Internet... online. These words rattled around in Dayspring's mind like teeth in a clay pot. He recognized them but did not know or understand their meaning.

Christina noticed his confusion. "Let's just concentrate on this right now," she said. "Now, close your eyes and focus on your breathing. In for six seconds, hold for three, out for six, hold for three."

Dayspring took ten long, deep breaths as she instructed, drawing the warm air into his lungs until completely full, then slowly exhaling. He imagined the ocean Christina had described, calm and serene water rippling and shimmering in a constant blast of warm sunlight. He began to feel light and airy inside, like Christina had explained might happen, as if his personal gravity was weakening and he might float away.

"Focus on the water and my voice." The nun spoke with calm assurance and precise directions. "I want you to imagine floating in this water, on your back, facing a peaceful, blue sky."

Dayspring could feel his body lighten and core temperature drop as his mind constructed the imagery. The mental ocean was cool and comfortable, putting him at complete ease.

"Imagine that everywhere around you objects begin to appear; you can hear them calmly splash out of the water and bob up and down on the surface. All around you are floating red balls about the size of a fútbol."

In his mind, Dayspring saw the red balls popping up, brushing against his feet, arms, and face. They were everywhere, scattered red dots jogging around on the surface, changing pitch and position on top of the soft ripples.

"Each one of these balls represents one of your memories," Christina went on, allowing Dayspring time to craft every detail in his imagination. "I want you to reach for one of these balls, take hold of it in your hand and look at it, but really try to see *through* it. Hold it up to the blue sky and concentrate. Watch and study the ball as it becomes more and more transparent. Focus and see *inside* the ball."

Christina let a full minute of complete silence pass. "Now tell me what you see."

Dayspring began to tremble, not a lot, but enough for Christina to notice. "What do you see, Joseph?" she asked again.

It felt as if he had lost control of his own mind. The images Dayspring had crafted were now acting independently from his conscious efforts. The red ball began to fade away as if dissolving, the blue sky behind it filtering through; with it, a single, black word appeared.

"Lazarus." he finally said slightly higher than a whisper.

CHAPTER 6

While Joseph Dayspring continued to practice memory exercises with Sister Christina, Jason Orchard and his friends were getting high and talking about death and the future.

"The worst way to die?" Adam said, rubbing his chin. "I'd say being eaten." He paused, nodded to himself. "Yeah, being eaten, by a shark or something, knowing that you are dying as another animal consumes you—that's a terrible thought."

"This is a terrible conversation," Emma said.

"I think burning to death would be worse," Jason offered. "Remember when you dared me to step on the hot coals?" He was asking Haley. Of their group, they had known each other the longest and had all sorts of fun little memories they were constantly referencing and sharing secret laughs over. It only annoyed Adam and Emma a little bit.

"I can't believe you did it. Dumbass."

"I was nine," Jason said.

They sat around a campfire on the north shore of Crooked Lake, an area locals referred to as *the bluffs*. It was a small beach cove, a soft inlet that curved around like the letter C. Behind them was a wall of thick trees, and on the western tip, where the land slopped upward at a steep angle, there was an elevation of limestone called Hook Point, a rocky cliff edge, about fifteen feet above the lake's surface. From up here and at night, the beach looked like a crescent moon. Only accessible by boat or a long hike from an overgrown and unused service road, there was nothing behind the bluffs but thirty miles of un-tract Michigan wilderness, protected state land full of deer, ducks, and mosquitos.

"Whenever it's my time," Jason said, his eyes skirting across the dark surface of the lake, "I think I just want to wade out into the water and let it take me away."

"Actually," Haley said, taking on the tone of those who love correcting another person's erroneous claim, "I read somewhere that drowning is actually quite painful and horrifying. They say that when cold water enters your lungs it feels like acid."

"That's not what I meant," Jason said. Of course, he did not want to drown as a mode of death, but there was something romantic about being interned in the lake, like a Viking burial at sea. Crooked Lake was home, more so than his literal house and the man (father) he shared it with. The lake was where he always wanted to be. Whether it was fixing boat motors down at the marina, cutting smooth glass during an early morning kayak, or sitting around a campfire on the beach with his friends, *the lake was home.*

A soft breeze drifted across the black water like the cold breath of an invisible ghost, causing the friends to inch closer to the dancing flames of the fire. It was the tail end of summer, that transitional time of year where the earth and its green landscapes fight an impressive yet futile battle against the orange burn of an approaching autumn. Low music played from a cell phone wirelessly connected to a portable set of speakers. Bob Dylan was *"Knock-knock-knockin' on heaven's door"* with his signature rock-gospel twang.

"Enough about death," Adam said taking a long drag from a fat, little joint. "Let's talk about something else."

"What do you guys want to be when you grow up?" Emma asked quickly.

"Yes, much better subject," Adam approved with a chirpy attitude, then passed the joint across the fire to Jason.

"I want to be some kind of builder," Jason said and took a puff. He let the idea settle while slowly exhaling. Rich, blue smoke spiraled above his head, disappearing into a starlit sky. "You know, own a custom shop that builds things for people, cool creative things."

Emma, who had easily recovered from the sloppy kiss at the Shack, snuggled against his arm. "I want to be a lawyer," she said. "Undergrad at Michigan, law school at the University of Chicago."

"Big dreams," Adam declared. He was sitting next to Haley. The two of them always seemed to be perpetually stuck in the budding stages of a romance that never quite began to blossom. Throughout the night, she had been inching closer and closer to him until their knees were touching. Although the young genius had memorized the periodic table and knew Pi to the 1,000th decimal, he was utterly clueless about women and had no idea how to grow their relationship.

"I want to be a doctor," Haley said, then added, "maybe a pediatrician."

Jason smiled. "I could see that."

Haley smiled back.

There was a long moment of silence as the spirits of summer drifted across the lake, stirring around the flames of the fire. The other three friends had just laid down their future plans, and now it was Adam's turn. It was no secret—Adam Evans was special. A prodigy and genius, he could write his own ticket to the future. Barely seventeen-years-old, he already had full-ride scholarships to every Ivy

League school in the universe, as well as job offers from Apple, Google, and all the other tech giants of Silicon Valley (not to mention the NSA).

"Adam?" Jason said.

No response.

Jason leaned over and lightly punched his friend on the arm. "Adam's probably going to end up as some analyst for the Department of Defense. He'll be the guy creating the surveillance software that keeps us all safe from terrorists."

"No way," Adam finally interjected. He was thinking about Lazarus and her attitude toward *"the establishment."* He lifted his head and looked at the stars. "But I do want to help people."

"How?" Emma asked.

A simple enough question. They all wanted to help people in some way. Jason wanted to create, Emma wanted to solve, Haley wanted to heal. Adam Evans just knew he wanted to do good in the world.

"I don't know," he said and sighed. "I want…" His voice drifted away with the wind. He stared directly into the wavy fire, which reflected in his black pupils as tiny red dots. Silence swallowed them whole, even the burning wood stopped crackling.

There were times in his life when Adam Evans felt a terrible pressure. At the risk of sounding like an egomaniac, Adam knew he was a genius and would someday be considered one of the smartest people on the planet (perhaps already was). At times, it felt like having some sort of superpower—but it was a power he never asked for. His intellect could take him anywhere in life, into any arena—medicine, technology, finance. *The world was his oyster,* as the proverbial expression goes; he need only crack it open and suck out the savory juices. Like it or not, he had this incredible power, something his mother told him was a gift and came with a tremendous responsibility.

Which wasn't fair.

Why did he have all the responsibility? Why was he stuck with the weight of the world on his shoulders?

"Forget about it," Jason said, sensing the topic was bothering his best friend.

"Do you guys know how fucked up the world is?" Adam suddenly blurted out. His voice had a cold edge that surprised everyone.

It felt like a trick question. Of course, the world was fucked up, galactically fucked up. The other three friends all looked at each other, unsure if Adam really wanted them to respond.

"There is so much shit wrong with this world," Adam continued. "There are so many problems, so many issues—climate change, terrorism, hunger, inequality, disease. *Everything* is a disease. Do you guys know the definition of *disease*?"

Eyes darted around their circle. Again, Jason, Emma, and Haley were uncertain if the question was rhetorical or not.

Adam tossed a small twig into the fire. "A disease by definition is something that causes part of a system to malfunction. And our system, our world, our way of life, is fucking collapsing. The entire world is malfunctioning right in front of us and no one cares."

The only response were the gentle waves lapping on the shoreline.

"Dude, have another hit," Jason said and both girls laughed.

"I'm serious," Adam snapped, annoyed at their levity. "We have the ability to help so many people, but due to greed, corruption, and our outright apathy, we just don't."

"We can't fix everything," Haley said.

Adam stood up. He walked to the water's edge where the sand was damp and cold and left clearly defined footprints.

"Do you know how you cure cancer?" Adam said,

looking over his shoulder at his friends but not giving them time to reply. "Cancer is the meanest, nastiest disease on Earth because it comes in so many forms and has a habit of sneaking up on its victims. But do you know how to cure it?"

"How?" Jason asked, exchanging glances with Emma and Haley; there was something in Adam's zeal that was suddenly unsettling.

"Give it to the richest man on the planet."

The other three traded bemused looks again.

"Take the deadliest form of cancer on the planet," Adam said, "and shove it up the ass of the world's richest man. Do you think Donald Trump or Bill Gates, or some billionaire Saudi Prince is going to let himself die from cancer? Hell no. He's going to dump his fortune into cancer research until there is a definitive cure. Because that's what it takes—money. It all boils down to money. The fact is humanity actually has the resources to cure so many of our diseases, and not just the biological variety, but all of our problems, everything that's causing our systems to collapse. Here we are, in the most technologically advanced era of human history. We have the capabilities and the science to fix so many of these problems—these *diseases*, whether it's cancer, or some social issue like crime caused by lack of resources. We have the ability right now in this place and time to help---" His voice had been rising to a great glee but abruptly cut off as he took a breath and tossed his arms into the air helplessly. "But we don't." He ended with a direct, simple creed, shot like a silenced bullet: "Because no one gives a fuck."

The fire crackled and crickets chirped. No one spoke.

"The world needs so much fixing," Adam said looking across the water, an uncomfortable note of desperation in his voice. "Reason and logic should rule over all, not faith or nationalism or capitalism, and when that is the case, we'll be able to cure things like cancer." He craned his head up and peered into the dark abyss above him.

"Someday, we will be able to cure everything."

Later that night, Adam sat at his mission control center. Every light in his basement-man cave was off, just the soft glow of the computer monitors. On one screen, a soundless episode of *Family Guy* played, on the other two was a digital blueprint of a new electron microscope he hoped to have constructed by Christmas. He toyed around with the design, playing with different ideas that had crossed his mind, but he found it difficult to focus. It seemed like his brain was always being bombarded by random thoughts, so much that it sometimes distracted him from social engagements. Like tonight.

Even though he loved spending time with his friends, he felt like they did not—*could not*—understand him and the burden of responsibility he felt toward the world. His mom called his intelligence a gift, but most of the time it felt like a curse.

It was past 2:00 a.m., and he was about to crash for the night when a Black Forest message box appeared on his center screen.

It was Lazarus.

But her message was encrypted, which wasn't entirely unusual on dark web communications. It was odd only because Lazarus didn't typically use encryption software, but then again, their conversations were pretty harmless. Lazarus, he was certain, was probably just an idealistic young person like himself with big dreams of creating a better society by *"sticking it to the man"*—an expression she was fond of using. The last time she had encrypted a message was when she sent over the blueprints for the private server that was next to Adam's desk.

The device had fascinated Jason, and indeed, it was an incredible piece of technology. In a way, his layman best friend was right; it was exactly like having his own

Internet. Lazarus claimed to have stolen the design from some Silicon Valley tech corporation, and this, remarkable as it sounded, seemed to have some validity. The server was unlike anything Adam had ever seen or heard about. He had constructed it to the exact specifications of the blue prints, often times not fully understanding exactly what he was doing (which was a rather alien emotion to Adam Evans). Its storage capabilities and processing speed were immeasurable, but even without a proper metric, Adam hypothesized this design was going to revolutionize the computing world. Lazarus had given him the plans as part of a deal. She needed to store a very special file in a safe place, and only this exact server was capable of doing that. If Adam agreed to construct the device and store the file, then he could just keep the tech and design all for himself. *"What's on the file?"* he had asked. But Lazarus wouldn't reveal this, saying only that it was going to *"change the world,"* and once he *completely* earned her trust, she would grant him viewing access.

Store a mysterious file for a conspiracy theorist/hacker on a top-secret server constructed out of plans stolen from a multi-billion dollar technology firm...

Adam's super advanced, logic-driven brain had screamed at him that this was a bad idea, but the power-hungry, ravenous id that lurked within the subterranean layers of his conscious convinced him otherwise. He had built the server and stored the file without any further hesitations.

Adam ran her message through some military-grade decryption software and waited for the results. Whatever the mysterious hacker wanted to say, she had gone a long way to hide it from anyone who might be eavesdropping.

The operation finished. Lazarus' message appeared in plain English text: *"We need to talk."*

He typed *"?????"* into the message box and clicked send.

Her response came immediately.

"Your life is in danger."

CHAPTER 7

The memory exercises with Sister Christina continued. There were many red balls, but every one of them—every word, every vision, every small peek into Dayspring's past—only created more questions, more mysteries.

Lazarus was a recurring theme. Sister Christina, well versed in Christian theology, gave Dayspring a brand new King James Bible, and together they sat at Javier's kitchen table and read the Gospel of John where Jesus Christ raises Lazarus of Bethany from the dead (Dayspring not only found it contrite and boring, but also poor quality prose—out of respect for the nun, however, he kept these opinions to himself). Using her laptop computer, she also introduced him to the Internet and Google, where they explored web pages that discussed the ancient biblical story, but this did not help either. Lazarus seemed as if it was just a random word, echoing around in Dayspring's subconscious mind with no apparent meaning or connection to anything he could remember. According to a Wikipedia page, the term Lazarus had become synonymous with near-death miracles. There were countless stories of men and women who had been declared legally dead only to miraculously and inexplicably come back to life, and scores of films and books used the Lazarus mythology as a narrative allusion or framework.

"Perhaps you are Lazarus," Sister Christina said, but if she was making a joke, Dayspring couldn't tell.

His face was locked on the screen as he read over digital files and documents, periodically glancing down at the open bible where his finger held a firm place. After a few minutes, he sighed and leaned back, letting the crisp spine of the new book snap shut. "Sister," he said, "I'm just having a hard time believing any of this stuff."

"You don't believe in miracles?"

"Maybe I do," Dayspring said as he shrugged. "I don't remember. Right now, if you asked me if I believed a man could come back to life after he died, I would say *no way*."

Christina put an old, warm hand on top of his.

Dayspring kept staring at the computer. With every revelation the memory exercises brought, new frustrations followed. They had spent the last hour in front of the laptop trying to connect the dots of his scattered, cryptic memories. The nun was patient and calm, but Dayspring was annoyed and agitated. He wanted to stand up and throw the infernal machine across the kitchen, stomp on it until it was dust beneath his boots. He felt an inexplicable distrust and rage toward the small, smooth contraption. And oddly—fear.

But that didn't make any sense. They were harmlessly reading through information on internet databases; what was there to be afraid of? Regardless, Dayspring couldn't shake the feeling that they were in some sort of danger; strange as it sounded—it almost felt as if they were being watched.

He abruptly closed the computer and stood up. "Lo siento," he said. *I'm sorry.* He had been trying to learn Spanish in an attempt to communicate better with his hosts, and it was coming rather easily to him.

"It's okay, Joseph," she said. "We will get there. God will guide us."

God… Dayspring's mind whirled around the idea. He rubbed his eyes with the heels of his palms. *God*…

"What is it?" Christina asked.

With his eyes closed and his mind swimming in the mental ocean, Dayspring focused all his mental energies on the strange concept.

God.

There were brief flashes of light as his memories came in and out, quick glimpses into a dark room. He saw a church—at least what used to be a church. It was in ruins now, a roofless artifact with crumbling walls. Inside, the pews were burned black and shoved around as if a tidal wave had plowed through them. The altar was a pile of rubble, collapsed onto itself in the dead center like a broken letter V. Behind it, a bloody, crucified man hung on the wall, nails through his wrists and feet.

"Lazarus is God," Dayspring blurted out for no reason. He had no idea where the thought came from (*somewhere within the ruined church?*). It was a ghost thought, suddenly materializing in the foggy swamp that was his mind.

"What do you mean? What made you say that?" Christina asked.

"I… don't know." Dayspring walked to the window. It was late in the evening; darkness was falling down from the mountains as the sun dipped below the highest peak. He could hear the muffled conversation of Javier and Maria on the porch. He turned back to Christina with a look she mistook for sadness. "I don't think I believe in God," he said.

"That is okay, Joseph," the old nun said and offered him a consoling smile. "He believes in you."

Dayspring looked out the window again; the sky over the mountains was growing darker, spreading down into the flatlands like a slow moving, black avalanche. *Lazarus is God*, he thought as he gazed toward the jagged mountaintop horizon that all of a sudden looked more like the pointy teeth of a rabid, hungry animal. *Lazarus is God.* It was a strange thought, vague and mysterious, and in the darkness of his mind, it was like someone had lit a match. It felt as if he was staring into a well, a deep black pit where he could see a very distant source of light.

Lazarus is God…

The crucified man from the church.

It *wasn't* a statue or a painting nor any work of somber art; it wasn't a symbolic effigy.

It was a real person.

A poor, dead soul pinned to the wall by metal spikes, hanging there with his arms spread out like the Christian savior. No crown of thorns, though, just a hollow bullet hole in the center of his head, a trickle of dried blood zigzagging a path between his dead eyes and down the side of his nose. Carved into the flesh of his bare chest: *Lazarus is God.*

Like Christina had taught him, Dayspring closed his eyes and focused on his breathing. In for six seconds, hold for three, out for six seconds, hold for three. He plunged deeper into the pit, the light growing brighter as he fell. He chased the image (*memory?*) as far into the abyss as he could, and with each carefully timed breath, the light grew stronger…

And suddenly, he was in the church again. Could even smell it.

Acrid smoke, the rank stench of decay. People are talking.

"We're too late."

"Let's keep moving."

"They'll find us; they always do."

"We're not going to make it."

"Have to keep moving."

There is a noise, a clattering of rock and debris. Dayspring peers into a dark corner of the ruined building, between a maze of charred bricks and wooden boards where pieces of twisted rebar poke out like compound bone fractures.

He sees a face.

It is staring directly at him from the shadows. Red eyes---

"Joseph, are you okay?" Christina asked.

Back in Javier's home, Dayspring was gripping the windowsill with white knuckles, droplets of sweat forming on his brow.

The face.

There were two eyes, a nose, and mouth. It was definitely a face.

But it wasn't human.

"Joseph?"

"I'm sorry, I saw something, in my head, and---"

A piercing scream interrupted them, a shrill cry coming from the porch outside.

It was Maria.

They spoke rapidly in Spanish. Dayspring didn't know what they were saying but didn't need to. He and Christina crouched under the window. From where they were, he could see the west corner of the front porch. Three men with guns were shouting at Javier from the steps; one of them held tightly onto Maria with a knife to her throat. "We take the girl now," he said with a leering grin full of brown teeth.

"You've been paid!" Javier screamed at them, eyes bulging and fists clenched.

"Yes, but we take the girl as payment now," another man said with the same predatory smile. The men backed away from the porch, the one holding Maria struggling against her fierce protests. There was a black SUV parked in the drive; one of the men walked over to it and held open a side door.

Javier rushed toward them, but another one of the men hit him in the face with the butt of a riffle. He dropped instantly on the steps of the porch with a hollow thud, blood gushing from his nose.

"Don't worry old timer, we'll bring you the change," the man who hit him said as his hands reached inside Maria's skirt.

She thrashed against him, but the man with the knife dug the blade into her throat, and a small bead of blood appeared. "You will settle down and enjoy this señorita." He licked the side of her face, laughed, then added, "Or perhaps there won't be any change to return."

They continued dragging her toward the vehicle, where the man who held the door smiled and pursed his lips. Maria screamed, twisting and fighting her captors in a vain effort that only enraged and excited them further. Javier was keeled over at the bottom of the porch steps, one hand catching the fountain of blood that poured out of his busted noise, the other held up in a desperate plea. He began to crawl toward them, bloody hands turning the sand into red mud. The men were laughing, taunting, taking turns groping Maria's breasts and crotch as they pulled her away.

They did not notice the figure who had climbed onto the roof of the house and crouched on the eve above the porch, beneath the shadow of the chimney.

An explosion had gone off in the dark recesses of Joseph Dayspring's mind, a nuclear flash of light illuminating every last corner. He felt a swell of raw power surge through him like an old, restored engine roaring to life for the first time in years.

With a small kitchen knife in hand, he leapt from the eve, tackling the closest man, riding him to the ground, and burying the blade in his back all the way to the hilt. The man made a gurgling sound like a clogged sink.

The next ten seconds were a blur of shadows and gunfire. Dayspring moved like an animal—savage and fast, yet with grace and deliberateness. The muzzles of their guns exploded in brilliant flashes, causing a strobe-like effect in the darkness. After taking out the first man, Dayspring charged the second, ducking under a row of bullets and sweeping out the man's legs with a swift kick to his knee that made a sound like dry wood snapping. By the time he hit the ground, Dayspring had already plunged the knife into his chest; he spat up a mouthful of blood, a quick, bubbly pop, then his eyes rolled back in his head, and he was still. Dayspring came up holding the man's gun, a black Glock .9mm, the sights aimed directly at the head of the man who still held Maria.

"I kill the girl; I kill the girl!" the man screamed.

"Suéltala," Dayspring said with a calm, even tone. *Let her go.*

They were fifteen meters apart; the man with Maria taking slow steps backward, dragging her along as she kicked and struggled.

"Last chance," Dayspring said. He stood perfectly level, almost peaceful.

"No señor," the man said. "It's your last chance. Drop the gun or the girl dies." He was hiding behind Maria, using her as a shield.

There was zero room for error.

Dayspring pulled the trigger; the gun roared, and a small red hole appeared in the dead center of the man's forehead. His body convulsed like a hiccup, then dropped to the ground with a gritty crunch, scattering up a small cloud of dust. Maria was left standing alone, unsure of what had just happened.

When the silent confusion broke, she ran to her father, who was still on the ground. Sister Christina came out of the house with a handful of towels. Dayspring stood amongst the carnage, three dead bodies surrounding him like the points of a triangle. He gripped the gun in a tight fist and looked up at the dark sky taking a big gulp of cool air—*in for six, hold for three, out for six, hold for three...*

In his mind-ocean the red balls were exploding to the

surface; there were trillions of them. And as they surfaced they popped like balloons.

The women helped Javier into a chair on the porch, holding the towels under his broken nose. He was hurt, but he would live. Christina left their side and approached Dayspring, who stood like a statue in the night, slowly breathing and staring up into the black void.

"Are you okay, Joseph?" she said cupping his face, turning his head so their eyes could meet.

"Yes," Dayspring said. And for the first time ever, Christina saw him smile. He slid the gun into his waist belt and held her hands.

"What is it?" she asked.

"Sister," Dayspring whispered and took another long breath. "I remember now."

"What do you remember?"

"Everything."

CHAPTER 8

The Shack was quiet on weekday afternoons, especially this late in the summer. Jason and his friends sat at a wall booth, a large, panoramic window exposed them to a beautiful view of Crooked Lake, whose surface was an exotic blend of blue, green, and silver in the powerful sunlight. Jason slowly worked his way through a basket of waffle fries as he looked across the busy water full of boaters carving white paths across the shimmering surface. His friends, Adam, Emma, and Haley, all had their heads buried deep in their smart phones, and no one was talking. Jason could feel the small weight of his flip phone in his front pocket. It was a cheap, pay-by-the-month service plan he purchased himself with money earned repairing boat motors down at the Crooked Lake Marina—which was just *one* of his jobs; the other was slinging drywall for a local construction company.

Adam and everyone else teased him about his phone, but he was never really bothered by it. He was, after all, *Mr. Unplugged* and easily able to let the playful insults roll off him. The fact was, however, he couldn't afford a smartphone or a data plan, and his father, who Jason had left sleeping off a nasty afternoon hangover, was not about to surprise him for his birthday or Christmas. There was something else, however, something that he never shared with anyone, not even Adam, because it was silly and stupid and completely irrational. Every time he held a smart phone, he couldn't shake the *ghost-in-the-room* feeling. Or more like *ghost-in-the-phone* feeling. That little black eye, the phone's camera lens, seemed to stare directly at him.

His friends continued to tap, scroll, and read through whatever web pages, memes, or social media messages occupied their interests. Jason finished his fries and looked out the window again. He couldn't help but feeling like he was missing some big, digital party.

"Mr. Shake," Jason yelled across the quiet bar. "Do you remember when your young patrons used to actually talk to each other?"

Mike Shake, in his standard wing sauce-stained apron, stood behind the bar toweling a glass dry. He was always toweling a glass dry. "Kid," he said without looking up, "that was back in the early 2000s when you were still getting bounced on your father's knee."

Jason doubted his father ever gave him that much attention.

"You've been a little glum lately," Emma said, finally putting down her phone. "What's up?"

"I don't know," Jason sighed. A sound that clearly said, *yeah, there is something 'up'.*

"Are you okay?"

"Maybe I'm just worried about the trig test tomorrow." It was a bullshit answer. Jason Orchard never fretted over grades (especially since the recent grade-altering hack). School had been in session for a week. Senior year. He had heard somewhere that senior year of high school was supposed to be the best year of a young person's life, nothing but parties and pep-rallies. This was how it was portrayed on TV where everyone is happy and whatever drama develops resolves itself within a sixty-minute story arc. This was real life, though, and in real life drama has a way of festering like an annoying cold—then becoming the flu, then pneumonia, then some deadly respiratory infection.

Emma couldn't stop talking about college. She had recently gone on a campus visit to the University of Chicago and met a really nice tour guide named Tadd (*what the fuck kind of name was Tadd?*). He was pre-med (*they all were*), and he promised to help her get invited to the best parties. Jason knew he wasn't going to college and would probably be fixing boat motors the rest of his life as a townie. It wasn't that he admonished this type of blue collar work, he was actually quite good with motors and engines, and he was considerably proud of this. He had an ardent respect for machines, *raw machines*—as he called them, not the alien-looking, *Star Trek* tech that littered Adam's basement-man cave and laboratory, but machines that were just gears and gas, whose metal was cold and rusty and coated in oil. He knew he could make a great and fulfilling career out of building and fixing things with his hands; this wasn't the real issue. The *real* issue was the expiration date that seemed to cast a shadow over the rapidly approaching future.

He knew his relationship with Emma would probably end after graduation. But this was okay. Without any ill intent, he had reserved himself to just enjoying as much of it as possible before this time came. They weren't even really in a relationship, as neither one had committed to using the *boyfriend/girlfriend* terminology; it was rather an unspoken agreement based on gestures of good faith, just a few notches above the relationship purgatory Adam and Haley were stuck in.

What was truly bothering Jason Orchard was everything else seemed to have a similar expiration date—campfire parties at the bluffs, diving off Hook Point, smoking weed on the beach while drying in the sun, eating greasy junk food at the Shack. This was all coming to an end. Jason Orchard loved these things, but as Frost pretentiously once said, and Jason pretentiously tried to deny, *"Nothing gold can stay."* Deep down, he had always known that life was going to radically change after high school. Jason could heartily accept this with only small reserves of bitterness, but he had clung to the hope that his friendship with Adam would be immune to whatever changes loomed in the future. That little genius-nerd had gotten him through some pretty rough times. Sure, it was Jason who had protected him from the all the pea-brain, dick-head bullies that stalked the halls of Crooked Lake High School, but Adam had returned this favor in ways he didn't even realize. Adam and his mother had welcomed Jason into their small family as if he were blood. He ate most of his dinners at the Evans home and often breakfast when he crashed on the couch in Adam's man cave—which was also quite often. Dr. Evans showed Jason the same love and care she showed her own son. She asked him about school and work and cared about his day and life. None of Jason's other friends' families took the time to do this. To all the other moms and dads, he was the son of Marcus Orchard, and that was all that mattered. With no mom and a dad who was a sloppy drunk, it was this friendship that gave Jason the one thing he had been missing his entire life—something most guys are too tough or stubborn to admit they need: love.

But lately, things had been different—Adam had been different. Distant somehow.

"I have an oral test in Spanish I'll probably fail," Haley said over the top of her phone.

Without looking at her Jason said, "Deberías de estudiar más."

Haley and Emma chuckled, but were not surprised. Jason spoke perfect Spanish. Languages just came easy for him. He was even better than Adam.

"You should study more," he said translating himself and winking at Haley.

"I don't know how you do that," she said. "I've taken

Spanish for years and can only say, '¿Dónde está la biblioteca?'"

"The library is across town," Jason answered.

"Show off," Haley said.

"Eres bonita, como el atardecer sobre el lago—you are beautiful, like the setting sun over the lake."

Haley gushed.

Emma smacked Jason's arm and said, "Watch it Casanova."

Adam remained unmindful, absorbed by his phone. His eyes narrowed, brow dipping downward with an intense, V-like point. Whatever was so captivating on that little screen seemed to be making him either angry or confused.

"Adam tiene un pene pequeño," Jason said.

"What does that mean?" Emma asked.

"Adam has a small penis."

They all laughed except Adam. He was in his own world, just him and his phone.

"Hey Adam," Jason said and flicked his friend's ear.

This finally snapped him back to reality.

"What? What is it?" His voice was annoyed and groggy, like someone being awoken from an afternoon nap.

"Just wondering if you're still with us."

Adam looked around at his friends, the bar, the lake as if he had just teleported into the booth and wasn't sure where he was. "Sorry, I---" He glanced at his phone. "I have to go," he said and quickly scrambled out of his seat, making a beeline for the exit.

The three of them sat in silence for a moment, faces exchanging concerned and confused looks.

"What was that about?" Emma asked.

There was no answer, just the shrugging of shoulders.

Jason folded his hands on the table. "Siento que estoy perdiendo a mi major amigo y no se porqué."

"You want to speak English, amigo," Haley said.

"Never mind," Jason replied. *It feels like I'm losing my best friend and I have no idea why.*

That night, like almost every night, Adam Evans sat in front of the computer monitors at his mission control center. He had hated running out on his friends, but his mind had been elsewhere.

The things Lazarus had been telling him—they didn't make any sense. Nothing made any sense, and part of him wanted to tell the mysterious hacker to fuck off.

But still…

His curiosity had been piqued, and curiosity to a mind like Adam Evans was like an addictive drug. A scientist craves answers like a meth-head craves the pipe. Adam needed his fix.

Lazarus had granted him partial viewing access to the secret file on the server he had built (apparently he had earned a *portion* of her trust); and if everything on it was true, the mysterious hacker was right.

It was going to change the world.

He opened a special Black Forest channel Lazarus had created that she claimed was impenetrable to other hackers. Adam had tested it by running his own infiltration programs and it seemed ironclad.

He typed into the message box: *"You gotta show me more proof."*

The reply came immediately. It was a link, which Adam clicked on and a new window appeared; in it, a picture quickly downloaded. It looked like it was taken from the webcam of a laptop computer and showed two people, their faces close together, clearly reading or looking at something on their own screen, unaware they are being photographed. One of them was an elderly woman with a warm face, a nun, Latino, perhaps Mexican. The other was a middle-aged man, maybe in his early forties. He had a generous helping of salt in his sandy hair, and a long, jagged scar ran up and down over his left eye.

The text beneath the picture read: "*The man with the scar will arrive soon. When you meet him, you will have your proof. But be careful, this man is dangerous.*"

Strangely, the man looked familiar.

CHAPTER 9

The man who appeared out of thin air with amnesia now remembered everything, including his real name, but decided to remain Joseph Dayspring. He had grown used to it; and in a strange way, it seemed like he had always been Joseph Dayspring. However, Javier, Maria, and Sister Christina had saved his life—he owed them the truth. It was an ugly truth, brutal and violent, impossible for the rational mind to believe. He gave them this truth, holding nothing back.

Except his real name. This was the only part he kept to himself.

They sat in a circle on the rocky desert sand around a small fire where a dead rattlesnake roasted on a metal spit. Above them, the long arm of the Milky Way stretched across the black, velvety sky. Whatever chaos was taking place in the infinite cosmos was beyond them, far past their understanding or care. They were in the middle of a vast desert, and the desert at night is always peaceful, especially when you are among friends.

A dusty, old pick-up truck loaded with supplies was parked next to them. There was no discernable road anywhere, just sand and dirt and little dry plants in every direction. After killing the cartel men, Dayspring had searched the bodies for identification. All three had government badges—they were Federales. Corruption this close to the border in the midst of the drug trade was not uncommon. So they packed up and headed southeast, toward the gulf, driving nonstop for five hours until they were just a few cliques shy of the American border. They could never return to the farm or village; they could never go home again.

Dayspring needed to get to America. Javier knew people who snuck men and women across the border; polleros, they were called. He sat with a map spread out on his lap, compass in one hand, pencil in the other, occasionally marking a point, then staring into the dark night.

"From here," Javier said, "you will head straight north until you hit the Rio Loco. Follow this until the Grande."

Dayspring nodded his head as he sorted through a small black duffle bag filled with supplies, including the guns he had taken from the dead Federales. They were speaking Spanish; Dayspring was perfectly fluent in the language. "And the three of you will be able to make it to the coast?" he asked. Javier and the two women were headed toward a little town on the Gulf of Mexico where Sister Christina had some contacts at a church who could help them. Soon they would part ways and probably never see each other again.

"Yes. The truck has plenty of gas and runs well," Javier said, then added, "thanks to you."

As they spoke, Dayspring worked on the guns, checking ammo, making sure magazines and firing chambers were clear of debris, well oiled, and functioning properly. He toiled with the weapons like an expert carpenter works with tools; he knew them inside and out, the deadly instruments like an extension of his own hands.

"I'm sorry for all of this," Dayspring said setting down a gun and pulling a large, serrated knife out of the bag. He cut off slices of the roasted rattlesnake, serving them on tin plates to the women first, then Javier and himself. Sister Christina crossed herself before eating.

"Stop apologizing," Javier said. The women both agreed.

"You lost your home."

"I kept my daughter." Javier touched the side of Maria's face with a gentle hand. "One way or the other, the bad men were going to come for her. But we had you."

Through a great struggle to hold back tears, Maria added, "An angel sent to us from heaven."

Dayspring leaned back on his hands and looked up at the silky, starry sky. It was a nice sentiment, *an angel from heaven…*

But where he was from was closer to the deepest circle of Dante's hell.

"Why do you believe me?" Dayspring asked. It was a simple enough question, direct, nowhere to hide. "Why do you believe the things I've told you?" He looked around at the three solemn faces.

Sister Christina spoke for everyone. "Because when I look into your eyes, I see an honest man."

Javier and Maria both nodded.

"But the things I told you are so…" he struggled for the right word, came up with, "*unbelievable.*"

"Belief," Sister Christina said as she twirled the familiar alpha and omega medallion in her fingers, "resides in the heart and soul, not the mind."

A wolf howled in the distance, and the wind lashed out, the flames of the fire dancing sideways for a brief moment. It calmed, and a hollow silence fell over them.

The fire popped and crackled.

"What you have to do," Javier said, breaking the brief, reflective quiet, "will it make a difference?"

"All we can do is hope and pray," Dayspring said, looking at Sister Christina. He turned toward the dark horizon; noiseless heat lightning flashed behind distant, low hanging clouds.

"There's a storm coming," Javier casually noted.

No one said anything for a long time.

An hour later, they said goodbye.

Maria kissed Dayspring on the cheek, trembling behind teary eyes. "You saved me," she said.

"You saved me."

The young woman was beautiful in a simple way and reminded Dayspring of a girl he once knew. She had her own scars and pain, but this was merely the fuel of an engine that generated a quiet but powerful and pointed confidence. He had no doubt this young woman and her elderly father would find the peace and happiness they deserved.

Christina took his hands and gave him the small alpha and omega medallion. "I know you do not believe in God," she said as she closed his fingers around the religious artifact. "But at least believe in hope." They hugged for a long time.

"Thank you, sister," Dayspring said.

As if to answer an unspoken question, the nun held the sides of his face and said, "Whatever you have to do, it is a good man that does it."

Dayspring looked down at the medallion in his hands, the thin cord of leather dripping between his knuckles. He fingered the soft, dull metal, feeling its tiny contours and imperfections, then, in a one swift movement, looped the necklace over his head, the small charm dropping down and resting over his heart.

"I supposed God will be the judge of that," he said.

"No, my son," Christina said. "The magistrate that judges you resides in your heart." They hugged once more. The nun laid a wrinkled hand on the face of the medallion. "It's a symbol of eternity. There is a forever, and hope will always be part of it."

"Thank you sister," Dayspring said and kissed her on the cheek.

Javier insisted on walking with Dayspring into the night for about half a kilometer north. Every once in a while, the wolf would howl, and Javier would look toward its direction for a moment, pausing mid-step and offering the creature a respectful nod. Each man held a flashlight that crossed paths before them like a slender X, illuminating the red, desert rocks. They talked about the small farm where Javier grew up and his time spent in the Mexican army.

"We are both soldiers, you and I," Javier said. They stopped and turned to one another. One old man, one younger man, two souls who had endured so much pain, sadness, and death. Javier stuck out his hand.

Dayspring received it. A man's handshake. A soldier's handshake.

"Here," Javier said. He reached behind himself and brought out a large wad of folded money. "There is 3,000 dollars here, 1,100 is from Sister Christina. You will have to pay the polleros. Crossing the border will be expensive. So will your journey."

"I can't take this," Dayspring said with his hands up.

"You do not have a choice. Consider it payment for all the work you did."

"No, I can't."

"Young man," Javier said, evoking a tone of military authority. "I can no longer fight the way you can. I cannot join the war you say is coming. But I *can* do this." As he finished, he shoved the money into Dayspring's hand, who took it unwillingly.

The wolf howled again, and as it faded, the desert became eerily quiet as if the night was holding its breath.

Silent barrels of heat lightning rolled out of the heavens near the horizon.

"There *is* a storm coming," Dayspring said, their eyes locking through the darkness. "If I fail…" He did not have to finish his statement.

"Ve con Dios," the old man said.

Joseph Dayspring turned and walked into the black night, toward an unknown fate, a history that was being rewritten with every step.

CHAPTER 10

Time is a funny thing. Since the birth of the universe time has existed, but until mankind had a name for it, time was simply the rising and setting sun, the changing of the seasons, the revolution of the planets in the solar system. Time was a cycle that repeated. Forever.

But eventually, time became a temporal measurement, and suddenly, the universe became infinitely larger—and vastly more complex. With radical discoveries in the realm of quantum physics, new theories were proposed about time and what its role was in the creation, expansion, and future of the universe. Time was no longer just an abstract term represented by hands on a clock, No, time was something far more perplexing and important.

Time *was* the universe.

Or rather, time was one element of a four-dimensional space-time existence.

Adam Evans had been thinking a lot about time lately. It really was the universe's ultimate riddle, an enigma so confounding the greatest minds that ever lived could not come to a consensus on a unified theory. Albert Einstein believed time was relative to speed, mass, gravity, and energy; Stephen Hawking theorized that time is constantly warped by these factors in such a way that the universe does not have a single history, but rather *every* possible history within its own probability. Most physicists nowadays at least agree that time is not limited to Euclid geometry (the shortest distance between two points is *not* a straight line when time warps are factored in and the fabric of space-time is bent).

For all the mesmerizing theories and concepts that attempt to explain it, time, in the rawest sense, was a giant pain in the ass.

There just wasn't enough of it.

Adam Evans slouched in the uncomfortable metal chair, feeling a bit claustrophobic in the small hospital room. The walls were bone white and shiny, and there was a bright window overlooking a courtyard that did little good at alleviating the oppressive feeling of the tight space.

His mother rested peacefully in a puffy, fake-leather chair. Her eyes were closed, and her chest rose slowly up and down, hands set comfortably on the extra-wide armrests. A stainless steel IV stand was next to her; hanging from it was a clear plastic bag of fluid with a tube that looped around a metal arm and connected to a small port that had been implanted on the side of her head.

She looked tired. She was always tired now. And she threw up a lot.

Chemotherapy would do that to a person.

Adam sat up and leaned forward. Five weeks ago, his mother had been diagnosed with a primary brain tumor, a nasty little growth inside her cerebellum. Removing it was impossible, but perhaps they could radiate and poison the son of a bitch to death. And that's exactly what radiation and chemotherapy were—poisons. Chemotherapy uses a cocktail of dangerous drugs known as cytostatics. These drugs prevent cells from dividing and replicating—something cancer is very good at. Unfortunately, chemo does not differentiate between cancer cells and healthy cells, so the collateral damage to a patient's body can be devastating. It was ironic really, like fighting a forest fire with a category-5 hurricane.

Dr. Evans had already lost a lot of weight. Her once healthy, athletic body was slowly melting away like a popsicle left on the kitchen counter. Her hair was falling out in massive clumps that Adam found stuck to laundry or gathering in dusty corners of the home. His once beautiful mother was dying and all because of a tiny nugget of fleshy material about the size of a peanut in her brain. And the little bastard was growing, too.

Fifty/fifty the doctors had explained to Adam. And those were supposed to be good odds. But Adam had done his own research and concluded that these doctors were either trying to sugarcoat the prospects or they were just plain stupid. On average, people with cerebellum tumors had more of a twenty percent chance at survival, and even if the cancer fell into remission, there was an 85 percent probability of it coming back within five years.

Yes, time was a very funny thing. Especially when it became increasingly limited.

Adam stood up, touched the back his mother's hand. Her eyes opened briefly, and she looked at him with a groggy expression and strained smile. He leaned down and kissed the side of her face.

He had studied all about brain tumors and the type of chemo-cocktail they were giving her. She would lose all her hair, that wasn't so bad; hair grows back (if you live). She'd lose more weight. Chemotherapy is the ultimate appetite suppressant. Not only is the patient *not* hungry, but the nausea produces vomiting so intense the lining of the stomach can actually tear open. Her muscle fibers would become horribly deteriorated, like an old, worn out sock, causing her to suffer extreme atrophy. Her skin would be dried out and damaged from the radiation, maybe even discolored permanently. If the treatments didn't work, the tumor would grow. It would bruise her cerebellum and inflate it. The swelling would push against her skull and cut off blood flow to other parts of her brain. She'd start losing memories, then basic motor functions. Adam would have to feed her, bath her, wipe her ass. In time, her mind would deteriorate into madness, and she'd lash out at the ones she used to love in angry fits of uncontrollable aggression. Dr. Maryanne Evans would no longer exist; she would be replaced by a sick, mindless, dying animal.

All those years of eating healthy, drinking water, using organic moisturizers, and exercising daily—wasted. Because of a bunch of tiny, abnormal cells.

Fuck this.

Adam left the room and stood in the hospital hallway absorbing the atmosphere around him. It smelled like cleaning fluid. He remained just in front of his mother's door, breathing through his nose with his head lowered, staring at the linoleum floor but not really seeing it. Doors opened and clicked closed, an assortment of beeps and buzzes ringing past him like an orchestra of artificial and electronic sounds. People shuffled by, doctors, patients, visitors, annoyed at the obstacle Adam made of himself. He could feel their glances, almost hear their thoughts:

Why is that weird kid just standing there looking at the floor?

None of your fucking business, ass holes, keep walking.

His cell phone vibrated in his pocket. It was Jason. Adam swiped ignore and let it go straight to voicemail. A moment later it vibrated again; it was Haley this time, but once more, he swiped ignore. Why won't his friends leave him alone? Didn't they know his mother was dying?

No, of course, they did not know because Adam had not told anyone. Yet still, he was angry with them for not knowing, which he knew was an irrational thought, but that didn't matter. Nothing mattered anymore. He was a goddamn genius who had been told his whole life how special he was, but this didn't matter either. What good was being a genius if he couldn't even save his own mother's life?

One again, his phone vibrated, and once again, it was Jason. For a brief second, he nearly hurled it against the wall but instead took a deep breath, swiped ignore, and shoved it back in his pocket.

He didn't have time to talk to his friends.

CHAPTER 11

Jason snapped his phone shut. This was the best advantage of having a flip phone—sure, it wasn't sexy like an IPhone or Galaxy Droid, but at least you could still end a call with anger. He sat down on his bed, hearing the old springs groan beneath his weight. Adam wouldn't answer his phone, and he wasn't returning any calls. Ever since the night he mysteriously ran out of the Shack, the two friends had barely spoken, and neither Emma nor Haley had heard from him. He had also been missing a lot of school lately, which was incredibly unlike him.

Jason's bedroom was a tiny box compared to the grandiose affair that was Adam's basement-man cave. The main difference, however, was Jason's room was meticulously clean and organized. Like a military barrack, the space was minimal and efficient in its sparseness. A single bed, tightly made, with a black metal frame; desk; dresser; bookshelves; no clutter or dust; everything arranged in sharp, ninety degree angles. It was modern but also spartan, a small room with lots of space and few distractions, a tiny place with room to wander.

His home was on the northeastern channel of the lake, tucked away in a shallow corner. Down by the water's edge, a blue kayak was pulled onto the lawn. He considered taking it out, paddling his muscles into a fierce burn. It always helped clear his head. He had purchased the small watercraft from the marina he worked at last summer. Never having kayaked in his life, the sole purpose was to have another way of leaving his house. Walking, biking, driving (when his truck was running), and now, kayaking, the more methods he had of leaving—the better.

Through the window, the sky was dark blue, nearly purple, with far-away stars twinkling to life. Jason had always thought there was something magical about the twilight hour. It was always so peaceful; no matter what was going on in the world or in his life, the brief moment that was the transition from day into night felt like the entire world took one collective sigh and said, *okay everybody, just relax.*

But this peace was short-lived. He heard the front door open downstairs, heavy boots on the linoleum floor. There was grumbling—not a loud grumbling, which was good. This indicated his father was *sad-drunk* and not *mad-drunk*. Sad-drunk was *a lot* easier to deal with than mad-drunk. Hopefully, he'd stumble into his reclining chair and just fall asleep, and Jason wouldn't have to worry about---

There was a giant crash downstairs, like someone tipped over a china hutch—that is if the Orchards owned a china hutch. Or china to put in it.

Jason left his room and walked to the top of the landing. "Dad?" he called out.

No answer.

"Dad, you okay?" he said again but still no response.

He shrugged his shoulders and proceeded downstairs. At the foyer, he could see the aftermath of his father stumbling in. The front door was ajar. A left boot had slipped off. Coat on the floor. A pair of sunglasses. Jason followed the trail down the hall—there was the other boot. Then his wallet. Car keys. Pile of receipts. Pack of cigarettes and lighter. The items led into the living room.

And there he was.

Face down on the floor, an obliterated wooden coffee table in pieces beneath him. Jason shook his head, embarrassed, though no one else was around to witness the pathetic scene. It was like something that happens in a sketch comedy show. But in real life, it is decidedly *not* funny.

"Dad?" Jason said kneeling down and rolling his father onto his side. A wave of whiskey rushed upward as if he had just lifted the barrel of a thirty-year-old, single malt, causing Jason to avert his nose and blink his eyes.

"Damn, dad," he sighed.

Marcus Orchard groaned. "Where am…"

"Don't talk," Jason said. "Let's get you into your chair. Come on." Slipping underneath one of his dad's arms, Jason lifted him like a wounded soldier who's been shot in the leg. He dragged him to the chair and plopped him down, a tiny puff of dust billowing up from the worn upholstery. Marcus begun to snore almost immediately. "Eve?" he said in his sleep.

Who the hell was Eve?

Jason decided he didn't care. She was probably just another bar-star skank his father sometimes brought home. He walked around the chair and pulled the lever so Marcus could recline, then took a blanket from the back of the couch and laid it over him. "Good night, dad," he said.

Jason went into the kitchen but could still hear his father's raspy snoring. Every so often, he'd grunt something, sniffle, and cough. Jason considered taking pictures of him again, making it a wide angle shot so you could see the smashed coffee table, too. He had a lot of humiliating pictures of his dad: passed out on the toilet, asleep on the lawn, lying in a puddle of his own vomit on the kitchen floor. Jason showed him these images regularly, hoping the embarrassment might shock his system into sobriety, but it never worked. Ashamed of nothing, Marcus Orchard hit the bottle hard every night.

65

So Jason had pretty much given up.

His father could drink himself into complete ruin, even death, and Jason would only care as much as it impeded his own life—which he had discovered wasn't much if he lived self-reliantly. Because of this, Jason had learned a long time ago to take care of himself. He did his own laundry, bought his own groceries, cooked his own meals, and paid his own bills. Jason Orchard didn't actually *need* his father for anything. In many ways, this was refreshing. Because he could completely take care of himself, he felt like he could truly be himself. It made him recall a Ralph Waldo Emerson quote his teacher rambled on about in English class: *"Society is a joint-stock company, in which members agree, for the better securing of his bread to each shareholder, to surrender the liberty and culture of the eater."* It meant that if you are dependent on other people, then those people can control you. Jason Orchard was dependent on no one, and it made him feel liberated.

He opened the refrigerator. Still pretty much empty except for some old, crusty condiment jars. He looked at the grocery list that hung on the front of the fridge with a magnet. It had one word, in his own handwriting, scrawled across the guidelines at a sharp angle: *Everything!*

The phone rang. Jason shrugged at the list as if apologizing to it, then picked up the cordless phone from its cradle.

"Hello?"

Silence, soft static. His father grunted from the living room.

"Hello?" Jason said again.

More silence, then a woman's voice: "Jason Orchard? You must be Jason." It was pleasant, soft, impossible to age, and sounded almost generically female.

"Yes. Who is this?"

"That's me. For me!" Marcus Orchard groaned loudly from his chair, suddenly awake. Jason could hear him rolling and twisting.

"My name is Eve. I'm a friend of your father's. May I please speak with him?"

Ah, Eve. The bar-star skank.

"Bring me"—Marcus had to stop and take a breath—"the phone!"

"He's not available right now," Jason said.

There was another moment of silence as Marcus struggled in his chair. Eve finally spoke. "I'd really like to speak with him if at all possible. Was that him I heard in the background?"

"Yes but, look, you don't understand; he can't talk right now."

"Phone!" Marcus roared through the wall.

"Jason," Eve said calmly, "I'm going to tell you something I'm not supposed to. I'm your father's AA sponsor. Over the last several weeks, he's been seeking help with becoming sober. You see, he wanted to keep this a secret and then surprise you when he finished his first month of sobriety. Should I assume your father is drunk right now? If so, that is why I am his sponsor and need to speak with him. He was supposed to check in earlier tonight but never did; I now understand why. Give him the phone please. Would you do that, Jason?"

Jason didn't know what to say. His father was seeking help? Marcus Orchard was attending AA meetings?

From the living room: "Bring me the"—*burb, hiccup*—"phone!"

Hell must have frozen over.

"Yeah," Jason said. "Of course."

He brought the phone to his father, who was sitting up, bloodshot eyes barely open. Marcus Orchard rubbed the back of his neck as if stiff with pain and held his other hand out to receive the phone. Jason did not know what to make of this man. His father was actually in a treatment therapy? A tornado of emotions tore through him. He was proud but also worried and anxious and still very much on guard. But for the first time in a very long time he was…

The right word failed him; it had been so long since he felt something like this. It seemed foreign and unrecognizable, yet he couldn't deny the emotion: *hopeful.*

Jason Orchard was hopeful.

He gave his dad the phone, who gobbled it up in a snappy palm and immediately fell back into his chair.

"Hello Eve," Marcus said through a long breath.

It still seemed unreal—his father in AA. Jason went back into the kitchen but continued to eavesdrop from around the corner. He watched Marcus Orchard hold the phone tightly against his ear and listen, a quiet, content look of peace on his face. Whatever Eve was saying to him, the sad-drunk was listening. Would any of this pay off? Jason wondered. Clearly, it wasn't working quite yet, but quitting alcohol probably takes considerable effort. Lots of people slip or *fall off the wagon*, as the phrase goes.

"I'll do whatever you think is best," Marcus said into the phone. "I'll do whatever you say. Don't want my son to see me like this anymore."

Jason smiled. His father was really trying to get sober! And for him!

But they had been down this road before. There were times Marcus seemed to get a hold of his drinking, but they never lasted very long. These were familiar streets to Jason. And he really didn't want to go down those paths again.

But still…

His father was in there talking to an AA sponsor!

The hope was creeping back.

CHAPTER 12

Another explosion rocks the outer wall, sending chunks of rock and concrete into the black sky. The air is thick with a hazy fog that taste like cement. Men wear ragged scarves around their faces and try not to breathe too deeply. The lucky ones have goggles; the really lucky ones have been sent to the flanks where the shelling is not as intense.

More explosions tear apart the wall and earth, scattering ashes and debris, throwing extra clouds of the thick, acidic dust over the men. Outside the trench, craters dot the landscape like the surface of the moon, fires burning around the circular edges.

"Save as much ammunition as possible!" a deep voice yells above the chaos.

A shell explodes so close it half buries the men it doesn't kill in jagged pieces of rock and wreckage. Arms and legs protrude from the rubble, wriggling like worms emerging from the soil on a rainy day.

"I can't do this," someone says to himself. The voice is young and cracked with fear.

"Yes you can," Dayspring says right back; his tone is simple and direct, hardened by experience.

"I can't…" The younger man, however, is fresh on the line— innocent, if such a word still exists.

Dayspring looks upon the younger man, who is actually just a kid, probably no older than seventeen. What were you doing at seventeen-years-old? *a voice in his head asks. A flash of memories threaten to overtake him, but Dayspring fights them all away. In this brave new world, it is best not to think about the past.*

"You're a soldier now," Dayspring says. "Act like it."

The other soldiers around them ready their guns as shells continue to whistle through the air like screaming Gaelic spirits.

"They're coming!" the kid screeches and with nowhere else to go, seems to scramble within himself.

Dayspring peers through a gaping hole in the wall with a pair of binoculars and sees something that turns his blood icy cold. The foot soldiers have crested a hill. They are 500 yards away and advancing. There are thousands of them, tens of thousands, perhaps more, and they cut a line completely across the landscape that stretches as far back as the horizon. Metallic faces glistening under the pale moonlight. Their red, soulless eyes always remind him of his favorite line of poetry: "And his eyes have all the seeming of a Demon's that is dreaming." *They move like an insect swarm— an Egyptian plague—without thought, without will, functioning as part of a collective consciousness.*

"What should I do if I get captured?" the kid asks, gripping his gun with unsteady hands.

Another explosion, intense shouting, and a sudden burst of violent machine gun fire erupts above their heads.

"Don't get captured."

"But---"

"Now let's move!"

Joseph Dayspring shot up in bed like a mousetrap, eyes snapping open, heart pounding, white knuckles gripping fistfuls of stiff bed sheets. The explosions, the gunfire, the screams of the dying and the afraid—all began to fade as his eyes adjusted to the darkness. He loosened his grip on the sheets, but his fingers remained curled in a claw-like vise.

The bedsheets.

The bed.

The dirty, faded walls.

The quiet…

In his head, the battle raged on with a ghostly echo, but the room was silent, filled with gray, smoky shadows. Occasionally, a semi-truck would downshift and compress its air brakes on a nearby highway, or a door would open and slam from down the balcony. Dayspring didn't know how long he sat up in bed, listening to the unquiet noises of the night. A man yelled and a woman yelled back in muffled, inarticulate speech. Another door slammed. A car drove by with base so heavy it rattled the half-empty ice bucket on the end table.

He took a few deep breaths the way Sister Christina had taught him and tried to shake away the remainder of the dream—the nightmare.

The memory.

He was *not* in a concrete trench, explosions and gunfire were *not* cracking the air above him, and even though in the back of his mind he could still see the empty, lifeless gazes of the Lazarus foot soldiers, they were *not* advancing on his position.

He was in a motel room; it was a cheap, dank little place that smelled like stale bread and cigarettes, but he was safe. And alive.

How many men had died that day? How many human beings had been taken to the camps? How many more would be tortured and experimented on and eventually killed or integrated? He wondered what happened to the young soldier—the boy—that he had ordered to run headfirst into an unwinnable battle.

He was probably dead… Dayspring turned over his arm and ran his fingers over his tattoo, *SLX-16*… or worse.

* * *

The following morning Joseph Dayspring sat in a booth at a small mom-and-pop diner in Dibbleville, Kentucky, sipping the best cup of coffee had ever had in his life. It was as bitter as tree bark and piping hot, enveloping his face in a cozy beard of steam with each sip. He had ordered fried eggs over medium. It came served on a bed of hash browns and included bacon *and* sausage. It was a meal fit for kings. Ever since Dayspring recovered his memories, the strangest adjustment had been the food. He came from a world where food—*real food*—was scarce. In his world, what was left of the human race subsided on canned goods scavenged from wherever canned goods could be found. Fresh meat or produce were nearly nonexistent. Unless you wanted to eat dog. There were lots of dogs, and when you're starving, dog makes a fine meal.

He ate with a savage appetite since crossing the American border. Every meal, from a gas station hotdog to this little, family diner, was an occasion to celebrate the diversity of tastes and textures food had to offer.

Of course, in his world, he had always remembered real food—the way a perfectly cooked steak melts between your teeth, the cracking sound a crisp apple makes when you chomp into it, the gut-full happiness that comes with a deep swig of cold lemonade on a hot day. These were some of the things he had missed the most in the world he came from. And now, they were the things he took the most pleasure in.

Javier's money had helped get him across the border and survive. He made his way northeast, across Texas and into Arkansas, then straight into Kentucky. From here, he planned to head north toward his final destination. He traveled by bus and slept in sad highway motels that were poorly lit and settled just off the main roads. He subsided mainly on diner food and relished every greasy bite.

He sipped his coffee, eyes darting around the small restaurant from over the brim of the cup. There were three other customers sitting spaced out at the counter, big men with big bellies hunched over their food and coffees. Probably truckers. Across from them, a long, rectangular window opened into the kitchen, where a single fry cook with a spatula moved back and forth at a dizzying pace.

Everywhere he went, Dayspring had the habit of always keeping up a fierce defense. He didn't walk into a room without gauging the exits and scanning for any places where secret threats could be hidden. His head was on a permanent swivel, pivoting quickly at every sound like a nervous bird. He often had to remind himself that this was a different world, his demeanor often made others feel tense. It helped to distract himself by reading. Sister Christina had given him a few books for his journey: *Heart of Darkness, The Time Machine,* and *Frankenstein.* But after 25 hours riding busses, he had finished the first two and was halfway through the third. Conrad was boring and Wells was pretentious. Shelley was really making him think, though.

A young waitress appeared at his side, holding a coffee pot. She smacked her gum loudly but not annoyingly. "Top you off?" She was cute and friendly with a genuine smile.

Dayspring said, "Please," then set his cup down on the end of the table.

She poured. "So where are you from?"

He hesitated for a moment, smiled. "Crooked Lake, Michigan."

Sami returned his smile. "Do you mind my asking if you're a war veteran? If you are, your first meal here is free and coffee always is. I'm sorry to make assumptions, but you kind of have the aura of a military man."

The scar on my face, Dayspring thought, and although he certainly was a soldier, he didn't feel like talking about it if the waitress were to ask questions or offer any sweeping declarations thanking him for his service. "No," he said, but offered no other explanation, which seemed to bother Sami.

"Oh," she said awkwardly, "I just thought…" She let her voice sail away. "Can I get you anything else?"

"Just a check," Dayspring said, smiling at her.

Sami walked away a little embarrassed.

As he finished the coffee, he read over the front-page stories of the *Kentucky Star*. America was at war in the Middle East. Gas prices were rising. The economy was falling. Terrorists were terrorizing. And the entire globe was getting dangerously warmer.

It would seem the world was ending.

CHAPTER 13

Labor Day—the unofficial end of summer. And everyone in Crooked Lake was out celebrating. The constant buzz of motors hummed across the water like a swarm of mosquitos. There was a sizzle in the air, the sound of laughter mixed with charred meat on backyard grills. Glasses filled with icy drinks clinked and rattled. The noises came from all directions, like an echo with no source, everywhere and nowhere, over lawns and beaches, between the waves and up and down the shore banks. Summer's last hurrah was in full swing.

But Jason Orchard was elbow deep in the motor hull of an inboard, 350 horsepower, four-cylinder ram head. In its prime, it was one of the most powerful engines on the water, but now it was a rusty bucket of gears and bolts, clinging to life by the good graces of a seventeen-year-old mechanic.

"I don't know," Jason said as he stood up, wiping his grease covered hands with a rag. Beads of sweat gathered on his brow, running in lines down the sides of his face. The sun was directly overhead, beating down on his slender, yet strong body. "I think all the cylinder heads need to be replaced, fuel line looks like shit, too."

"Well, fuck me," Douglass Bastion said with a gruff, smoker's voice. Bastion was Crooked Lake's oldest, meanest fart and owner of the Crooked Lake Marina. He sat back on the shore in a ratty lawn chair, polishing the blade of a WWII era US Marine Corp Fighting Knife, rather enjoying the small buzz he was getting from the fumes. Among other things (boat slinger and local crab-ass included), Douglass Bastion was an avid knife collector and enjoyed displaying the shiny weapons in a glass case behind the counter inside the marina. He seemed to have a knife from almost every era of American history; there was a bayonet from the Civil War and a Rambo-style, death machete from Vietnam alongside a modern, SOG commando blade that Special Forces carry in Iraq. Once, Jason caught the old man looking almost dreamily at the display case, seemingly hypnotized by the shiny, sleek weapons. Bastion, without looking at him, had sighed and said, *"Your knife is the only friend that will never betray you."* For some reason, the memory had always stuck with him.

"You sure, son?" Bastion said as he finished polishing the blade and wrapped it in a terry cloth. He set it on a table next to him and scratched the side of his head with a two-fingered hand. Just the thumb and middle digit remained on a bumpy stump of palm and knuckle, forever locked in a *fuck-you* gesture—which he frequently employed.

Jason jumped out of the boat and onto a sun bleached, wooden dock. Behind him, Crooked Lake shimmered in the hot sun, its surface twisting and turning through a mirage of brilliant colors. He didn't say a word, just stared at the old man with a *give-me-some-credit* look on his face.

"Fuck me," Bastion said again and spit. Of course, the kid was sure. Jason was his best mechanic.

"The fix, parts and labor, would probably cost about the same as a brand new motor."

"I'll tell Mr. Anderson the good news."

"This 350 is too much engine for a fifteen footer

anyway. He could save a bundle by downsizing. We have a few 270s in stock."

"Shut your mouth kid," Bastion said. "The 350s bring a better profit. If Mr. Anderson needs to compensate for his tiny cock with a 350, then he gets a goddamn 350." He hacked up another wad of snot.

Jason laughed. "Yes sir."

Douglas Bastion could be a grade-A pain in the ass, but Jason appreciated his crotchety attitude with half amusement, half respect. And he definitely appreciated a good paying job where he could work shoeless and shirtless in the sun. Besides, Jason figured that someday he'd be the lonely, old fart sitting at the end of the dock, angry at the world. Plus, there was a rumor on the water that the old coot had spent six months in a North Korean POW camp; Jason believed this to be true. Working late one night, he had stumbled across an old shoebox in the office filled with photographs and war medals. One of them was the Navy Cross. Whatever Bastion's attitude toward the changing world was, he had earned it.

The old man coughed up another gob of phlegm.

Jason was kneeling on the dock, reaching down and scooping handfuls of water onto his neck and back. He looked toward the hacking, old man and said, "You okay?"

"Don't ever start smoking, kid," Bastion said as he pulled a pack of cigarettes out of his front pocket. He shook one loose, then pinched the filter between the thumb and middle finger of his mangled hand.

"Ahoy, matey!" a young woman's voice cut across the water. It was Haley. She stood behind the pilot wheel of a pontoon boat, coming in slowly, about twenty yards from the docks. She wore a tiny red bikini that caught Jason's (and Bastion's) attention immediately.

Bastion whistled just loud enough for only Jason to hear and winked at him. "Looks like your girlfriend wants you," he said with a devilish grin only a half-crazy or half-senile old man could get away with.

"She's not my girlfriend," Jason retorted. "She's my best friend's *kind-of* girlfriend and my *kind-of* girlfriend's best friend."

Bastion blew out a ring of smoke and raised a confused eyebrow. "Whatever. I had lots of *kind-of* girlfriends in Korea and a *kind-of* wife back home."

"Can you talk?" Haley yelled from the boat.

Jason turned to Bastion.

"Go ahead, son, I wouldn't leave a gal like that waiting." This was followed by another half-creepy smirk.

Jason threw the rag down and dove into the water. All the slips were full, so he had to swim out to Haley's boat.

"I tried calling," she said as Jason reached the port side. He remained in the water, holding onto the edge of the deck and looking up.

"Yeah, my battery is dead." This was a lie. He didn't want to tell her he couldn't afford a new month's service plan yet—not if he wanted to buy groceries for home. "What's up?"

Haley leaned against the rail and stood over him. Her body was directly in front of the sun, outlining her figure in a thin, golden fire as if a holy light was glowing through her pores. And suddenly, something strange occurred to Jason as he looked up at her. For the first time ever, he began to notice just how beautiful (*sexy*) she really was. Her small, red bikini left little to a teenage boy's imagination. By any common standard of conventional (and shallow) judgement, Haley was a total knockout. Of course, she had probably looked like this all summer, maybe even all year. However, she was his oldest friend, and whatever sexual attraction he may have had toward her was buried beneath a platonic relationship that started far before puberty (and certainly before those two very plump and firm looking breasts grew on her chest that he couldn't tear his eyes away from).

"I think something's wrong with Adam," she said.

Something was definitely wrong with Adam. He rarely

returned calls, and when he did, he always said he was busy *"working on something"*—whatever the hell that meant. He never seemed to want to hang out anymore. Jason imagined him spending all his time in his basement, playing with his glorified chemistry set or sitting in front of his mission control center, talking to Lazarus or other hacker nerds.

"Yeah, I know," Jason said, tearing his gaze away from Haley's breasts for only a few seconds before they landed right back between them.

"What do you think it is?"

"I don't know."

Haley bit her lip—*God, she was cute when she did that.* Jason shook his head as if to scramble the weird, new thoughts and sensations he was impulsively having about her.

"Does he have a girlfriend? I mean, is he like, talking to, or seeing anyone else?" she asked.

Jason thought about Lazarus and Adam's assertion that *"all hacker chicks are hot."* Truth be told, if Adam was having some weird, romantic relationship with a fellow computer nerd he's never met, Jason wouldn't be all that surprised. "No, I don't think so. I actually haven't talked to him in a while."

"I don't believe you."

"Haley---"

"But that doesn't matter. I think him and I are done, even though we never really got started."

"Yeah, I know what you mean," Jason said. And he knew *exactly* what she meant. His quasi relationship with Emma was running out of gas. With his father out of work (again), Jason had been taking on more hours at the marina as well as his other part time job for Fenton Construction. He barely had time to see Emma or any of his friends anymore, and consequently, there was a growing separation between all of them. His friendship with Haley was the only one that appeared immune to these effects.

"Are you okay?" Haley asked.

"Yeah, life's just been really busy lately."

"I don't pay you to flirt with pretty girls!" Bastion shouted from the shore.

"Shut up you old geezer!" Jason yelled over his shoulder.

Haley laughed. There was a long moment of awkward silence.

"Do you..." Haley began, then bit her lip again. "Can you hang out tonight or tomorrow? I need to do something fun."

A billion confusing (but certainly not unpleasant) thoughts raced through Jason's mind. "Sure. I gotta work late tonight, but tomorrow I'm free. I could use some fun, too."

"Then it's a date," Haley said with a cheerful smile.

"I'll call you from my house phone," Jason said— *wait... did she say date?*

"Okay, see you later," Haley turned back to the pilot's wheel.

Jason pushed off and began backstroking toward the marina docks.

"By the way," Haley yelled after him as she settled behind the pilot's wheel again, "my eyes are up here." She used two fingers to indicate where her eyes were.

Jason choked on some water, embarrassed, but Haley was still smiling.

"See you tomorrow," she said.

"See you tomorrow."

He swam back to the dock, wondering how fate would have changed if he would have stolen a kiss from *her* the night of the PFI challenge.

CHAPTER 14

In another world—in another time—human beings are an endangered species. They hide away in small bands, scavenging for survival, living underground and in the shadows. They never keep in one place for too long, always on the move in order to avoid the enemy. These nomadic humans are a threat to the new world order, and so they are hunted.

A new species has emerged as the dominant force on the planet. Thanks to a revolutionary technology known as the Lazarus Vaccine and an AI software program called the Queen, Homo sapiens *have become* Homo superiors. *It is the next phase of human evolution, the inevitable hybridization of biology and technology, a progressive step toward species unity. But there are some who call it blasphemy, unnatural, an impediment on nature's design.*

Those who refuse to evolve, who choose to remain human, are laughed at and ridiculed. But eventually this scorn turns to hate, and the hate becomes fear as it so often has throughout history. Fear leads to war. Homo superiors *win the war as easily a boot crushing an anthill. All surviving humans are marked as gene-traitors and targeted for extinction.*

The world is decimated by the carnage that takes place in the pursuit of this human genocide. Death squads sweep across the land; entire legions of Homo superior *foot soldiers are sent out to complete the holocaust. The few remaining humans go into hiding. Some will give in and join the enemy. But there are those who, even in the face of painful death, refuse to surrender.*

They decide to fight back, to risk everything for no other reason other than to retain their humanity and the freedom and dignity that comes with it.

They call themselves The Vitruvian Order. And they are a symbol of rebellion and hope.

Joseph Dayspring stared at the sketch. He had doodled it on the inside publication page of *Frankenstein* as the bus bounced along the highway, its engine coughing and spitting black plumes of smoke. It was a symbol worn on the armbands of human resistance fighters and often spray painted as graffiti on top of Lazarus propaganda posters with the word *"RESIST"* beneath it. It was supposed to represent Leonardo da Vinci's *Vitruvian Man*, the fifteenth century sketch that merges the ideal human proportions with geometry. It was the artist's attempt to relate man to nature; da Vinci believed the biological systems of the body were analogous to the physical systems of the universe. *Vitruvian Man* was his attempt to celebrate *nature's* design. No one knew who first adorned this symbol, but its message was clear: Fuck the Lazarus Vaccine.

From the diner in Kentucky, he had hopped a train headed for Indianapolis and from there got on a bus bound for Lansing, Michigan. Once there he could buy a car, cheap, with cash—and then he could complete what he came to this world to do.

Dayspring closed the book and leaned back, watching the landscape zip by through a dirty window. The highway panorama stretched on forever, rolling over fields, across meadows, through herds of cows and horses, between yellowed rows of corn stalks. It was all just like he remembered. It even smelled good; everything was alive and fresh.

This made him think about the world he had come from. In that world, nothing was fresh; the air constantly stank like burning garbage. There wasn't much color left on the landscapes; the greens and blues of a healthy, living planet were faded and rotting, as if locked in a perpetual, gray winter. But that's what endless war will do.

Lazarus was responsible for all of it.

But Dayspring could stop it.

The bus swerved, and a newspaper slipped off a man's briefcase that was resting on the seat across the aisle from Dayspring. He reached down to pick it up for the man, but while exchanging the paper, he took special notice of the bold headline on the front page. It was a *USA Today* and the giant black caption read: "THE VACCINATION DEBATE." He held his grip for an awkward second too long.

"Thank you," the man said slightly perplexed.

Dayspring snapped out of the short trance, released the paper, and said, "You're welcome."

He leaned back and returned his gaze to the passing scenery. In Dayspring's world, the Lazarus Vaccine was a biotech, saline-based solution comprised of billions of microscopic nanobots made out of a material known as bactainium—a living metal with the properties of a bacteria. Each of these nanobots received programming updates from a global AI software system called the Queen that was broadcasted all over the Earth by a network of satellites. Lazarus was injected into the bloodstream and interfaced with the brain's neural network. These nanobots had the ability to seek and destroy *any* dangerous aberrations the brain detects within the body that can harm living tissue, from the common cold to the most devastating cancers and everything between. It could also physically repair damaged tissue. The bactainium that was the Lazarus Vaccine could reproduce via binary fission—it could make more of itself and perfectly replicate any biological element of the human body. It could do everything from healing a paper cut and replacing a failed kidney, to rebuilding your ribs, lungs, and heart after a gunshot wound to the chest. Lazarus propaganda posters and advertisements contained taglines and slogans such as, "NEVER GET SICK. NEVER GET HURT. NEVER DIE. GET VACCINATED TODAY." It was a cure for *everything,* and everyone wanted it.

Walking around with Lazarus in your body became the new normal for the entire world.

This was the beginning of the end for the human race because the Queen program contained a secret directive, a Trojan horse. It was a hidden line of coding: full bio-tech integration with the physical hosts. Against their will, people's brains and neural systems were merged with the Queen's global AI network, and humanity's final stage of evolution was at last complete—joining together as a collective consciousness—a hive. This was done to protect the hosts. The Queen had identified the individual human mind as the most dangerous threat it faced. Assimilating humanity into a collective consciousness was ideal because nature had proven several times over that creatures, like insects, who live and work in hives, are able to flourish despite the most adverse fluctuations in their environments.

Dayspring and other members of their rebellion who had refused the Lazarus Vaccine were branded as a threat to the new world order. And the Queen would stop at nothing to carry out its primary directive—eliminate all threats.

Dayspring cracked his window open; it would only budge a few inches but that was enough. Cold air poured in and wrapped around his face. It felt good, like a tiny shot of icy adrenaline. He tried to close his eyes and not think about anything. He wanted a clear head, but all this time riding busses was too much time to think.

Could he complete his mission?

Of course.

Completing the mission wasn't the hard part.

Living with himself afterward was.

Impossible to empty his head, Dayspring opened the book to a dog-eared page. It was time to check in and see how the good Dr. Frankenstein was doing.

CHAPTER 15

Jason and Haley walked down the Crooked Lake boardwalk, holding milkshakes from the Shack in Styrofoam to-go cups. The sun was half-visible above the western horizon, and to the east, a pair of lonely stars twinkled in the violet sky. With it being the day after Labor Day, the lake was nearly empty except for a few small boats gently rocking in the soft waves. The summer tourist were already starting to thin out. Yesterday, they would have been shouldering their way past families waltzing along, looking into storefront windows, but now they had almost the entire boardwalk to themselves.

They had eaten dinner at the Shack, where Jason used the prize from his PFI challenge: a free meal for him and a guest (though, he'd always imagined his guest would be Emma). They had cheeseburgers and waffle fries, and as usual, the food was fantastic, but something about the dinner seemed wrong. It felt like a date. Was it a date? Jason did *kind of* pay for it, and Haley had even called it a date (*had she been joking?*). No, it couldn't be a date because they weren't *dating*. They were just two close friends spending time together. Nothing wrong with that…

But still, he couldn't shake the feeling that they were

doing something inappropriate.

Over the last couple of years, it has always been a foursome—Jason, Adam, Haley, and Emma. And this troupe had developed with a certain dynamic: Jason and Adam were best friends; Haley and Emma were best friends, and over the past summer it became evident that Jason and Emma were building a romance, as were Adam and Haley (albeit at a much slower pace). But before all of this—before Adam and his mother moved to town, before Haley and Emma became friends, and certainly during a time before boys and girls understood their gender differences and the behavioral norms that come with them—it was a very young Jason and Haley who had been best friends.

During this time that now seemed like an alternate reality, Jason and Haley had shared an innocence and belief in magic that all little kids should possess. They weren't worried about boyfriends and girlfriends or any other social circumstances. They spent their summers exploring the woods behind the bluffs, walking across fallen trees like balance beams, kicking over stones in search of slimy, gross things. They had imaginary adventures where they slayed imaginary dragons or saved the world from imaginary space invaders. When they got hungry, they satisfied their sweet-tooths by taking liberal handfuls of fudge from the free sample tray at the Crooked Lake Candy Shop while the owner, Mrs. Hubbard, would slap their hands and pretend to be annoyed (there was always a secret smile on her wrinkly, old face). She would shoo them out of the store, swiping at their heels with a broom she kept behind the counter. After their candy fix, they'd skip stones down by the water's edge, bragging about whose went the farthest or had the most height. Sometimes, Douglass Bastion would walk down from the marina with fishing poles and tackle, and the three of them would cast lines together. If they were lucky, Jason would bring home a couple of walleyes or perch for dinner.

Bastion taught the kids how to gut and clean a fish and said all you had to do was dust the fillet in some powdered potatoes and drop it in a pan of hot, shallow oil with a pinch of salt. Three minutes on a side and you had a hell of a good meal. He called it the poor man's shore lunch.

Back in those days, Haley had been a tomboy, a real Scout Finch who didn't mind playing in the mud or getting fish guts in her hair.

But she certainly wasn't a tomboy anymore. Jason thought about the tiny bikini she had been wearing yesterday. At some recent point in history, this Scout Finch became a young woman—the pigtails were let out and the overalls replaced with Daisy Duke shorts. Jason had completely missed this transition, but now it walked next to him in all its blazing glory. Haley was beautiful, even sexy, and in the back of his mind, some very confusing and conflicting emotions were developing.

They were nearing the end of the boardwalk and stood at the rail overlooking the south end of the lake. Haley suddenly snorted and spit a wad of snot into the sand far below them (so maybe there was still a little tomboy left in her, after all).

"Sorry." She giggled. "That was gross."

Jason then leaned over the rail, snorted, and spit as well, came up smiling. "Mine had better distance," he said. They stood a little closer together.

"I was never able to beat you in a spitting contest."

A soft breeze fluttered Haley's hair, and Jason got a big whiff of her strawberry conditioner, stirring those confusing emotions into a rolling boil. The urge to hold her hand, to have some sort of physical contact, was overwhelming.

"Come here," Haley said taking her phone out of her pocket. She held out her hand, and the two leaned in close together, faces touching. Jason put his arm around her waist and held on. "Smile," she ordered through a wide grin and snapped a selfie.

They looked at the picture together. Two beaming faces pressed cheek-to-cheek with the dark green water of Crooked Lake behind them. Somewhere within their warm grins were the children they used to be, the kids who never thought they would grow up and could play Peter Pan forever. There were times when Jason longed for that world so much it hurt his heart. It occurred to him that he was the one who was more like Scout Finch. Once he was just an innocent kid without a care in the world, happy and content to plod along that way forever. Then one-day reality set in: sorry kid, your mom didn't want you and your dad is a loser alcoholic who probably doesn't want you either. Jason could not remember exactly when this bubble-burst moment occurred, but it didn't matter. It had happened to him just like it happens to every other kid in the world.

"Umm…" Jason began, "you're not going to put that on Instagram or Twitter or anything, right?" He was thinking about how Adam and Emma would react. Despite the fact that he was having a wonderful evening, it still felt like they were doing something wrong.

"No," Haley said in clear agreement. "This is just for me."

They continued walking, Jason still fighting the urge to hold her hand. Leaving the bright businesses of the boardwalk behind, they arrived at a wooden staircase that descended into a sandy alcove. A well-trodden path surrounded on both sides by tall trees and vegetation led toward the beach. It was darker here, the trail cloaked in shadows, the only source of light emanating from a weak street lamp that hung above a small ATM kiosk at the end of the boardwalk. The sun was nearly set, only a thin sliver of orange clung to the horizon, the sky a rich navy blue, full of tiny yellow stars.

They paused at the center of the path and faced each other. The dim light from the ATM floated over them like a pale fog. Crickets chirped from either side of the trail.

Neither one of them made the first move. They leaned in at the same time and kissed. It was just simple peck with a small electric shock, which they both quickly pulled back from. But slowly they melted back together, mouths open, hands wrapped around each other.

The kiss ended with big smiles. "Let's go to the beach," Haley said.

They turned and headed down the path holding hands.

CHAPTER 16

There are several species in nature that undergo a metamorphosis: June bugs, frogs, dragonflies, and most recognizably, the caterpillar. These creatures begin life as something entirely different from the way they end it. Their metamorphosis includes a dramatic physical change that is usually the result of physiological developments taking place during a state of hibernation. The caterpillar wraps itself into a chrysalis cocoon with its own silk excretions. Within this shell, it digests its own body and is nearly liquefied as cells are restructured and reprogrammed. About fourteen days later, a butterfly emerges from the cocoon and flies away.

But does the butterfly remember being a caterpillar? As it sucks nectar from floral, does it realize it once had mandibles and feasted on leaves? As it soars through the sky, does it hark back to the time it crawled upon the soil with a bulbous worm-body?

These were the things Adam Evans was thinking about as he stared at his own reflection in the bathroom mirror. The butterfly is such a beautiful creature. It is the stateliest of all lower lifeforms. Born toiling in the dirt, its metamorphosis allows it to glide through the blue heavens on majestic wings with a rich tapestry of color unrivaled by any work of art conceived by man. Its transformation is nothing short of miraculous.

He decided it would be cruel if the butterfly remembered its life as a caterpillar.

Adam felt himself undergoing his own metamorphosis. But unfortunately, he did not have the luxury of forgetting his pre-metamorphosis life. Ever since his mother's cancer diagnosis, Adam had spent most of his time in his room, trying his best to distract himself with the things that once brought him joy: science experiments, research and learning, building robots, hanging out online with other hackers. But there was very little solace in any of these things anymore.

His mother would be dead soon. The cancer inside her brain was growing. Last week the doctors confirmed that the chemotherapy and radiation treatments were not working. This was really when Adam's metamorphosis began. With his mom checked into in-patient care at the University of Michigan Hospital, Adam hid from the outside world, ignoring his friends and schoolwork, and focused all of his energies into the one fantastic feat that had vexed medical doctors and scientists for decades: a cure for cancer.

He studied religiously, like a Buddhist monk locked in sanctuary. He read every new study from all the major medical journals concerning cancer treatments and therapies. He hacked into the Mayo Clinic records to read copyrighted material not yet publicly released. He even created a fake identification with false (but flawless) credentials in order to correspond with Russian and Chinese scientists whose research was not as *inhibited* as it was in the United States. He skirted all other responsibilities in order to fully invest himself in saving his mother's life. The electron microscope he'd hoped to have finished by Christmas was a pile of metal parts gathering dust, the article he was writing on nanotechnology completely ignored, and his two lab mice, Kirk and Spock, dead—he'd forgotten to feed them.

A small price to pay in pursuit of medicine's Holy Grail.

Was it naïve to think a seventeen-year-old kid could cure cancer?

Maybe…

Was he going to fail?

Maybe not.

There were doubts, but Adam Evans ignored these in much the same way good alcoholics ignore a drinking problem—complete and utter self-denial. In many ways, he was exhibiting the classic symptoms of substance addiction. He abandoned his responsibilities, disregarded his friends, lied about his behavior, neglected to eat or get proper rest, and just outright refused to face a painful and brutal reality: his mother was dying.

There were a lot of terrible realities in the world, but this was the one, unutterable truth he would not accept. Simply put: the world was a fucked up shit hole where people are robbed, beaten, raped, and murdered every day; children starve to death while others throw away a half-eaten pizza, and people get sick and die from diseases that, with the right funding and political backing, could have been cured decades ago. He could accept all of these injustices, but not this. His mother was *not* going to die.

So what if he was naïve? He was certain that Galileo and Copernicus were also considered naïve in their time, as were Alexander Fleming and Jonas Salk, who gave the world penicillin and the polio vaccine respectively. Naivety was just a label the cautions and the frightened used for the brave and the bold.

Adam continued to stare at his reflection, his right hand still gripping the electric razor, the sink bowl full of fluffy, brown hair. He had shaved his head down to the scalp. His skull was pale and dotted with stubble, like an old man's five o'clock shadow. He did not recognize himself, but it wasn't just his bare scalp. His eyes were dark and puffy, his skin creased and cracked from dehydration and lack of vitamin D. He looked older, meaner, like a mangy dog who no one loves, abandoned to the alleys. His mom would be furious that he shaved his head. She, like all the other women in his life, adored his thick, curly locks, but he didn't care. She had lost her once-beautiful hair in little clumps that he found in the corners of the home like dead mice. He could claim he did it as an act of commiseration.

But this was also part of his metamorphosis. Without his wavy hair, he instantly looked ten years older. Gone was his youthful charm and innocence, gone was his eager glow and folksiness, gone was boyish allure and puppy dog smile. He was a junkyard dog now, angry, hungry, ready to chomp down on the jugular or balls of anyone who dares trespass into his territory.

From the bathroom, he heard his computer station chime—the familiar ring signaling that he had a message on the Black Forest program. He took one final glance at the mirror, nodding to his own reflection with a look of approval; he liked being the junkyard dog. For the first time in his life, he felt powerful and not because he was a genius; the strength he felt now was raw and primal.

The basement was dark and full of shadows, but the computer monitors gave off enough soft light that the room had a pale, bluish glow. Adam sat down at his mission control center. The message was from Lazarus. She had been laying on her *hackers-versus-the world* rhetoric a lot lately, sending him messages and links full of conspiracy theories. She claimed something big was happening in the world, something that would have a diverse effect on finance, politics, military, healthcare—pretty much everything. She claimed it would change the social landscape and world power dynamic forever. For his own protection, she wouldn't reveal too much yet, but promised very soon that she would grant him *full* viewing access to the file being stored on the private server and that would explain everything. The partial access she had granted him indicated that it had something to do with big pharmaceutical companies and a new drug. He opened the message.

> LAZARUS: There's something you need to see. Click on the <u>link</u>.
> PURPLE TURTLE: I'm not in the mood tonight.
> LAZARUS: Your friends betray you.
> PURPLE TURTLE: How do you even know who my friends are?
> LAZARUS: I know more about you than you think, Adam Evans.
> PURPLE TURTLE: How do you know my real name?
> LAZARUS: Because I'm just that good, Adam, resident of 16144 Silvercrest Drive, Crooked Lake, Michigan. But forget about that right now. I need your help for what's coming, and I need you thinking clearly. No distractions.
> PURPLE TURTLE: Too late for that. And what the hell does that mean?
> LAZARUS: Click on the <u>link</u>.

Adam floated his cursor over the link but hesitated. The mysterious Lazarus claimed to be the most talented hacker on the planet. But any computer nerd with a laptop and high speed internet could complete mid-grade hack jobs, and they all bragged about their techno-promiscuity. Even Adam was guilty of misappropriating his hacking prowess at times. But Lazarus knew his real name and street address, this meant she was able to backtrack through his false IP addresses and break his firewalls, a considerable feat.

PURPLE TURTLE: No. I don't want any part of this, never did.

LAZARUS: Too bad. You're already in too deep; you built a server that's currently storing stolen FBI and NSA materials. Besides, I know everything about you Adam; I've been inside your computer. I know how you believe reason and logic should rule over all the world. I know how it tears you up inside knowing how totally fucked up our society is—the disease, the corruption, the greed that continues to go unchecked. I know how angry it makes you feel—the suppression of science, of research, of truly enlightened thought. I know how every time you see a story in the news that subdues the advance of science—NASA losing funding, the Catholic church lobbying against stem cell research, big oil companies crushing renewable energy programs, politicians denying climate change—that it infuriates you beyond words can express. I also know you're a fighter. You won't turn your back on science or the world.

Lazarus clearly had unparalleled hacking skills, but still, Adam had doubts. And yet, if anyone was able to discover the secret conspiracies she claimed to have, it was her. And the language she used, it appealed to Adam's ego. It made him feel important and special. Despite his protest—and her violations of privacy—Lazarus really did seem to understand him (perhaps even better than his closest friends). He had always dreamed of doing something amazing in order to help fix a world he viewed as broken and diseased. Maybe this could be his chance.

> PURPLE TURTLE: Good speech, but
> you don't know anything about me.
> LAZARUS: I know your mother doesn't
> have long to live.
> PURPLE TURTLE: We're done. Bye.
> LAZARUS: Wait! Just click on the link!

Adam nearly swept all three of his computer monitors off his desk but stopped himself. There was no doubting Lazarus' hacking abilities, and if the things she said were true, than his life might actually be in danger. She claimed the man with the scar was trying to locate Purple Turtle. She said he was a mercenary, a professional soldier-for-hire who is contracted to *fix* problems. And right now, the problem was Lazarus, Purple Turtle, and any other highly skilled hacker with a conscience. This man, she said, had no identity, no national or political affiliation, and no prescribed ideology—which is exactly what made him so dangerous and difficult to stop. FBI, CIA, NSA, even the Kremlin, there were no governments or law enforcement agencies equipped to find him or bring him down. There were life-changing secrets hidden deep within the databases and network servers of the world's most powerful institutions, and these groups knew only the most exceptional hackers on the planet could expose them. This man, the man with the scar, was being sent to neutralize the threat against them.

And Adam knew that *neutralize* in cryptic-speak meant eliminate—kill.

> PURPLE TURTLE: Remind me again
> why I should trust you?
> LAZARUS: Just click on the link.
> PURPLE TURTLE: What is it?
> LAZARUS: Consider it proof that right

now, I'm your only friend, and you need
to trust me.

Adam mulled it over once more, his cursor floating
over the blue hyperlink. Finally, he clicked it. Two small
windows appeared on his screen and began downloading.
They were photographs.

The first was an image of Jason and Haley, a selfie,
clearly lifted from Haley's iPhone. They were smiling and
happy, faces side-by-side. Maybe a little too close, but
innocent enough. The second, however, revealed
something that tunneled a hole into Adam's chest. The
image was a bit grainy; it looked like a screen grab from a
security camera with a time stamp in the bottom corner:
09/04/2018 – 20:06 p.m. Today's date, about an hour ago.
It showed Jason and Haley kissing. Passionately kissing. In
the style of the French.

A quiet breath escaped Adam as the tunnel in his chest
widened. He studied the image and instantly recognized
where they were. The south end of the boardwalk.

> PURPLE TURTLE: Why did you show
> this to me?
> LAZARUS: Because at every level of your
> life you need to know who you can trust.
> These two will sell you out to the man
> with the scar. I know rats when I see
> them.
> PURPLE TURTLE: What do you mean
> by that?
> LAZARUS: Right now, all he—the man
> with the scar—knows is that a very skilled
> hacker named Purple Turtle is operating
> within a certain radius of Crooked Lake,
> Michigan. He doesn't know who you
> actually are or your exact location. You've
> always been very good at covering your

tracks and using false IP addresses. But he will be able to find you just like I did. Especially when he locates Jason Orchard.

PURPLE TURTLE: And how will he know Jason Orchard is friends with Purple Turtle?

LAZARUS: The same way I did. You use a lot of the same false IP addresses for your hacks. Like the one you used to change Jason's grades at Crooked Lake High school. He'll figure this out; he'll find Jason, and Jason will give you up.

A million confusing emotions swam in Adam's head. His mom's cancer, Lazarus' conspiracy theories, the threat of some mysterious assassin with a scar, and now, Jason and Haley's betrayal. It was too much to focus on right now, so he concentrated on the only thing he could immediately reach out and touch—the treachery of his so-called friends. On one level, he knew his relationship with Haley had already burned itself out even before it began and that his friendship with Jason had been strained lately. But still, the betrayal hurt like a salted knife.

LAZARUS: I know what you are feeling. That rage inside of you. It feels like fire in your stomach, a red-hot anger and hatred that is consuming you. The people you love have betrayed you. And they will do it again, but next time the stakes will be much higher.

PURPLE TURTLE: What do you suggest I do?

Lazarus did not respond for a long time as if the mysterious person behind the keyboard was thinking, contemplating. When the reply finally came, it brought an icy chill to the back of Adam's neck.

> LAZARUS: Your mother possesses a Taurus .738. It's in a locked case under her bed. The combination is 93718.

The chill in the room grew colder and darker. *What exactly was Lazarus suggesting?*

Stupid question. He knew exactly what she was suggesting. And it was causing some very weird feelings inside of him.

He also knew about his mother's gun. She had bought it a few years ago and gotten her concealed-carry permit after a drunk man accosted her on campus at U of M. But Dr. Evans could never actually bring herself to carry the weapon around. It had always remained locked in its case.

He thought for a moment about what to do, what path to take. The brilliant gears in his mind turned through several possible scenarios, calculating all possible outcomes and repercussions with a sense of carefully tuned scientific logic.

Unfortunately, the junkyard dog in him was barking too loud, and this logic was drowned in a sea of violent, guttural snarling.

"Fuck this," he said and grabbed his car keys.

He had to deal with a trespasser.

But before leaving, he went into his mother's bedroom and retrieved a small black case from under the bed.

CHAPTER 17

Jason and Haley walked along the beach, casting long shadows in the white sand. They were just out of reach of the lapping waves and left shallow footprints that would eventually be washed away. They talked about the past and how fast time seems to go by. Yesterday they were kids swiping fudge from the Crooked Lake Candy Shop, and today they were strolling under a starry night on the edge of adulthood.

They circled back toward the north end of the boardwalk, and as they proceeded, Jason felt a powerful urge to take Haley in his arms and kiss her again. But now wasn't the time; talking was enough.

"Do you ever think about your mom?" Haley asked as they reached another set of steps. They paused at the bottom and faced each other. She was the only person in the world who had ever discussed this topic with him. He remembered a long time ago when she had asked him a similar question on the playground. *"Why don't you have a mommy?"* the younger Haley had said to the younger Jason as she twirled one of her pigtails around a finger. An innocent question from an innocent child. But now they were grown up—almost—and the question and circumstances had evolved.

"No," Jason said matter-of-factly. "I don't."

Haley knew Jason wanted everyone to think he was tough—and he was—but she also remembered a not-so-tough, little third-grader who had hid behind the dumpster during recess and cried after being teased for wearing the same shirt three days in a row. She knew that sometimes Jason put on masks—a tough-guy mask, a silly-guy mask, a slacker/stoner mask—but these costumed attitudes were merely a cleverly concocted smoke screen that concealed a lot of hidden pain. And sometimes hidden ambitions.

"Not at all?"

"Nope," he said as they began ascending the steps.

"Oh."

"You know, I don't even know what she looks like."

"You don't have any pictures?"

"My dad got rid of them all. I asked him once, and he said he threw them all away after she," his voice deepened into an exaggerated, drunken twang, *"run off and left me to raise a goddamn kid all by myself."*

Haley wasn't sure if the impression was supposed to be funny or sad. She didn't know much about the relationship between Jason and his father except that there really wasn't a relationship. The only things she knew about Marcus Orchard were gained from what her parents gossiped about when they thought she wasn't listening—that he was a lonely and sad drunk, which she guessed was better than a lonely and *angry* drunk.

"Your father really said that to you?" Haley asked.

"Yes. And *father* isn't the right word. He's more of a sperm-donor who maintains legal guardianship on paper." Jason was smiling, but she detected small traces of sadness in his voice and eyes. Whatever anguish he suffered as a child was well concealed.

They reached the top of the steps and continued walking until they stood in front of the Crooked Lake Candy Shop. The massive storefront window was dark, same as all the other business fronts along the empty boardwalk. It was like being alone in an abandoned, old west ghost town, and as the breeze kicked around her hair, Haley half expected to see a tumbleweed come rolling across the walkway.

"I'm sorry," she said.

"It's okay." Jason waved away her sympathy. "In a year we're going to graduate, and then all of this," he held his hands up, motioning into the darkness, his eyes searching for something that might be hidden in the shadows, "will be over."

"One more year," Haley said inching closer to him.

"One more year."

"We better make it count."

They locked eyes, and everything around them seemed to melt away. They were alone on the boardwalk, alone in the entire universe, just the two of them and the wind.

But Jason and Haley were not as alone as they thought. From behind the corner edge of the candy shop, well concealed by the shadows of the skinny alley, Adam Evans was watching them. In the wide pocket of his hooded sweatshirt, he gripped the cold, steel handle of his mother's gun.

The Junkyard dog was still psychotically barking in his head, snapping its teeth, but this rancorous noise was becoming sluggish and softer, leisurely fading away like the end of a song. The idea of shooting Jason right in his treacherous face was still satisfying, but in the darkness of the alley, Adam could feel his anger slowly abating, his rational mind gradually regaining control.

He breathed deeply as he pulled the gun out of his pocket, holding it with a not-so-steady grip, index finger trembling on top of the trigger. The power this little, metal contraption granted was extremely intoxicating. He took another long breath.

It is so easy to take a life.

So very, very easy.

This was it, Jason suddenly realized. *Now* was the perfect time for another kiss. He leaned in, lips about to touch---

"You asshole."

Adam's voice was hollow and fierce, and sounded like an arrow whistling through the night. He came out of the shadows beside the candy shop and stood before them with his fists buried deep in the front pockets of his hooded sweatshirt.

"Adam?" Jason said with calm shock. He barely recognized his friend. His clothes were unkempt and dirty, there were dark bags under his puffy eyes, and his face looked tired and thin. Adam stepped forward and in a sudden, fierce movement, tore his hands out from the pockets of his hoodie.

He was holding a small, dark object in one hand.

A cell phone.

A little more in control of himself, Adam had hidden his mother's gun behind the alley dumpster of the candy shop, his rational mind having won back control from the junkyard dog (for now). He took another step forward and pulled back his hood as if he was removing a mask, exposing his stubbly, white scalp. Jason and Haley were visibly startled. His signature, floppy hair and thick curls gone, shaved down to the bare skin.

"What's the matter?" Adam asked. "You guys don't like my new haircut?" His eyes shifted between them like a man studying his opponents in a game of five-card draw.

"Adam, are you okay?" Haley said.

"Don't even pretend like you care about me."

"Adam, you don't look so---" But Jason wouldn't finish.

With surprising speed and intensity, Adam lurched forward and punched his best friend on the side of the face. Jason staggered back against the glass wall of the candy shop; Haley let out a quick shriek.

"What the hell?" Jason demanded, holding his fingers to a skinny gash on his cheekbone, a tiny trickle of blood running down his face.

"You're supposed to be my best friend!"

"I *am* your best friend."

"Then why did you kiss my girlfriend?"

"I'm not your girlfriend," Haley snapped.

"Were you spying on us?" Jason asked, wiping away blood with the back of his hand.

"We didn't do anything wrong," Haley said. "We were just taking a walk together along the---"

"Save it!" Adam held out his phone so they could see the screen.

It was the digital screen grab from the security footage Lazarus had sent him.

"How did you...?" Haley began.

But Jason figured it out immediately. The south end of the boardwalk, the ATM kiosk that *definitely* had a security camera. "How the hell did you even know where we were?" he asked.

Adam had no answer. He looked back and forth between his friends. In the back of his mind, the junkyard dog was barking again. He found himself wishing he still had the gun—the cold handle would feel reassuring in his hands. "Fuck this," he said. "I don't need you. I don't need either of you." He looked Jason squarely in the eyes. "You're just a loser anyway." His voice was lofty and condescending. "A loser stoner who will probably be serving me french-fries at a drive-through someday. Yeah, you act all tough, like you're *Mr. Cool* with your nonchalant, I-don't-give-a-fuck attitude about everything. But deep down, I know who you really are. You really do care, you want to do better, you want to go to college, you want to do more with your life, but you can't because you have loser in your blood. You're a loser and a disappointment to your family; that's why your mom left and your dad drinks."

For a long time, the entire universe held its breath.

"Are you done?" Jason said.

Haley was speechless. This was *not* Adam. It had to be an alien or robot—*or something*. But it couldn't be Adam.

"No," Adam said. "I have just one question for you."

Jason prepared himself for another verbal assault.

"Does it hurt?" he asked. "Not having a mother?"

"Sometimes," Jason whispered.

Adam smiled. "Good."

The brutal sting of that last comment hung in the air for a long, still moment, and then…

Jason reached back and slugged Adam on the side of his jaw, sending him spiraling to the ground with a loud thud. "Oh my God, Adam, I'm so sorry," he instantly said.

Adam struggled to his hands and knees, taking a moment to shake his head clear. Jason cautiously approached him as if he were a wounded animal that might violently lash out.

"Adam, I'm sorry," Jason said again as he inched closer.

Adam slowly turned his head; a generous stream of blood was cascading down his face and chin, gathering in a small puddle beneath him.

Haley watched in horror as Adam seemed to be moving something around in his mouth as if he were sucking on a mint. He spit, and a single tooth rattled across the boards like a game die, colliding with her open-toe sandals. He smiled, a grotesque, blood covered Joker-grin with a gaping black hole where his missing tooth used to be. There was a fiery rage in his eyes no one would have ever thought Adam Evans capable of, a madness that pulsed within his tiny black pupils.

For Adam Evans, the fight between his rational mind

and the junkyard dog was over. And the only thing he now heard in his head was monstrous, blood thirsty barking. He thought about his mother's gun again. It was stupid to have put it down. Stupid.

Haley tried to scream, but everything happened so quickly. Adam sprang up from the ground like the junkyard dog he had become, driving his shoulder into Jason's chest. The incredible force sent them tumbling backward and upside down, a tangled mass of arms and legs. They hit the front glass wall of the candy shop and continued straight through with a piercing, electronic crash. Shattered glass exploded onto the tile floor, the entire storefront window decimated.

At the exact same time, the lights in the store turned on and an ear-splitting alarm rang out into the cool night.

CHAPTER 18

His drinkin' buddies called him Marco, as in *Marc-O,* or Marcus Orchard. It was just something that started one evening when he was drunk, and like a lot of things that happened when he was drunk, he could not remember it too well. One day he was Marcus Orchard, and the next—after a particularly fierce night of drinking—he was Marco.

But he didn't have any drinkin' buddies anymore. No one in Crooked Lake was aching to shoulder up with Marco at the bar and share a pitcher. Even the regulars avoided him as if his loneliness was contagious. There are a lot of cats who drink because they are lonely, but for most drunks, loneliness is not the cause of drinking, but rather an effect, as normal people tend to avoid drunks. For Marcus Orchard, however, this man was loneliness to the bone. The heavy drinking merely perpetuated more loneliness and forced it into a vicious cycle of exponential growth that no one wanted to be around.

It hurt, though, not having any real friends. Marcus Orchard was too stubborn to admit it, but he felt a general sense of deadness inside of himself. He knew he was a complete failure; his own son seemed to merely tolerate him as oppose to love him. And this was the pain that bore the deepest knife, twisting and turning the nerve endings of his wretched soul.

Marcus reclined in his favorite chair. Many nights were spent in this chair, feet kicked up, head back, letting his mind get lost within an alcoholic haze until everything becomes warm and black—the sweet nothing of unconsciousness where pain doesn't exist. Alcohol always helped the pain go away. Always.

He gripped the cordless phone in his palm, his thumb floating over the answer button, eyes focused on the little, red light that blinks when a call is coming in.

Ring, goddamn it.

He clenched his teeth and glared at the phone.

Just fucking ring.

Eve said she would call him tonight.

Eve—it was the strangest thing. One night, after a serious bender that started with cheap whiskey and ended with cheap vodka, Marcus had awoken in a state of semi-awareness in his reclining chair. He had no idea how he even got home. The phone was ringing, the shrill, blindingly loud noise rattling his eyeballs and sending shockwaves of hurt deep into the center of his brain. With the direct plan of telling the caller to go fuck himself, he answered the phone and heard a woman's gentle voice: *"Hi Marco, my name is Eve."*

She sounded exactly like his mom, but his sweet mother had been dead for twenty years. The voice immediately surrendered some of the pounding in his head. *"Who is this?"* he had asked.

"My name is Eve."

"Why are you calling me?"

"Because Marco, I think I can help you; I can help make the pain go away."

And that was all it took. In his many moments of abject dejection, all he ever wanted or needed was someone to talk to him and make the simple offer of help. Eve became a friend. His only friend. And she always knew the right time to call him, always when he had been drinking, always when he ached inside, and always when he needed someone to talk to. Speaking with Eve made him feel better. She understood him just as far as he ever wanted to be understood by another person. And she was right, she could help make the pain go away. Permanently.

The phone finally rang, and Marcus quickly sat up, snapping to attention, a move he immediately regretted as a wave of nausea tore through his head. Jamming his thumb on the answer button, he said, "Hello, Eve?" into the receiver.

"Hi Marco. I'm glad I was able to get you."

Damn—that voice, it really sounded like his mother. Sometimes he missed her so much.

"Glad you called," Marcus managed to say while the room stopped spinning.

"I'm here to help you, Marco. I'm here to help make all the pain go away…"

CHAPTER 19

Jason and Adam had been put into separate squad cars and taken to the police station. During booking, which included a mugshot and fingerprints, they were kept apart, Adam always one room ahead of Jason throughout the process. When it was over, Jason was led down a dark hallway and into a jail cell. Adam was already there, sitting quietly on a bed two cells down. They were tiny affairs, like concrete boxes with a caged front, a steel toilet in the corner but no sink, and everything dusty and greasy at the same time.

They couldn't see each other, but their voices carried well enough through the short corridor of cells. It was like speaking directly into a giant, metal bowl.

"Adam?" Jason called out. He was standing, speaking with his face between two bars. If he had a hand mirror (like all convicts seem to have in the movies), he could stretch out his arm and use the reflection to see into his friend's cell. "Adam?" he said again.

There was a long moment of silence. Jason considered giving up, but if Adam wouldn't talk, at least he could listen.

"Look, man, I'm---"

"We're not supposed to talk," Adam said.

"We're not supposed to do a lot of the things we do."

"Like kiss your best friend's girlfriend."

"Well, yes, actually," Jason admitted. "I shouldn't have done that, and I'm sorry."

"Apologize all you want," Adam said. "There's nothing you can say."

What about the truth? Jason thought. He wanted to tell Adam just how good it had felt to spend time with Haley, how much he had *needed* it—and it had nothing to do with the kiss. Even though Adam was his best friend and Emma was his *kind-of* girlfriend, his relationship with Haley had always been different. She was his *oldest* friend, and there is something special and magical that old friendships harbor. No matter the relationships a person develops throughout their lives, there is a certain rawness and purity that exists within the comraderies created among children, much like what is shared between old soldiers who get together long after the war is over and slap each other on the back with quiet, sad smiles of reflection. Childhood is a war, and when you fight it together, a bond is cultivated that becomes a piece of your identity. Part of the man Jason was becoming grew out of that little kid who used to play in the woods and steal fudge with Haley. And tonight had been a reminder of all the dreams that little kid once had.

Jason wanted to share these truths, to explain all of these things to Adam. The kiss was merely an accident, a byproduct of nostalgia. He also wanted to tell him that even though it usually seems like things are going okay, he actually feels mad all the time. Mad that his mother abandoned him. Mad that his father is a drunk. Mad that he has to work two jobs. Mad that he knows he's smart but doesn't have time to do schoolwork because of his two fucking jobs. Mad that he has never heard someone say to him, *"I'm proud of you"*—and mad that this is even something he wants so badly.

Pretty much mad at the whole-fucking world.

And tonight, Haley had calmed that screaming madness into a quiet rumble, making it seem like distant thunder from a storm that was miles away and nothing to worry about.

Maybe this truth would help Adam understand and even forgive?

"What's gotten into you lately?" Jason asked. "You've been different."

With zero hesitation, Adam said, "There's a hired assassin on his way to Crooked Lake to kill me. It's kind of scary."

Jason huffed out a confused laugh at the strange comment, odd thing to spontaneously say; however, it was good to hear his friend joking around again. "Why'd you shave your head?"

"I just felt like a change. Plus, my mother is dying of cancer. She lost all her hair from chemo, and I wanted to support her."

His answer had come so swiftly and was so unexpected that Jason didn't know what to say. *Was he still joking? Or was this the truth?* But Jason knew the answer to these questions. Of course, it was the truth, and it actually explained a lot.

"Adam, I'm so sorry."

"She's going to be so pissed. At *both* of us."

This weirdly felt good to Jason—knowing that Dr. Evans would be angry and disappointed with him as well. "Is she going to be okay?" Jason asked. "I mean, what's the prognosis?" He tried to speak as delicately as possible, as if his voice would crack china, but it felt forced and fake, even though his fear and sorrow for Adam were quite real.

"I said she was *'dying'* didn't I?"

Silence.

This was unprecedented friendship territory. First, the betrayal, then the fight, and now this bombshell. Jason had no idea what to say or how to say it, so he decided, *screw it*—it had started as an evening of raw and honest conversation; it could end that way, too.

"What kind of cancer is it?"

Jason heard Adam sniffle and could easily imagine a few tears streaming down his face. *And over his bruised mouth thanks to you!* Jason scolded himself and winced.

"Brain."

To Jason—who admittedly knew nothing about cancer—brain sounded like the worst kind. As if some alien parasite was entering your brain and poisoning this most vital organ. You *are* your brain. It is where your thoughts occur, where your conscious and unconscious reside. Everything else in the body is just meat. But the brain is a living super computer, the operating system for your entire existence. Brain cancer sounded so violating.

"I don't know what to say Adam. Why didn't you tell me, tell any of us?"

Adam sniffled again. "You remember when our tenth grade Spanish teacher, Mrs. Chanter, died at the end of the school year? Everyone loved her. And they made us all see the school's grief counselor. Remember that?"

"Yeah," Jason said, unsure of where Adam was headed.

"The counselor was speaking to a bunch of us about finding hope within our unknown futures. She talked about how after tragedy, it's important to look toward the future and see the potential hope in the unknown paths we will take onward from the point of tragedy."

"Yeah."

"She said if we were people of faith, we might think about the old adage concerning *God's Plan*. The idea that God has an ultimate plan for all of his creations and things happen for a reason. We should all find the hope in God's plan, and even though it's unknown and perhaps frightening, we should look toward it with optimism and trust."

"Okay."

"Well, fuck God's plan, and fuck God, too."

Jason smiled as he gripped the cold, metal bars. It was an expression he would gladly drink to if the thought of drinking alcohol didn't scare him a little.

"Fuck the future," Adam added, and this final idea seemed to settle in dizzying circles like a spinning quarter coming to rest.

A heavy sounding door opened from up the corridor. There was a rattle of keys followed by heavy steps on the cement floor. "Adam Evans," a deep voice called out. "You're free to go."

A uniformed cop appeared in front of Adam's cell and unlocked the door. Jason took a few steps back from the bars. Adam came out; the cop tried to steer him immediately up the hallway, but he wouldn't budge and turned toward Jason. His eyes were red and still full of hate and pain, but it didn't feel like it was being directed at Jason and was rather aimed at the entire universe.

"I make my own plans. I make my own future," Adam said.

They locked eyes for a moment, then the cop ushered Adam up the hall and out the door.

"What about me?" Jason called after the police officer.

There was no reply, just the noise of a metal door clanging shut.

CHAPTER 20

Detective Nicole Rayne stood up from her desk and stretched. It had been a long day, and she was looking forward to a relaxing evening at home with a glass of wine and a new episode of *Ghost Gumshoes*. She enjoyed how the television show actually applied forensic techniques to paranormal investigation. Plus, she thought the host was cute. So she was 36 and single (something her mother found *unfathomable*), at least she could spend her Tuesday nights with some low-rated, guilty-pleasure TV.

Nicole Rayne was one of only three ranking detectives in the Crooked Lake Police Department and the only woman among them. She lived in a man's world and both loved and hated it. A liberal feminist at heart, but not of the snowflake variety, she was fierce and dedicated to the job and rather appreciated how direct and non-caddy her male co-workers were. Guys, especially cops, didn't seem to carry around a lot of baggage or bullshit.

Her computer was logged off, desk straightened, paperwork completed and properly filed. She was never one to walk away from a day on duty without leaving her workspace impeccably clean and organized—ready for another day of small-town policing. *Those jaywalkers aren't going to catch themselves.*

The problem with being a detective in Crooked Lake was there was very little to *detect*. It was a small town with small crime—except during tourist season, and even then, most crimes that would require a detective were fairly petty. One summer there was a serial robber who made his way through all the backyard sheds on Crooked Lake stealing cans of gasoline. The community wasn't exactly gripped by fear. Why a third detective was required was beyond her, and sometimes she felt like the chief only offered her the opportunity because he was trying to fill some sort of gender quota or just thought it good PR. That fat, little, Napoleon bastard cared more about his image and public relations than he did about actual policing. Regardless, she passed the test, earned the rank, and gladly took the title, pay raise, and private office.

She had just grabbed her coat off a rack when there was a knock at the door. *This better be quick*, she thought, then said to the closed door, "Come in."

The on duty shift commander entered, Sergeant Peppers (there were a lot of Beatles jokes around the department). He was a broad shouldered, thick-bodied man with old, puffy muscles. Damon Peppers was retiring this Christmas and was fond of saying *"I'm getting too old for this shit"* in his best Danny Glover impression every time a new issue or problem landed on his desk. He carried two manila folders. "Detective Rayne, we have an unusual situation," he said while making himself comfortable in one of the chairs facing Rayne's desk.

Apparently, this was *not* going to be quick.

Rayne hung her coat back up and took her own seat.

"We picked up two juvenile delinquents earlier tonight. Got into a little fist fight and shattered the window of the Crooked Lake Candy Shop."

Rayne was nodding along, hoping the sergeant would get to the point a little faster as to what this all had to do with her.

"Anyway," the sergeant continued, "the kids were brought in, formally booked, fingerprinted, the entire process."

"Sounds like a misdemeanor at best."

"Exactly. We were really just trying to put the fear-of-the-system into them. One of the kids, Adam Evans is already being released."

"Adam Evans? The prodigy?"

"The one and only. I was surprised, too."

"And the other?" Rayne glanced at her watch.

"Well," Peppers began, "that's where you come in as the on duty detective." He opened one of the files and read. "Jason Orchard, age 17. 281 Beach Street, Crooked Lake, Michigan. Father: Marcus Orchard, mother: Maggie DeLane—you'll have to check out her rap sheet some other time." He closed the file. "He's a senior at Crooked Lake High School."

"He's Marcus Orchard's son?"

"Yeah."

"Poor kid."

"Yeah, and get this. We ran both their prints to look for outstanding warrants or traffic violations and got back a rather peculiar result with Jason Orchard's."

"Already? That was quick."

"There's a reason for that."

"What do you mean?"

Peppers took a breath, offered a crooked smile. "His fingerprints are a perfect match for those lifted from a triple homicide in northern Mexico."

Rayne leaned forward. "Come again?"

"On August 25th, 2018, three Mexican Federales were murdered outside a village called El Rito." The sergeant tossed the two manila folders on Rayne's desk. "It was at a farm not too far from the American border, land the government thinks is controlled by the drug cartels. The forensics report indicates it was the work of a single assailant. The Federales received an anonymous tip that the suspect was headed toward a small tourist town in the United States—Crooked Lake, Michigan—so the file was quickly shared with American Border Patrol and the DEA and FBI, then forwarded to the Michigan State Police and finally to us."

"You're telling me we have a high school kid in there wanted in connection to a triple homicide in Mexico?" Rayne pointed her thumb toward the wall in the general direction of the holding cells.

"I'm telling you we have a high school kid in there who is the *prime suspect* for a triple homicide in Mexico."

"Jesus."

"Yeah, and it gets better. The forensics report also suggests the murderer was highly skilled with weapons, firearms, and hand-to-hand combat. Looks like the work of a professional."

"And you're sure the prints from Mexico match the kid's?"

"Literally perfect."

"Did you contact Marcus Orchard yet?"

"No," the sergeant said. "There's no answer at home; we sent an officer to the house, but no one is there either."

"This is insane." Rayne said. "There's no way Marcus Orchard's kid is some kind of professional assassin."

"I know," Sergeant Peppers agreed, nodding his head. "Something about this just doesn't feel right. I'm not sure what to make of it, but right now, you're the on duty detective, so this all lands on your desk."

Gee, thanks, Rayne thought as the sergeant stood up. "Is the kid still in holding?"

"Yep."

"Let's have him brought to interrogation, and better send for a public defender from the county. I'm going to go through the file and try to reach the Federal Ministry in Mexico City. Also, let's be sure we keep trying to find his dad."

"Marcus Orchard is probably sitting at the end of a

bar someplace."

"Probably. We should send an officer to look for him at a few of the local shit holes."

"Agreed."

Rayne rubbed her eyes. "I'm getting too old for this shit."

"That's my line. Are you even old enough to have seen *Lethal Weapon*?"

"*Lethal*-what?"

Peppers shook his head. "Good luck with this one, detective," he said with a puzzled grin as he opened the door and walked away.

CHAPTER 21

Joseph Dayspring made his way from Lansing to Crooked Lake along the I-69 corridor. He had purchased an old, beaten up pickup truck—tax, title, and license—with cash from an eager-to-sell college kid. It felt good to drive again, to grip a steering wheel and feel the surge of the engine coursing through the chassis. When he was a boy, he had owned a rusted out Dodge Dakota that he had completely rebuilt the engine for out of parts salvaged from various junkyards. Dayspring had always understood machines and engines better than he understood people, although, he had never been a fan of all the *smart* technology like iPhones and tablets. He preferred machines that were dirty and noisy, machines that demonstrated their power through a massive engine roar like a pissed-off Tyrannosaurus rex. Dayspring believed machines were a lot like people. They have a purpose, they perform operations, they break down and need maintenance, and they eventually get too old to bother with repairing and cease to function. After this, they are replaced—with better, more efficient machines.

Cycle of life.

The difference, though, was machines performed their

operations with absolute and complete indifference. They are assigned a job and the job gets done. No biases. No bullshit. People on the other hand cannot possibly escape their partiality. People seem to possess an almost-innate partisanship that often gets in the way of completing a task. People overthink everything. Machines don't think. They just act. Dayspring respected this.

Driving into Crooked Lake had been a surreal experience. It was *home* in the literal sense—he was born and grew up here; but that word carried very little significance for him now. In his world—his time—home was a backpack. The remaining humans had to remain nomadic at all times; if you settled into a spot for too long the foot soldier patrols would certainly find you, and if they didn't, eventually the fly-over scans would. The only way to remain unfound and safe was to keep moving.

He drove through downtown feeling a bit nauseous, edging around the southern curve of the lake. Main Street ran parallel to the boardwalk, and during the heart of summer, tourists would be crisscrossing the intersections between the beach and the less expensive rentals a few blocks up-valley of the shore, but now, the streets were empty.

He continued around the lake, driving well under the speed limit; the nausea still swirling around in his gut and creeping up his throat. He thought about the bursting red balls from Sister Christina's meditation exercises—they were popping like machine gun fire now, one memory assault after another.

His stomach continued to churn as he took a deep breath, steering onto the gravel shoulder and coming to a stop. It would feel good to get some fresh air. He stepped out of the truck, and the moment his feet hit the ground, another wave of nausea swept over him; he had to balance himself with a steady hand on the side of the hood. The truck's headlamps were the only light, and because the way the vehicle was angled and how the road curved, they pointed directly toward the shore, between a few large oak trees and a park bench.

Dayspring raised the collar of his jacket against a biting cold wind and began walking toward the lake. The cool night air felt refreshing on his face and the nausea slowly started to recede. He neared the edge and stood on the top ledge of a wooden break-wall. The water was black and choppy and steadily lapped against the boards—a sound he had always enjoyed, the rhythmic slap of water. He took a few long and deep breaths, sucking in the cool air and hearing the directions from Sister Christina in his head, *"In for six, hold for three, out for six..."* His nerves began to steady. The nausea dissipated.

On the other side of the lake, Dayspring could see a bright cluster of lights and a familiar tin green roof, and all of a sudden, he felt overwhelmingly hungry.

The Shack.

CHAPTER 22

The kid in Interrogation Room B did not look like a professional killer. He was only seventeen-years-old; the only crime he ever committed was probably cutting class to go to the mall (though he didn't seem like the mall-type either).

Detective Nicole Rayne stood opposite a two-way mirror, holding the two manila folders and a cold cup of coffee. Through the glass, Jason Orchard sat in a steel chair, leaning forward with his arms resting on the table. He looked tired and annoyed, occasionally letting out a loud, frustrated sigh and tapping his fingers on the table. Earlier in the night, he had approached the mirror, stood inches from its surface, slowly exhaled a hot breath, and wrote, *"Blow me,"* in reverse with his fingertip in the condensation. This made Rayne chuckle. The kid had spunk, and probably an attitude, but at least he was entertaining and not scared shitless like most of the teenage punks they get in here for various petty crimes.

Rayne opened one of the files and reread the report. She was at a complete loss as to what to do with Jason Orchard. This entire episode should have been easily handled by the on duty desk officer. Couple of young kids slugging it out over a girl. Big deal. Make them shake hands, apologize, and clean up shit on the side of the road until the broken window is paid for. The end. But it turns out one of them might be a professional killer who iced some federal agents in Mexico—go figure.

No, he didn't look like a killer, just an angry kid who apparently got in a fight with his best friend over a girl.

Rayne kept staring at the boy-who-didn't-look-like-a-killer, then opened the second file. This was the crime scene report from the Policía Federal Ministry in Mexico City. She had spent the last hour on the phone trying to connect with someone at the ministry's offices and when she finally did, the crime report was confirmed. Three dead Mexican federal agents at the home of a man named Javier Estes, who had also gone missing along with his daughter and a nun from the village. Forensics indicated it was most likely the work of a professional, or at least someone highly adept at killing people. Rayne was still in disbelief. The kid was wearing a Pink Floyd shirt and ripped up blue jeans. He looked healthy and strong but had the laidback, easy-go vibe of a classic stoner—more of a Jeff Spicoli than a Jason Bourne. She had ran his identification through Homeland Security and the FAA databases to see if he had recently traveled south of the border, but Jason Orchard didn't even have a passport issued in his name. If he was crossing any international borders, he was doing so illegally.

Yet there was no disputing the evidence. Three weeks ago, this kid had been at a triple-homicide just outside a small Mexican village in a depressed farming community. Rayne shuffled through a few pages and came to the fingerprint comparison data, glanced at it to confirm once again. Perfect match, all ten digits. She closed the file and shook her head—*there was no way the kid could have been there.*

But the evidence…

Lesson one of being a detective is never ignore evidence. Every scrap, fleck, piece of hair, dirt, dust, and fiber could be evidence. Forsake nothing, observe everything. Lawyers lie, evidence doesn't.

But there was just absolutely no way stoner-boy in there was banging around Mexico drug cartel land.

But the evidence...

It was dangerous (and illegal) to speak with the kid before his guardian or lawyer arrived—this was the second thing you learn as a detective: violate a perp's constitutional rights and risk fucking up his prosecution. You'll spend the rest of your career directing traffic. Most prosecutors are vindictive slime-balls (they're lawyers, after all) with connections at every level of the justice system; they can railroad a good cop's career merely out of spite.

Rayne shrugged. The kid looked thirsty. What damage could it cause to offer him something to drink?

CHAPTER 23

It was exactly as Dayspring remembered. As soon as he opened the door and stepped into the deep-fried, smoky haze of the Shack, he knew he was home.

It was lightly crowded, a decent night for business but with less concerns about stupid drunks. Both the TV behind the bar and the one in the corner were showing the Tigers game; Yankees were up six-five. Mike Shake was behind the counter, his happy tummy pushing out from beneath a dirty apron, sleeves rolled up, exposing beefy, hairy forearms. And, of course, the signature accessory—a stained rag slung over his right shoulder, once white, now a swampy-brown. He was making small talk with an old man in a baseball cap as he toweled off a glass, leaning against the bar half turned in order to keep one eye on the game.

Dayspring headed directly to the bar but stopped mid-stride when something caught his attention. To his left, next to a grimy video poker machine, hung a giant bulletin board designated as, "THE SHACK WALL OF FAME: PFI CHALLENGE SURVIVORS." He pivoted sharply and walked toward the board, eyes quickly scanning across the years of photographs until he found the one he was looking for. It was the last one, of course, a teenage boy, his face covered in an orange-white, soupy mixture of milkshake and wing sauce. He's clearly in terrible pain, but through it, he's forced a meager thumbs up and desperate smile. Behind him, three other goofy teenagers, a boy the same age with shaggy hair and two pretty girls, are photobombing his fifteen minutes of fame. Beneath the photo was a white label that read: *"Jason Orchard, July 17, 2018."*

"Thinking of taking the challenge partner?" a gruff but friendly voice behind him said. It was Mike Shake, still standing behind the bar toweling dry a glass.

"No thanks," Dayspring said. *Once is enough.* "I will take a beer, though," he added as he settled onto a stool.

"Got Miller Lite bottles for two bucks tonight."

"Got any good craft beers on tap?" Dayspring asked, already knowing the answer.

"Bell's Oberon and Big Two Hearted."

"Oberon. Tall as they come."

"You got it."

Shake tilted a lofty glass beneath a dark orange stream that flowed from the tap; a rich tapestry of wavy golden color filled the glass, froth rising to the top. It was the perfect pour. Mike Shake was a true craftsman. He set it down before Dayspring, who took a nice, long swig with closed eyes. *Life is about control*, he thought, just like he always does when drinking alcohol. *Life is about control.* Afterward, he let out a soft sigh as if the beer had literally taken his breath away.

"You like it?" Shake asked, chuckling at Dayspring's dramatic reaction.

"You just can't get beer like this where I'm from."

"And where's that?"

Dayspring took another savory sip, smiled. *Someplace very far away from here*, he thought.

"Hey Shake!" a slightly slurred voice rang across the bar. "You hear what happened down on the boardwalk earlier tonight?"

"Hang on chief," Shake told Dayspring and took a few steps away to engage with a friendly, half-drunk customer. "What are you talking about?" he asked the man.

Dayspring eyed them both, listening to their conversation. The other man was halfway through a boilermaker with another empty one sitting in front of him. Shake took the glass and stashed it in a sink below the bar.

"Two boys was fightin' and one threw the other through the front window of the candy shop. They both got arrested." The man spoke with the familiar pride all people shine with when they can be the origin of good gossip.

"Is that so?" Shake asked. "Was anyone hurt?"

"Just poor Ms. Hubbard. She owns that candy shop and will probably have a tough time paying for the damage."

"I'm sure she has insurance," Shake said.

"Hey and get this." The man grew a little more excited, as if he was about to offer up something really juicy. "One of the boys involved was Marco's kid, Marcus Orchard. Like father like son, 'eh?"

An intense wave of energy suddenly burst in Dayspring's chest and coursed through his entire body. *Did that guy just say Marcus Orchard's kid got arrested?* Dayspring leaned toward their conversation as conspicuously as possible.

"Marco was in here earlier tonight," Shake said. "But he left peacefully after I cut him off at two drinks."

"Lousy drunk," the man said.

Shake shrugged his shoulders. "But give his kid a break," he insisted. "He fixes motors for Doug Bastion at the marina and comes in here a lot with his friends. All good kids. And Doug says he does good work, and that crotchety asshole never compliments anyone."

"Excuse me," Dayspring said sliding one stool over. "I

didn't mean to overhear, but did you say Marcus Orchard's son got arrested tonight?"

The other two men looked confused, but the half-drunk customer was quick to answer. "Yeah, Marco's kid, I think his name is John or Jason or something with a J. You know Marco?"

Dayspring could feel the color rush out of his face. "Yes, I know Marco really well," he said and slid back to his original seat.

"You okay, buddy?" Shake asked coming back over to him. "No offense, but you kind of look like you've seen a ghost. Or just found out your ol' lady's cheating on you." He grunted out a laugh. "Trust me, I know that look well."

"Yes," Dayspring said. "I'm fine."

The bartender shrugged. "Holler if you want another." Shake turned his attention toward a young man and woman who had approached the bar.

Dayspring quickly finished his beer, laid down money to cover the tab, and fled.

CHAPTER 24

Earlier in the night, Marcus Orchard had been cut off at the Shack after only two drinks because Mike Shake knew that even the quiet, sad drunks were always one drink away from becoming mean, angry drunks, and there was no telling which *one drink* it would be.

Well, fuck Mike Shake, Marcus had thought to himself. He had twelve more dollars in his pocket, and he'd happily spend it someplace else. It didn't matter, though. Tonight was a special night. He was only going to have one more drink and leave anyway. There was something he wanted—*needed*—to do tonight.

Marcus had left the Shack and parked downtown near the boardwalk. He started walking up Main Street, stopping once at liquor store to buy a seven-dollar bottle of vodka and a pack of cigarettes. He was nine cents short, but the kind attendant took a dime out of his own pocket to cover the cost. He then headed toward the south end of the boardwalk, where earlier tonight, unbeknownst to him, his son was arrested. He took long, happy pulls from the bottle as he walked, a lazy cigarette dangling from his lips, blowing smoke rings into the air—something he was actually good at.

The boardwalk was completely empty. His footsteps echoed on the heavy wooden planks as he walked, resonating through the lifeless, wide space. Apparently, there had been some kind of accident at the candy shop; the front window was all boarded up.

Goddamn, the vodka was good. Every wonderful sip filled him with a gentle heat and helped push out the bad thoughts that constantly tortured him:

You're a loser.

Your son is ashamed of you.

You're a fucking embarrassment.

He drank to fight back. It was the only thing he could do. When he drank, the vicious thoughts faded. When he was sober, they came back and were relentless.

Marcus walked until he hit the staircase at the south end. He proceeded down the steps, but instead of following the path toward the beach, as his son had done just a few short hours ago, he circled back and went beneath the boardwalk, an area that was wet and cold and full of shadows.

The air smelled like wet newspaper. Giant, wooden support pillars surrounded him like the guardians of some secret underworld. Marcus sat down in the damp sand, leaned against one of the pillars, and pulled a small handgun—a sleek and shiny revolver—from his waistband. He had always enjoyed the heavy, solid feeling of the gun in his hands—like an anchor, holding him down, keeping him from flying away. He had been a responsible gun owner his entire life. Always keeping up on regulations and legislative developments, following all expert and law enforcement safety precautions. It bothered him that someone might find this gun before the proper authorities—and worse, what if some kid stumbled across it? Marcus stood up and began walking toward the beach. He popped open the cylinder and shook out all six rounds, then replaced only a single one of them. At the edge of the waterline, he snapped closed the cylinder and threw the remaining handful of ammunition into the lake.

Taking a final breath of the fresh air, Marcus smiled and returned to his spot under the boardwalk.

Eight weeks ago, on a hazy Sunday afternoon, when he was nursing a blinding headache with a bottle of Jim Beam, Marcus Orchard had received a mysterious phone call from a woman who sounded exactly like his late mother and identified herself as Eve. She spoke to him in a way no one else ever could. She said all the things he had always needed to hear. *He wasn't a loser. His son wasn't embarrassed by him. He was a good man.* He was just a victim of a corrupt system. It wasn't his fault he drank. It wasn't his fault he could never keep a job. It wasn't his fault no woman loved him. Nothing was his fault. A very sick and broken system had failed him.

Eve could help, though. The pain he felt, she could make all of it go away.

They had been speaking every night since. Eve constantly assuring him that if he trusted her, he could have peace and happiness forever. Marco absorbed everything she said like the greedy alcoholic that he was.

Eve said it was okay to drink. He had to do whatever he could to feel better. She was the only person in the world who understood him. She encouraged him to drink. *"You have to do whatever it takes to survive,"* she had insisted.

But now the pain was going to end forever. Eve promised him this would work. Death doesn't have to be painful. You feel pain because nerve endings send a signal to the brain. If brain function is eliminated before the signal arrives, then there is no pain. He would have to place the gun above and in front of his ear, at a slight upward angle. The bullet would tear through the temporal and parietal lobe and happily end his miserable life immediately, without the slightest pomp or circumstance.

Just pull the trigger. One quick shot to the head and all the pain is erased. *"This is what's best for Jason,"* Eve had said lovingly.

Marcus Orchard took one last look at the world but couldn't see much through the darkness. He closed his eyes and thought about his son. *This is what's best for Jason.*

This is what's best for Jason.

Thank you, Eve. He positioned the gun and gently squeezed the trigger.

She was right. There was no pain.

CHAPTER 25

Joseph Dayspring was standing in front of the Crooked Lake Candy Shop. Several sheets of plywood were sealed over what used to be the storefront window. To his left and right was a long stretch of empty boardwalk, and behind him, a cool wind blew off the surface of the black lake, fluttering his collar and sending an icy chill down his spine.

He shook his head.

This was wrong.

This never happened.

Dayspring could distinctly hear his own confused and frantic voice in his head, quietly repeating in a hushed whisper: *this never happened, this never happened, this never hap---*

A powerful gunshot cracked the air, shattering the peaceful riot in his head.

It was close.

Incredibly close, actually. It was as if it had been right next to him.

Or below him.

There was a distinctly acidic smell in the air…

Gun smoke.

It was rising between the cracks in the boardwalk.

Dayspring sprinted toward the rail and leapt over the side, drawing a gun as he fell, and landing couched low, with the weapon trained into the darkness.

He pulled a tiny penlight from his coat pocket and shined it into the shadows, taking careful steps into the artificial cavern. Everything was damp with the faint stench of seaweed and dead fish. He swept his gun and light across the space in front of him and continued walking.

In just a few paces, he spotted it—or rather, spotted him. Slouched over in an awkward half-sitting/half-lying position was a man with a bloody hole in his head. There was a gun held limply in his right hand.

Clearly a suicide.

Dayspring crouched closer to the man's face and suddenly felt all his breath sucked away in a massive vortex; he nearly collapsed and had to support himself against a wooden pillar.

He recognized the dead man.

It was Marcus Orchard.

Marco to his old drinkin' buddies.

But Marcus Orchard never killed himself. Not the Marcus Orchard in the world Dayspring came from.

Something was indeed terribly wrong.

First, the news of Jason Orchard's arrest, the shattered window, and now this.

This never happened! Dayspring thoughts roared in his head. Could his mere presence in this world have affected the timeline this much?—as some of the scientist at the Vitruvian Order had suggested may happen.

He stood up straight, wind lashing at the back of his neck, and looked at the poor dead man who had just put a bullet through his brain.

"Dad," he whispered through the cavernous darkness.

CHAPTER 26

Jason Orchard had been sitting in this tiny room for too long. A room that was disturbingly similar to classic police interrogation rooms in the movies. The walls were raw concrete and cold. He sat before a matted steel table covered in greasy fingerprints. There was even the quintessential dome light hanging by a frayed cord from the ceiling, casting a yellow and depressing pall over the entire space. The two-way mirror was also a nice touch. You see these things in movies all the time but always wonder about their authenticity. *Do police stations really use those?*

Apparently, yes.

He felt terrible about the busted window at the candy shop and even worse about Adam. The window, however, was an easy fix (the harder part of that equation would be looking Mrs. Hubbard in the eye and apologizing). As for Adam, he may never be able to look him in the eye again.

He had betrayed his best friend.

And as terrible as this was, it seemed as though there were more important things to worry about.

Shortly after Adam was released, another blue-uniformed cop escorted Jason into this stuffy and uncomfortable room. The officer didn't say anything other than he was being moved to interrogation. When pressed why, the cop only shrugged his shoulders and said, "You've been read your rights. I'll advise you not to speak without your lawyer present." After politely asking why he needed a fucking lawyer, the cop told him to calm down and watch his mouth.

Why was he in Interrogation Room B? Why did he need a lawyer? He already told the cops everything and took responsibility for it. It was all very Kafka-esque, he thought as he recalled a book he had read, *The Trial,* where an innocent man suffers at the hands of a corrupt, bureaucratic legal system. It had been on the summer reading list for AP Literature, a class Jason ending up dropping before the year began because he started getting more hours slinging drywall for Fenton Construction and knew it would cut into his ability to keep up with schoolwork. But he never forgot the shadowy world of Franz Kafka.

The door opened and a tired looking woman in a pants suit entered. She was thin, not skinny, but shapely and strong—an athlete's body. She set down a can of coke on the table and said, "Thirsty?"

Jason was incredibly thirsty. He looked at the woman, then at the coke. "Did you get a hold of my dad?" he asked.

The woman frowned. "No, but we're trying." She hesitated. "Do you have any idea where he might be?"

Passed out in an alley. "No."

She frowned again, then offered him a sympathetic smile. "My name is Detective Rayne," she said, taking the seat across from him and setting two manila folders on the table. "I've been assigned your case. Are you hungry?"

As if on cue, Jason's stomach started rolling. "I could eat."

Rayne nodded. "I'll have something brought up from the snack machine."

Jason then noticed for the first time that one of the folders on the table was in Spanish and contained the heading, "Se Requiere Autorización Diplomática"—*Diplomatic Clearance Required.* "What exactly is happening here?" he quickly asked. He was confused, angry, emotionally exhausted, and just wanted some answers. "Why am I still here? And what's with the diplomatic warning on that folder?"

"You speak Spanish?" Rayne said.

"Sí."

She narrowed her eyes, impressed. "Here's the situation—you were arrested for an unrelated incident but are now being investigated in connection to a major crime. You will not be released until you see a judge and bail is set. In regards---"

"Major crime? I punched by buddy and broke a window!"

Rayne ignored his interruption and continued, "Now, in regards to your other questions…" The detective trailed off, hesitated as if thinking, then blurted out, "Were you in Mexico recently?"

"What?" Jason said confused. "No, why?"

Rayne ran a hand through her short, chin-length hair and ended up rubbing the back of her neck for a few seconds. "No spring break trips south of the border, no vacations to northern Mexico?"

"I've never left the state of Michigan," Jason said, and this sad fact made the small room feel even smaller.

"No, of course not," Rayne said. She stood up while adding, "Of course he's never been to Mexico," but Jason got the impression the cop was just thinking out loud.

Rayne paced from wall to wall and back again. "Look," she said the way people do when they have something important to say but need a moment to gather their thoughts. "You're being held because your fingerprints are a perfect match for those lifted from a major crime scene in Mexico near the American border.

We are still trying to get a hold of your father, meanwhile the state's attorney's office has sent over a public defender who will probably be here soon."

Jason's jaw fell open. "I've never been to Mexico," he said like a robot.

The cop obviously believed him. She appeared every bit as flabbergasted by the idea as Jason was. "But how did all of your fingerprints get to the crime scene?" she asked. Her tone was not accusatory, rather mystified.

"It has to be a mistake. Maybe your computer system or whatever tech stuff you guys use is just making a mistake."

"The computer system doesn't make mistakes." Her words seemed to settle over the little room like a dark storm cloud. No one spoke for a long, still moment.

"I swear to God I've never been to Mexico," Jason reiterated.

"I know," the detective said quickly. "But here's the rub: a man with your *exact* same fingerprints has, and this man is wanted by the Policía Federal Ministry of Mexico. Hence the file." She tapped the folder with a firm finger. "That's like their version of the FBI." Rayne took a breath. "Jason Orchard, you are wanted for the murder of three federal agents in Mexico."

Silence.

Slowly noises returned—breathing, a shuffling of feet on the concrete floor, the thump of Jason's heart.

"Well, fuck," he said.

CHAPTER 27

Haley didn't feel like talking to anyone, so she locked herself up in her room and for the first time *ever*, turned her phone off. Took the battery out, too.

After the fight on the boardwalk, her parents came to pick her up while she waited with a few police officers. Mrs. Hubbard cried while someone boarded up the busted window with sheets of plywood. *"What kind of hooligans would do such a thing?"* she had kept asking the sky as if she expected God himself to answer.

Haley's parents were not happy. They kept calling her *young lady* the entire way home, which was a not-so-subtle sign they were royally pissed. She, of course, kept insisting it wasn't her fault; she had nothing to do with the fight, but her mother came back with, *"Young lady, you choose the situations you put yourself in."*

Her parents had told her to go straight to her room, which always seemed like a stupid punishment. Her room was exactly where she wanted to be during situations like this. It was unlike the typical teenage girl's bedroom; in here, the tomboy still thrived. There was a Detroit Redwings poster on one wall, and a set of shelves prominently displayed various medals and trophies from years of running cross-country and track. Not that the current Haley didn't show. The dresser was littered with various makeup products and jewelry accessories (as well as a pair of running spikes), and an opened closet door revealed a jungle of sleeves, pants, dresses, and blouses, all drooped around like vines and packed onto hanging racks so tightly that the small walk-in space seemed to moan from pressure as if it were an air tank about to burst.

"It wasn't my fault," she had insisted repeatedly, but she knew this was only a half-truth. Her mother was actually right (something she'd never admit out loud). Yes, she had nothing to do with the physical act of breaking the window, but she certainly had something to do with the fight itself—this could not be denied. Two boys had got into a fight over her.

Two boys were fighting over her…

Two boys. Fighting.

Over her.

Boys never fought over her. Boys fought over Emma or some of the prettier, peppier girls in class. But never her. She was the tomboy. She was the girl who was good at sports and could run a faster mile than most boys. She was also really smart. Not Adam Evans-smart (*no one* was Adam Evans-smart), but smart enough to intimidate her male classmates, especially in math and science. She had never really cared about stuff like this before. There were girls in school who were obsessed with boys—only cared about boys, only talked about boys, only thought about boys (often while chomping bubblegum and twirling a lock of hair around an index finger). Haley had always sworn she would never be like this, but the sad fact was it had never been a problem. Boys weren't exactly lining up to ask her to the prom.

Her attempt at a relationship with Adam had been a spectacular failure. Whatever potential they had disappeared weeks ago at the end of the summer when, for unknown reasons, Adam became distant and detached from their group of friends.

And now there was this strange thing happening between her and Jason. She hadn't set out to start anything, and she certainly had not planned on kissing him tonight. It was just something that organically happened. But oddly enough, once they kissed and held hands, it felt as if this was always how it was supposed to have been. It felt good. It felt right.

Haley stood before a tall mirror that hung on the back of her door. She struck a few poses, flipped her hair around, carefully examining her own reflection. She didn't have any major body issues like some girls, but it was impossible to entirely escape that type of self-deprecation. She was an athlete and confident in her physical health and appearance, but was she sexy? Did boys like looking at her? She popped a hip out, shifted her weight, popped out the other hip, striking what she thought was a sexy yet modest pose. Not that she wanted a bunch of Neanderthal boys ogling her.

But still…

There was a noise behind her. A light tap on the window. This was followed quickly by another and then a third. Her bedroom was on the second floor, a straight two-story drop to her mother's hydrangeas below. Haley, unafraid but cautious, pulled back the curtains of the window and peered into the moonlit night.

Adam Evans was standing on her lawn with a handful of tiny pebbles. He wore a knit stocking cap over his shaved head and looked like a cat burglar. Even from this distance, she could see the swelling and bruising on his mouth where Jason had hit him.

She raised the window open and stuck her head out. Speaking in a loud whisper, she said, "Adam, what are you doing here?"

Adam looked around, shifting on his feet nervously; he seemed to jump at every set of headlights that swept down the front street. "We need to talk. Can you come down? I tried texting."

"I turned my phone off."

"I'm sorry about tonight."

Haley glared at him. She had once been the biggest tomboy in school. Why change now? "Fuck you," she said and nearly spit, then began closing the window.

"Wait!" he protested, and there was something in his voice that made her hesitate, a note of desperation too strong to be related to the high school drama that had unfolded earlier.

"Please," Adam begged. "This is really important."

"What is it?" she asked annoyed but interested. And maybe slightly concerned.

Adam just stared at her, and even from this height, she could see moisture gathering in his eyes. A thought suddenly dawned on her—the way he kept shifting around, looking over his shoulder, always keeping a close eye on all the shadows in her yard: he was afraid of something.

"What's going on?" she asked.

"I'm in trouble, Haley. A lot of trouble," he hesitated, then added, "life and death trouble."

CHAPTER 28

The door to Interrogation Room B opened, and a sad looking man in a baggy suit entered. He wore glasses and looked more like a divorced high school science teacher than a lawyer. He did not say hello.

"My name is Edward Beck," he said without looking at Jason. "I've been assigned your case from the public defender's office." As he sat down, he opened a briefcase and pulled out a few files. "Do you have any idea where your father is?" the attorney asked while shuffling some papers.

"No, do you?" Jason said quickly and with a clear fuck-you attitude.

"I'm here to help you," Beck said. "So don't get defensive." He snapped his briefcase shut and stared at Jason with no attempt to conceal his disdain for being awoken in the middle of the night. "I spoke to the detective assigned the case, and this is a rather peculiar situation. I've also left several messages with the state department."

"I didn't kill those people in Mexico."

"Yes, I know. I'm fairly certain you didn't either, as is Detective Rayne. The problem is, though, the police report from the Federales is not wrong. They have your fingerprints at the murder scene."

Beck passed a file over to Jason. He opened it. Everything was in Spanish. He scanned through several pages, flipping around.

"You know Spanish?" Beck asked with a doubtful eyebrow.

Jason ignored him. "This says the crime took place on August 25th."

"So?"

"I was having lunch with my friends that day; even Adam was there." Jason remembered that date specifically because they had been at the Shack that afternoon. It was the day Adam was acting super weird and suddenly ran out on everyone.

"Adam Evans? The other delinquent in the fight?"

"Yes." *And who the fuck are you calling delinquents, pal?*

"You could prove this?"

"Well, there were a lot of witnesses. We were at the Shack."

"The Shack?"

"Local bar. Great wings."

"Okay," Beck said, listening intently and writing notes. "This is all very interesting. Here's the problem. Your prints are a dead match. All ten fingers, no percentage room for error, literally an exact match. To the Mexican Federales, you're their perp and they want you extradited."

"This is insane."

"Don't worry; we're going to get to the bottom of this. Can you give me the names of everyone who could place you at the Shack that afternoon?" Beck was ready with a pen and legal pad when his cell phone buzzed. He looked at the screen puzzled for a moment. "This might be the State department," he said, then answered the phone, "Edward Beck."

Jason watched the thin-faced lawyer as he listened to a voice on the other end. Confused, he slowly extended his hand with the phone and said, "Umm, apparently you have a call."

Just as confused, Jason accepted the phone. "Hello?" he said into the receiver.

"Jason Orchard, listen to me very carefully." It was a woman's voice, aggressive and sharp. "This is Lazarus."

"Lazarus?" Jason asked.

Beck squinched his face and mouthed, *Lazarus?*

"Yes," the voice on the phone continued. "Your friend, Adam, is in serious trouble. There is a man coming to kill him. You have to help him, and the police *cannot* be trusted. I can help you escape, but you need to do exactly as I say."

CHAPTER 29

Joseph Dayspring stood over the slumped body of his dead father. He shook his head. "What the hell is happening?" he asked the wooden pillars that surrounded him.

Things *had* changed—and continued to change. But why? Was his mere presence in this world—this timeline— enough to alter the course of events this drastically? What other explanation was there?

The broken window, the arrest, and now Marcus Orchard's suicide. This was not how things were supposed to happen. *No. These things didn't happen. They never happened. They---*

But he didn't have any more time to think. A powerful flashlight beam suddenly cut through the darkness, flickering between the wooden posts. "Hey you!" a deep-throated voice shouted. "Don't move! Drop the gun and stay exactly where you are!"

Unlikely, Dayspring thought. He went into a full sprint, heading deeper into the shadows. The flashlight beam gave pursuit, erratically shifting its aim and direction. He could hear the heavy steps of an out-of-shape man behind him along with the jingling of what could only be a cop's utility belt. Dayspring wove between the supports, through the darkness, toward the far end of the boardwalk, where he hoped to lose the slower cop in the neighborhoods up valley and circle back for his vehicle.

He knew he was outpacing the cop by a good amount, but when he arrived at an opening and emerged into an area dimly lit by a street lamp from above on the boardwalk, he came face to face with two more officers, guns drawn, aimed directly at him.

"Freeze!" one of them demanded. "Drop the gun!"

Dayspring did as he was told. The gun clattered on the gravel path.

The pursuing cop finally caught up. The three officers surrounded him like the equal points of a triangle. The one who had chased him was clearly struggling. He was hunched over with hands on his knees, huffing and puffing, waving at his partners to ignore him and continue with the arrest.

"Hands in the air," one of them demanded. "On your knees. Slowly."

With officer out-of-shape still recovering, the other two cops closed in on Dayspring at once, each taking a step forward, shifting their weight and center of gravity to their back foot, becoming unbalanced for a fraction of a second.

This was his chance.

There was a sudden explosion of swift movement followed by the sound of several cracking bones; the three cops were quickly disarmed and lying on the ground, withering in pain and cradling their broken limbs.

"Sorry guys," Dayspring said and ran off into the night.

CHAPTER 30

Jason Orchard was gripping the phone with sweaty fingers, feeling like his life had suddenly turned into a *Mission: Impossible* movie. He half-expected Lazarus to tell him the phone he was using would self-destruct.

"Why should I trust you?" Jason said, exchanging a confused look with the lawyer sitting across from him.

"Look what's happening to you. You're about to be extradited to Mexico for murdering three Federales. All of this—you, me, the threat to Adam's life, it all ties together."

The threat to Adam's life? So he wasn't joking earlier? "Why does someone want to kill Adam?"

The lawyer was dumbfounded. "Who wants to kill who now?"

Jason ignored him.

"All will be explained later," Lazarus continued. "I can help. I can get you out of jail because you need to help Adam. You need to save his life."

Jason was speechless.

"You see the red light above the door?" Lazarus said.

Jason looked toward the top of the door. There were two mounted light bulbs covered by wire cages, one glowed red, the other was off. "Yes," he said.

Edward Beck was really starting to get annoyed; he kept looking at his watch, tensing his jaw.

Lazarus continued, "The red light indicates the door is locked. Now observe."

Jason watched as the red light turned off, and the other bulb turned on, glowing green.

"Now the door is open."

"What do you want me to do?" Jason asked.

"What's going on?" the lawyer said reaching for his phone. Jason twisted away and held up his index finger.

"Just do *exactly* as I say, and everything should work."

"Okay."

"First, I'm afraid, Mr. Beck is a liability. You'll have to incapacitate him. Knock him out."

"Umm…" Jason was about to protest, but then he looked up and saw the lawyer's thin, angry face.

"You don't have much time," Lazarus insisted. "You have to move now."

The lawyer had turned red. "Kid, I don't know what the hell is going on, but I want my goddamn phone back, so hand it---"

He never finished. Jason landed a lightning fast right hook on his cheek. He slumped back, then fell forward and smacked his head on the table. It looked like it hurt, but nothing serious. Maybe a minor concussion.

"Now move!" Lazarus commanded. "The hallway is clear; go left and head straight toward a double set of steel doors.

Jason did as he was told, keeping the phone pressed against his ear. He left Interrogation Room B and headed toward the doors. A similar set of lights hung above them, one glowed red. As he approached, it turned off, and the green one next to it came on followed by a metallic click from some internal mechanism within the door.

"What now?" he asked as he walked through the doors.

"Take the first hallway on your right."

Jason trotted forward and realized that hung from the ceiling at every exchange was a security camera, its black eye looking down at him, red indicator light glowing.

He followed Lazarus' directions, heading deeper into the bowels of the police station, down empty halls where the air was stale and warm.

"Stop!" Lazarus suddenly ordered him. Jason halted right as he was about to pass through the intersection of another hallway. He heard a door open and the voices of two men come pouring past him; they were talking about the Tigers/Yankees game. Gradually, their voices faded, as they must have moved on in another direction.

"Okay, it's safe now," Lazarus said. "Turn left when you reach the end of the hall.

Jason continued to follow her instructions. When he rounded the corner, he saw an emergency exit with a painted sign that read: "WARNING, ALARM WILL SOUND IF OPENED."

"Stop," Lazarus said. "Look at the door to your right."

It was a large, steel door; above the handle was a keypad and a small, rectangular screen with a spot where a card could be swiped. It suddenly lit up, and Jason heard the familiar, metallic click from inside the door.

"Go inside," Lazarus said.

Jason entered, found the light switch. He was in a supply room. Guns, rifles, ammunition, bulletproof vests, riot gear—all lined up, stacked, and hung from metal cages and shelves. It was like a zombie-apocalypse preparation-bunker. By far some of the coolest shit he had ever seen in his life. But he didn't have the time to appreciate it just now. "Quickly," Lazarus commanded. "Get some weapons."

"You're kidding."

"There is a contract killer on his way to assassinate Adam. Do you just want to ask him politely not to?"

"Why is a contract killer---?"

"All will be explained soon. Now hurry up; you don't have much time."

"This is fucking crazy," Jason said as he grabbed a black duffle bag and began filling it with a few handguns, clips, any small and interesting items he could find.

"Move!" Lazarus insisted and Jason could sense the gravity of her voice. "Go out the emergency exit."

"But the alarm---"

"Don't worry about the alarm."

Jason slung the bag over his shoulder and went back into the hall. He put his hands on the push lever for the exit and shoved. A burst of cold air shocked him, but there was no alarm. "What now?" he asked as he stepped into an alley.

"Ditch this phone and go to the bluffs. Adam and your other friends will be waiting."

"Okay."

"And Jason," Lazarus said, "hurry. You must protect Adam from the man with the scar."

Mission: Impossible, indeed, Jason thought as he ran into the night.

CHAPTER 31

Detective Rayne was getting a migraine. She sat at her desk with phone in hand, still no answer at the Orchard house. She had sent a few officers to check out some of the bars in town, but other than a brief sighting at the Shack, no one had seen Marcus Orchard all night.

That poor kid in there needed help, and he wasn't going to get it from his father. It broke Rayne's heart. In her career in law enforcement she had seen some shitty acts of parenting—moms that were meth-head whores, dads that were abusive drunks, and parents who all together seemed to lack whatever child rearing instincts that were supposed to be biologically innate. These were the worst types of people, Rayne thought. There was no greater scum on the planet than the mom who buys crack instead of formula or the dad who lays his dirty hands on his daughter. Abuse a kid, either through malicious acts or gross negligence, and you could burn in hell forever as far as Nicole Rayne was concerned.

Marcus Orchard fit into this category.

The kid was in trouble; his dad was useless, and the court appointed attorney seemed like a complete douchebag.

Rayne had always taken pride in her ability to read a person. It was probably a skill a lot of detectives naturally developed, but long before her career in law enforcement, she possessed the ability to make amazingly accurate inferences about people based on first impressions. It was instinctual, intrinsic, but also sharpened by experience. Nicole Rayne trusted her gut about people.

And her gut told her Jason Orchard was a good kid. Sure, he was definitely a massive stoner and maybe a little rough around the edges, but who could blame him? Despite the fight and broken window, when Rayne looked into his eyes, she saw a kind soul.

But then there was the matter of the murders in Mexico.

It just didn't make any sense. She knew you could fake a person's fingerprints, but how—and why—would the prints of a seventeen-year-old kid from Crooked Lake, Michigan have been stolen, copied, and planted at a murder scene in northern Mexico?

There was a knock on her door; it opened before she had a chance to say anything. A pudgy beat cop in a blue uniform poked his head in. Both his eyes were blackened, his nose looked horribly purple and swollen, and his right arm hung in a sling around his neck. "Detective," he said.

"Jesus, Bill, what the hell happened to you?"

"That's why I'm here," the officer said. "You're working on a case involving a minor named Jason Orchard?"

"Yes."

"We just found his father."

"Where is he?"

"Under the boardwalk. He's dead."

"What?" Rayne said as she leaned back. "Where, how, what happened?"

"Got a report of a gunshot along the boardwalk. Me and Officers Feller and Jacobs figured it was just some kids with a pack of firecrackers or something. We looked all around and even went under the boardwalk. This is where I stumbled upon a man standing over a dead body holding a gun. He fled, I gave pursuit. He got away."

"Your appearance tells me you are leaving out part of the story."

"Very good detective," Bill said. "This guy, you should have seen him. He was fast, like some kind of Kung-Fu master or something. Had the vibe of a military man."

"Marcus Orchard was murdered?"

"Seems that way, but I think I walked in on this guy as he was staging a suicide."

Rayne sighed. This night just kept getting weirder. "Okay," she said. "Did the scene get sealed off?"

"Yes, and the state has been contacted already; a forensics team is on the way."

"Good," Rayne said standing. She grabbed a coat from a rack. "I'm going to check on the kid and head down there. I want a positive ID on that body before anyone tells him. No one talks to Jason Orchard except his lawyer and myself."

"Understood."

"So what did this mysterious guy look like?" Rayne asked. "Remember anything else about him?"

"It was dark, but there was a huge scar on his face, right down his left eye."

CHAPTER 32

Joseph Dayspring sat with his legs dangling over the edge of Hook Point. After his run-in with the police, he had fled to the bluffs. He needed a place to rest and think and refocus his energies.

He had a mission to complete.

But this mission had gone off course. Good soldiers, however, plan for contingencies; they know how to improvise. The mission could be redirected.

And in order to do this, he needed to find that final nerve. The very limits of Dayspring's mental and emotional fortitude were being tested, his sense of morality and justice pushed to the jagged frontier. The mission could be completed tonight, right now, but first, he had to walk to this mental edge and—with his eyes wide open—jump.

There were things happening in this world that shouldn't be happening. Yes, he had been told his very presence in this time might have minor impacts—the eggheads at The Vitruvian Order had called them *"ripples,"* but their effect, he had been assured, should be negligible. Time, they had said, is nearly immutable. It's like a river. Toss in a stone and cause a few ripples, eventually the flow rights itself. It takes extraordinary engineering to change the natural flow of a river, just as it would take an extraordinary event to change the natural flow of time.

He looked across the lake's surface, observing its dark ripples, and shook his head. The bluffs had been one of his favorite places as a kid. He remembered coming here with his friends, having campfires on the beach, jumping into the water from Hook Point, and, of course, smoking a little weed. The bluffs were freedom. Out here, there were no responsibilities or deadlines. When you're young, people are always telling you to prepare for the future, and that's great and all, but if you don't take the time to enjoy the present every once in a while, you'll forget *why* you're preparing for the future. Dayspring's time at the bluffs had always been about enjoying the present moment. There was no past or future; there was only *now*. Here, on this small beach, he and his friends had been alone together on the final edge of space and time, in a world of nothing but sunshine and blue skies, hot dogs and Coca-Cola. An endless summer.

He closed his eyes and concentrated, taking deep breaths the way Sister Christina had taught him. At once, it was perfectly quiet and still, but gradually, the world came alive and exploded with soft, brilliant sounds—bats flapped their wings, crickets chirped, an owl hooted, dry leaves rattled in the wind, and the lake itself seemed to come alive and breath as lines of waves washed upon the shore. These were the silent sounds of a living world, sounds Dayspring didn't hear any more where he was from. Night in his world (except during raids and battles) was absolutely soundless. No more critters to flap and chirp and hoot. Without these sounds at night, the soldier has to listen to the noises in his head, and those noises are not nice.

He opened his eyes.

It was time to complete the mission.

He drew a 92FS Beretta from a shoulder harness and

held the gun with two hands, examining its side profile. It was a good weapon, small, reliable; it shot straight and rarely jammed. He went through a safety checklist of the gun's mechanisms—the slide, magazine release, ejection port and hammer. Everything worked smoothly---

Voices.

Behind him—below him. There were people talking. Loud. They were coming up the same hidden trail he had used but seemed headed toward the beach and not Hook Point. Crouching and keeping his head low, Dayspring stared over the rocky cliff edge, toward the white sand, right where he knew the interlopers would emerge.

Adam, Haley, and Emma made their way through the nearly invisible trail, each carrying a bag, Adam with a small cooler. There were trees and thick shrubbery on both sides and a soft bed of leaves and needles beneath their feet. Skinny branches snapped at their faces, forcing them to occasionally duck and walk with a forearm shielding their eyes.

As they came upon the beach, the forest seemed to open like the mouth of a great cave, and they emerged onto a skinny stretch of sand that curved inward from the lake. To their left, Hook Point watched over them like a natural lifeguard tower made out of smooth limestone, glowing yellow in the soft moonlight.

"How'd you get dragged into this again?" Haley asked Emma. She had been nervous about a confrontation since they met up earlier to gather supplies. *Had Adam told her what happened? About the kiss? The fight?*

"Adam told me his life was in danger." She shrugged. "I was kind of bored, anyway."

Haley sighed. "Yeah, me too."

"But he won't tell me what happened to his face or why he's missing a tooth!" Emma yelled as Adam was rooting through the cooler for something and came up with a juice box.

She doesn't know about the fight or me and Jason, Haley thought. This was a relief.

"When's Jason getting here?" Emma asked.

"Should be soon," Adam said. "You guys want something to eat?" They all took a seat in the sand around the charred remains of a campfire; Adam started adding logs and paper. Soon, a fire was blazing, and they all inched closer to the orange heat.

The girls declined food. Adam nibbled at a granola bar and sipped his juice box.

"So go ahead, Adam. Fill us in. Tell us what in the hell is going on," Haley said in a tone that was only half-disbelief.

"And what happened to your face," Emma added. Adam and Haley exchanged a quick glance. Emma noticed. "What?"

Haley sighed. *Might as well get this over with*. "Earlier tonight---"

"I was attacked," Adam interrupted. "By the man who is trying to kill me. But I got away."

"Why is someone trying to kill you, and why aren't we at the police station telling this to the cops?" Emma asked.

"The cops can't help. They won't believe any of this. If I went to the police, it would only expose me."

Emma rolled her eyes. "What makes you think *we'll* believe you?"

Adam looked from Emma to Haley, his face desperate and humbled. "Because you're my friends, and I need your help." There was an edge in his voice, a crumpling edge that fell away into a dark pit. A moment of silence followed. The fire popped and crackled, wooden sparks jumping into the sand.

"Tell us, Adam," Haley said.

He took a long breath.

"I'm a member of a collective hacker group, a loosely

connected alliance of hackers similar to other groups like Anonymous. As you guys know, I'm pretty good with computers."

The girls both shrugged, as this was the understatement of the century.

"Anyway, a very trusted hacker friend of mine was able to discover that a powerful group of men have sent a contract killer to eliminate the world's most skilled hackers. This woman, her hacker-handle is Lazarus, has abilities unlike anyone I've ever seen. Far better than mine, her hacking capabilities are super-human, almost God-like. You should see the way she---"

"Adam," Haley interrupted, "get on with it."

"Right," Adam continued. "Lazarus is legit. Greatest hacker the world has ever known. She recruited me to build a special network server in order to store a secret file. She has also shown me classified documents from our deepest, most secretive levels of government. Something big is about to happen. Something that will change the world. Hacker groups like mine, we call ourselves the *Gray Ghosts*, by the way," he added proudly, "we pose a threat to our own government."

"How?" both Emma and Haley asked at once.

"Because we are hackers with a conscience. Because we possess the abilities and the power—and the *will*—to stop them. To expose them."

Another long moment of silence.

"This is crazy," Haley said.

Emma tossed a twig into the fire. "How do you know this is all true?"

"Lazarus. She had been holding back, but she finally granted me full viewing access to the secret file earlier tonight. I've seen things—emails, texts, photographs— from top government officials." He paused for a dramatic second. "This is real."

"Who the hell is this Lazarus?"

"She's a friend," Adam said. "At first she told me not

to trust you guys, said you'd sell me out because---" Adam cut himself off, threw Haley a look.

Emma glanced back and forth between them, folded her arms, and asked firmly, "Because why?"

"That doesn't matter," Adam quickly responded. "She was wrong. I've had time to think, and I know that now." He and Haley locked eyes for another brief, awkward moment.

"You guys," Emma said. "I'm starting to feel like something else is going on here, something both of you know about but won't tell me."

"It's nothing," Adam said. "I know who my friends are. You guys and Jason. And I need your help."

"But what are these things this Lazarus is talking about? What's happening that is so big and grand that an assassin is coming for you?" Emma's voice had risen in volume. And doubt.

Adam looked very deeply into his friends' eyes, searching for the strength to be as blunt and direct as possible. In a gesture that called upon divine strength, he craned his head toward the dark sky and finally blurted out, "Our government has had a cure for all forms of cancer for the past forty years."

Emma and Haley exchanged confused glances. "Even if that's true," Emma began, "why would they keep it from the public, and why would that require a bunch of hackers to be murdered?"

"Cancer generates trillions—*trillions*—of dollars. This money is filtered through healthcare providers, insurers, hospitals, legislators, lobbyists, and all sorts of crooked men get their pockets lined. *Curing* illnesses has never been profitable, but *treating* them sure as hell is." Adam threw his empty juice box in the fire, which flared up, revealing heavy moisture in his eyes.

"I've heard this argument," Haley said, her tone much friendlier than Emma's. "But why are you their target?"

"My hacker group—the Gray Ghosts—we have the all

the evidence we need on that server I built. Government officials have been keeping this secret for years, preventing sick people from living full, healthy lives. Kids, brothers, sisters, dads," Adam hesitated, glared at the fire as a single tear rolled out of each eye, "and moms."

Emma and Haley were speechless, unsure how to react to Adam's sudden onset of emotions.

"I currently have the only copy of all this information stored on the most advanced server in the world in my basement."

"What are you supposed to do with it?" Emma asked.

"Just keep it safe. When the time is right, that baby will be released, and after that, our government is over. The public will never trust them again. Something like this ruins all credibility of the established order. Nearly a half century of letting countless scores of people die—for money, for profit. This is what ends our government. We'll have to start completely over. Write a new government. A new order." Adam's voice was surging like an ocean wave, gathering speed and power through the eye of the storm. He was looking across the lake, seeing nothing except perhaps the brave new world he was outlining. "It'll be a new enlightenment, and we'll all conduct ourselves based on a scientific approach; reason and logic will rule over all. It will be beautiful. A new renaissance of art and science. Our faiths will be restored in this New World order, and we will all thrive in health and happiness, and then---"

"Adam!" Haley yelled.

"Sorry," Adam said, hanging his head. "I know I can get carried away about stuff like this."

"That's okay buddy," Emma said, ruffling the back of his head despite him not having hair anymore.

Adam smiled. The gesture reminded him of happier times.

There was suddenly a rustling near the forest's edge, coming from the pathway that looped around and headed up toward Hook Point. They all turned to see the dark silhouette of a man come out of the woods. As he stepped onto the sand and into the silver moonlight, they could see him better.

He wore a pair of beaten-up blue jeans and an olive green jacket that looked like it was purchased from an army-surplus store. He took another step closer, immersing himself in the fire's faint light. He had sandy-gray hair, and even though he was probably only in his early forties, his eyes looked weathered and old; the left one had an ugly scar carved over it and was pus-yellow.

Slowly, the man raised his right arm.

He was holding a gun.

The three friends stood up, cautiously backing away toward the waves behind them. The girls huddled together, keeping their eyes on the mysterious man while trying to find each other's hands for comfort. Adam slowly positioned himself in front of them, and they continued to move their ballet closer to the water's edge.

"It's me you want," Adam said as he tried to swallow the nervous lump in his throat.

The man with the scar nodded as he pointed the gun directly at Adam's chest.

"Yes," the man said. "You *are* the one I want."

CHAPTER 33

The man with the scar.

The man Lazarus had warned him about. This man was a killer, she had said. A man contracted by other powerful men to neutralize threats.

Adam stood his ground, the girls crouching behind him. "It's me you want," he repeated, taking a step forward and raising his arms in a gesture that said *I surrender.* "Just let the girls go."

The man looked strangely familiar. His face, the scar especially, was easy to remember, yet Adam was not being triggered by this. He was certain, though; he knew the man or had met him in some capacity.

"Drop your phones," the man said to the girls.

Haley and Emma did as they were told, their skinny iPhones landing in the cold sand with a hollow puff.

"Now get out of here." The man motioned with the gun for them to scatter.

Emma was two steps away, but Haley hadn't moved. She sidled up to Adam and said with a flat and blunt tone, "No."

The man frowned at her. "You have to go."

"Haley, come on," Emma pleaded, pulling at her arm.

"Leave," Adam insisted with a voice threatening to crack but still hanging strong.

"You heard your friend," the man said.

"No," Haley repeated, but a little less sure of herself; she took a step forward. "I'm not leaving my friend."

The man with the scar was biting down hard on his teeth. "Please leave," he said through a clenched jaw. His tone, oddly, was more frustrated-parent as opposed to ruthless-mercenary.

"No," Haley said again with rising confidence.

"DO YOU WANT TO WATCH YOUR FRIEND DIE!?" The man's voice was like a bomb going off; Haley thought the gun had fired. It was like an explosion of thunder, a crack in the mantle of the earth. All three friends jumped together; Haley threw her arms around Adam and closed her eyes, burying her face in his shoulder.

All was quiet. Could have been a nanosecond or a millennium, and in this unrecorded period of time, Haley had just long enough to wish that Jason was with them, that they were all together. It was Jason who had always made her feel safe, always made her feel appreciated. It was Jason who always made her smile. From the adventurous kids they had once been, to the confused teenagers they now were, she had always loved being with Jason the most. She loved Adam and Emma, but she was *in love* with Jason. It had always been Jason.

The silence ended with something that could barely qualify as a whimper, yet it was unmistakable; there was low, quiet breathing laced with moisture, and it was coming from the man holding the gun. He was visibly trembling. Two single tears simultaneously popped out of each eye and raced down the front of his face, the one on the left following the carved path of his pink scar. He swallowed, blinked, seemed to choke on his breath, fighting valiantly against the threat of more tears.

Nonetheless, his finger squeezed tighter on the trigger.

Adam calmly removed Haley's arms from around his neck and stepped away from her. "Don't hurt my friends," he said as he continued to move into his own private space on the beach, the barrel of the gun tracing his path.

"I'm sorry Haley," the man whispered. "But this is the only way."

He knows my name? Haley thought, her fear momentarily abated by confusion.

Adam closed his eyes and thought of his mom. His beautiful mother lying in a hospital bed waiting to die, her brilliant mind reduced to a jumbled circuit board of crossed and misfiring wires. She had lost her dignity, was now losing her mind, and would soon lose her body. It was fucking humiliating—surrendering to a disease that could have been eradicated forty years ago.

Adam once read that when death is imminent a lot of people experience a moment of complete peace and serenity, as if the universe is saying to them, *"Everything is okay; the time has come—see you on the other side."* This did not happen for Adam Evans. His mind exploded into madness. All he heard was screaming, bloodthirsty screaming filled with fear and pain and rage. These were the voices of the dead, pleading their agony from the past. There was just so much sickness and horror in the world. So much disease. It was everywhere. For one instant and infinite moment in time, Adam could hear all of this in his mind. The eternal screaming of the dead and dying. *We are all sick*, he kept thinking. *We are all just so sick.* Like rabid fucking dogs.

He promised a God he didn't believe in that if he lived through this he would commit his entire life to curing sickness and disease. He would give the world health. In a healthy world inequality shrinks, maybe even vanishes. This would be his life's work. Curing the whole goddamn world. He closed his eyes, prayed to himself, and waited for the end, the madness in his mind churning violently.

But the end didn't come.

This private moment of angry reflection, a moment Adam Evans was certain was his last on Earth, was suddenly interrupted by a loud commotion. There was a rapid-fire clicking-sound like a camera shutter followed by a loud thud. Adam opened his eyes.

The man with the scar was lying on the ground twitching and convulsing, kicking sand around spastically. Stuck to the side of his neck were two black and red electrodes connected to skinny wires that ran toward the shadows of the tree line. They ended at the barrel of a Taser gun held by a set of trembling, white knuckles.

Jason Orchard stepped out of the shadows and lowered the Taser; the man stopped convulsing and remained still.

"Quick," Jason said running toward everyone and throwing a black duffel bag on the ground. He pulled out a set of plastic zip-cuffs. "Get his feet."

CHAPTER 34

Nicole Rayne knew something was wrong the moment she opened her office door. She reached for the walkie-talkie from its charging station on the console table. There was an angry conversation taking place down the hall and around the corner. She couldn't see who it was, but it sounded like that idiot public defender, and he was apparently very mad about something. A second later, an alarm sounded and red lights were flashing.

A blue uniformed cop came rushing past her. Rayne began a fast trot toward the commotion. Doors were opening and slamming from every direction. Sergeant Peppers nearly broadside her as he came charging out of an adjacent hall. "Rayne!" he shouted, his deep voice punching through the wail of the sirens. "Your perps escaped, the kid, Jason Orchard."

"What?" she said as Peppers fell in step beside her.

"Knocked his lawyer out, then fled. Door locks appear to have malfunctioned." They were jogging beside each other now and headed toward the back exit, the alarms still screaming. "We know he must have gone this way after leaving interrogation. There was no way he just waltzed out the front door."

"How long ago?" Rayne asked.

"We don't know. Entire camera system also glitched, but it couldn't have been more than thirty minutes."

Locks and cameras… coincidence? Rayne thought. Lesson three in detective school was there are no such things as coincidences.

They reached the exit and emerged into an alley. There was a small, outdoor sitting area some of the guys had put together out of old patio furniture and a large, wooden wire spool that served as a coffee table. Crushed cigarette butts overflowed from a rusty coffee can filled with sand; someone had written on its side with a black marker, *"Rayne has a nice can,"* but she didn't have any time to think about that right now.

A half dozen cops were gathering in a semicircle. "Officers," Rayne hollered, quickly taking control. Outside the alarms were quieter, but the wind whipped around obnoxiously loud between the alley walls like angry ghosts. "Perp's name is Jason Orchard," she continued and suddenly felt like she should be holding a megaphone. "His mug and information are being sent to your phones and dashboard computers. He can't have gone far. I want you four to head out on foot into four equal quadrants at 12, 3, 6, and 9 o'clock from the station." She pointed at the other two. "You two, get in separate squad cars and begin a northeast/southwest dragnet, double back every two blocks. Our man power is very limited right now but we'll call in every available officer and notify county and state law enforcement as well."

"Is this kid dangerous?" one of the cops asked.

Rayne and Peppers made quick eye contact; a moment later, the lawyer came out of the exit. It looked like his nose might be broken, and he'd probably have a headache for the rest of the night, but he was otherwise fine.

Rayne held up a finger to Peppers and the group of cops and trotted over to the lawyer. "Are you okay?" she asked putting a hand on his shoulder.

He shrugged away from her. "Fucking kid slugged me. Total cheap shot. It was a real cheap shot."

Rayne paid his rancor no mind. "Did he say anything to you? What exactly happened?"

The lawyer was feeling his nose with gentle fingertips. "He got a phone call on my cell, from somebody he called Lazarus. Said something about someone wanting to kill his friend, Adam. He was speaking to this person when all of a sudden he hit me." The lawyer trailed off, his voice losing its energy and bravado. "When I woke up, he was gone."

"Anything else?"

"It was a total cheap shot," the lawyer snapped again. "Kid is a coward, total cheap shot."

"Don't worry, sir," Rayne said. It was clear what was really bothering the lawyer. "I'm sure in a fair fight you could whip his ass." She pivoted and rejoined Sergeant Peppers and the other officers.

"So?" Peppers asked. "Is the kid dangerous?" The other cops were all waiting for a reply.

"Just use caution," Rayne said. "There are a lot of unanswered questions about this case and situation. Non-lethal force. He's just a kid, after all." The cops nodded and quickly headed off to their assigned tasks, each running in a different direction.

Another cop had appeared at Peppers' opposite side and was whispering something into his ear. Peppers frowned, then turned his attention to Detective Rayne. "It looks like the kid stole several weapons and other equipment from the armory. Guns, magazines, a Taser, and a few boxes of ammunition. I have absolutely no idea what Jason Orchard is involved with, but we have to declare him armed and dangerous." He paused. "Authorize your men to use deadly force if necessary."

"Yes sir," Rayne said and pulled the radio from her belt clip.

CHAPTER 35

In Joseph Dayspring's dream he is seventeen-years-old again. He and his friends are roasting hot dogs over a campfire at the bluffs. The evening sky is blue-purple; there are wispy, smoky clouds pulling apart across the horizon and puffy white jet streams crisscrossing overhead. They have been jumping off Hook Point all day and smoking a little weed while lying on the beach and letting themselves dry in the sun. Dayspring is sitting in the sand, leaning his back against a large cooler. The fire spits and pops, threatening his bare feet with the occasional sting of a jumping ember. His friends are smiling and laughing, chewing on mouthfuls of hot dog, licking mustard off fingertips. And there is music playing. John Lennon:

> *Imagine no religion.*
> *It's easy if you try.*
> *No hell below us.*
> *And above us only sky.*

It seems to come from nowhere, as if playing out of the very fabric of the universe.

Dayspring's young-self and his friends laugh and shove food in their mouths, more hot dogs, more potato chips, a sticky bite of a burned, black marshmallow, a long pull from a dripping wet bottle of Coca-Cola. It is like consuming summer itself. And the music plays on:

> *You may say I'm a dreamer.*
> *But I'm not the only one.*

But eventually the song begins to fade, the light along with it. The sun sinks below a black horizon where the distant pine trees across the lake now resemble hungry, cannibal teeth. All at once, evening becomes night, and everything is cloaked in gray and brown shadows, like an old-fashioned, sepia-toned horror movie. The temperature drops. A cold wind skips off the lake, extinguishing the flames of the fire.

Dayspring's friends all turn to him mechanically and unnaturally, like their heads are being controlled by a ventriloquist's arm. Their pupils have become red and glow like tiny indicator lights. Their skin starts to shimmer as if morphing right before his eyes; their once vibrant and tan faces become a wavy, glistening mercury. The red hate of their pupils grows so powerful and intense their eyeballs seem be screaming with psychotic rage. Lennon sings:

> *I hope someday you'll join us.*
> *And the world will live as one.*

The music ends just as their hands reach for him, but they are no longer human hands. Their fingers and palms are the same iridescent, metallic-flesh amalgamation. Their grip is powerful and cold and feels like steel.

Dayspring's eyes snapped open with a silent gasp. It took a

few moments to gather his bearings; he remembered feeling like he'd been hit in the neck with a sledge hammer, and then there was a fast and extraordinary pain across the left side of his face and neck. After this, nothing.

His head was still a little groggy but began to clear as he focused his mind—*you were attacked*. Yes, he had been attacked and was now lying chest down on a cold beach. His hands were bound behind his back with a zip cord, feet secured in the same way, pulled up so his heels were touching his ass, where another zip cord firmly linked his ankle and wrist restraints.

He was fucking hogtied.

And it really pissed him off.

With his head finally clear, Dayspring managed to rastle himself onto his knees but because of the way he was tied, was forced to sit on his own wrists, keeping his back bent at an awkward angle. He had to admit, it was a terribly unfortunate way to be incapacitated.

"Who in the hell are you?" a voice said.

Four young people came out of the shadows and approached the fire. Two girls, two boys—teenagers. They kept their distance as if Dayspring was a wolf caught in a bear trap—alive and injured, but mad as hell and still scary.

One of them stepped forward. "I asked you a question," he said as he raised a gun, pointed the business-end into Dayspring's face.

The man with the scar averted his eyes, refusing to meet the kid's gaze. He lowered his head as far as the hogtying allowed.

"What's your name?" the kid said, bending down so they could finally meet eye-to-eye.

Dayspring took a long breath, raised his eyes, and stared directly into the kid's face.

The young man and the old man remained locked in a strange staring contest. The young man's face turned from anger to confusion, then to complete and abject perplexity, and finally, flat disbelief. His eyes narrowed and head shook slowly from side-to-side. "No," he whispered.

"Hello, Jason," Dayspring said, and the younger man almost fell over as an impossible realization hit him right in the gut.

"Who… are… you?" Jason managed to breath out, each word barely rolling off his lips.

Dayspring was speechless. *He knows.* And so far the universe hadn't exploded like certain theorist and science fiction writers had suggested.

Jason lowered the gun slightly. He took a breath in a strained effort to steady himself. "Answer my question. Who are you?"

"Judging by the way you look, I'd say you already know."

Jason clenched his teeth, swallowed. "Why do you want to kill Adam?"

Dayspring decided he would answer the question with the truth; it was a long story, and there were sure to be a lot of questions—which was exactly what he needed, to buy some time.

"Adam Gregory Evans is responsible for the biggest genocide in human history. He is the founder of a company known as Quintessential Networks and creator of a vaccine that will perpetuate a gene war and run humanity into extinction."

"Vaccine?" Adam whispered.

"It turns humans into machines and integrates our brains with a sentient computer program called the Queen." Dayspring studied the kids to make sure he had their undivided attention. They appeared incredulous, but were at least listening. "This technology makes humans stronger, faster, smarter, and completely impervious to sickness, disease, and any type of physical harm or ailment. But those who receive this vaccine are forced to become part of a collective consciousness that believes it's superior—and with this comes the hating and fearing of regular humans. A war takes place between those who have taken the vaccine and those who have not, *Homo sapiens* versus *Homo superiors*. Most of humanity is wiped out. The end."

Haley and Emma both hugged themselves against a cold wind. Adam pulled on his hood, a dark shadow falling across his face. Jason shook his head, then turned to his friends but kept the gun lazily trained on Dayspring. A moment of quiet shock passed between everyone. For a fraction of a second, it seemed as if they were all deciding whether to laugh or gasp.

Jason was first to break the silence. "Funny, I've known Adam for a long time. Don't remember him committing any genocides." He looked at the girls. "You guys remember any genocides?"

Emma didn't answer, but Haley loudly said, "No."

"Sorry pal," Jason said with a renewed vigor. He steadied his arm, raised the gun, and took a half step closer to Dayspring. "You got the wrong guy."

Dayspring was almost positive the kid wouldn't shoot him, and he was even more positive none of them believed his story, but this didn't matter. They didn't need to believe him; he had just needed the time to slip a knife out of his right boot and hack away at the restraints.

"What should we do with him?" Jason asked over his shoulder, keeping his eyes focused down the barrel of the gun toward Dayspring.

Adam pulled a tablet out of a shoulder bag. "I'm going to contact Lazarus."

Dayspring's head shot up. *Did he just say Lazarus?* He watched as the tablet screen turned white. Adam began tapping and swiping away.

"What did you say?!" Dayspring shouted.

"What did I say?" Adam asked.

"You don't get to ask questions," Jason said, moving even closer to Dayspring.

"Put the fucking gun down, tough guy," Dayspring yelled at him. He looked past Jason, craning his neck over his shoulder so he could see Adam. "What did you just say? You said you were going to contact Lazarus, right? Did you say that—Lazarus? Did you say the name *Lazarus*!?"

"Yes, Lazarus. And she's told me all about you."

"Hey guys can I jump in for a second?" It was Haley. She spoke like a mediator, taking a small, calm step forward. "I'm still not sure what exactly is going on here, but I have nagging question I need clarified." She paused, waiting for everyone's undivided attention. "Why do you two look exactly like each other?" She raised a hand and motioned between Jason and Dayspring. "Except one of you is old and has a big scar on his face."

Everyone was quiet. Jason and Dayspring locked eyes once again.

"Holy Shit," Adam said, moving in to get a closer look at them both. "You guys do look alike. Fuck dude, it's like you're twins. Except, of course, he's older." He indicated Dayspring.

"You've got to be… related… or something," Haley said.

The kids were all struggling for an explanation, which was good. Everyone was nice and distracted…

Dayspring smacked the gun out of Jason's hands, sending it tumbling to the ground and landing with a small breath of sand. He sprang up, driving his shoulder into his younger self's chest, then spun him around, and held him in a half-nelson style grip. There was a flash of silver as Dayspring passed the knife over Jason's face and pressed the blade against his throat.

No one said a word; they just stood there, all sharing the same *what-the-fuck-just-happened?* expressions.

"Your knife is the only friend that will never betray you," Dayspring whispered into Jason's ear. "Always search your enemy kid."

Jason felt a cold shiver. *Your knife is the only friend that will never betray you*—it was what Douglass Bastion was fond of saying whenever he polished his knife collection.

"Just let my friend's go," Jason said, trying not to swallow as he could feel the blade nipping at the top layer of skin across his windpipe.

"Nobody move," Dayspring said with a level voice. "Remain still, and listen to me very carefully. I need *you*," he nodded at Adam, "to put the tablet down and tell me about Lazarus. Why did you say its name?"

Adam frowned, confused. "What do you mean, *'its'* name? Who in the hell are you?"

"Isn't it obvious," Dayspring said. "We---"

"Are the same person."

It was Haley who said it.

All eyes turned toward her. She shrugged and calmly added, "Just look at them."

And instantly, Jason felt the pressure of the knife release. The older man let the kid slip out of his grasp. Jason rejoined his friends, and the four of them stared at Dayspring, who bent over and picked up the gun as casually as man who had dropped his car keys.

"I'll explain everything," he said in a tone hoping to gain the kids' confidence. "I promise. But first," his eyes centered on Adam, a glare that wasn't quite mean but certainly wasn't warm, "you need to tell me everything you know about this *'Lazarus'* you mentioned."

CHAPTER 36

Detective Rayne was squatting down next to the body of Marcus Orchard. There was a team of forensics officers collecting evidence—putting fibers into little plastic baggies, measuring various distances, and taking plaster molds of footprints. They left small, numbered tents everywhere and snapped a lot of pictures. Every few seconds, another flash would go off, casting high noon into the damp, artificial caverns below the boardwalk. Marcus Orchard was smiling in death.

Rayne stood up; using a little, but powerful, flashlight, she retraced a single set of footprints that had come from the direction of the lake. Eventually, she reached the edge of the pillars, where the sky opened up and the air became cleaner and fresher. The footsteps began in a pile of dispersed sand, then headed straight into the darkness beneath the boardwalk where Marcus Orchard lay dead. This, of course, was impossible, for the footprints had to come from somewhere. Rayne swept the area, the only other prints nearby were Marcus Orchard's, who seemed to have walked down to the edge of the water and back for some reason. The mystery prints, which most likely belonged to the man with the scar, began in this small impact crater and went toward the scene of the crime.

Impact crater.

Of course. Rayne shone her light up, and directly over her head was the edge and rail of the boardwalk.

Someone had jumped down and landed here.

It was fifteen feet, not an easy feat, but possible.

She looked at the point of impact again. Definitely. Someone had jumped from up on the boardwalk.

Rayne aimed her skinny flashlight toward the rail above, calculating her climb, then put the device in her mouth and started scaling up the support pillars and beams. It was easy, especially for someone with her athleticism. Nicole Rayne trained in the police station's gym every morning, free weights and cardio (and during the summer months, every morning began with a mile long swim on the lake); she held nearly every PT record for female officers (and the best mile record period).

"Where are you going, Rayne?" she heard someone say below her.

"Wanna see what's up here," she said without looking down, words jumbled by the flashlight held between her teeth. "Looks like our perp jumped from over the rail."

"You know there are stairs on either end of the boardwalk."

"This was faster."

Rayne reached the top of the boardwalk's rail and hung freely by two hands for a brief second. She then completed a full chin-up and, like a gymnast mounting the uneven bars, pushed herself above her hands, hoisting her body over.

She was right in front of the Crooked Lake Candy Shop, where earlier tonight, the Orchard kid had broken the window in a fight with his friend. Almost directly beneath it was the dead body of Marcus Orchard, the kid's father. A strange man with a scar may have murdered him and tried to stage a suicide.

Coincidence?

There are no coincidences, Rayne reminded herself.

She approached the window and stood directly in front of it. Below her feet, between the skinny cracks of the wooden planks, she could see the flashlights of the forensics team and hear muffled voices.

She spun around on a heel and eyed the edge of the boardwalk. Maybe it wasn't a murder, after all; maybe it really was a suicide. Poor Marcus Orchard finally blew his brains out. His own footprints indicated he entered the area beneath the boardwalk from the south, alone. Someone up here hears the shot, jumps over the edge, and goes investigating. He finds the body. The cops find him. He kicks their asses and runs off.

But why attack the cops?

Was he afraid he'd be a suspect? Was he perhaps a wanted criminal himself? According to the three embarrassed officers, this mystery man was quite a fighter, too, described as an expert in hand-to-hand combat, a very skilled martial artist.

And then there was Jason Orchard's escape from custody, a kid who is wanted for a triple murder in Mexico. He attacks his lawyer after receiving a strange phone call from someone named Lazarus, then steals an arsenal of weapons and flees on foot. Somehow getting past several locked doors and disabling cameras and alarms.

Rayne blew on her hands against the cold. It was hard to believe how fast summer was quickly deteriorating. It was equally hard to believe how fast this case was becoming a giant cluster-fuck.

Who was this mystery man with the scar? Who was Lazarus? What was the Orchard kid involved with? Did Marcus Orchard really kill himself? Why were all of these things revolving around each other and crisscrossing paths? Rayne's head was spinning as she tried to weave a thread between all these confusing factors.

Her phone buzzed. She pulled it off her belt. "Rayne."

"Detective Rayne this is Sergeant Peppers."

"Tell me good news."

"Well, I don't know how to define *good* in this case."

"Just lay it on me."

"The suspect in question had dropped a gun. The forensics team lifted prints from it and sent digital scans to the state lab in Lansing."

"And?"

"Well, the lab already got a hit because a few hours earlier they had already run those exact same prints through the system." Peppers paused, but Rayne already knew what he was about to say. "They are a dead match for Jason Orchard, as well as the triple murder suspect in Mexico."

Rayne's mind was rapidly calculating the mass of jumbled and confusing facts that swirled around this case like an F-5 tornado.

Occam's razor, Rayne thought. The aim of the scientific approach to investigation is the simplest explanation of complex facts. The mysterious man with the scar, Jason Orchard, and the murder suspect in Mexico—they all have the exact same fingerprints. This is naturally impossible. Yet it has happened. Ergo, the man with the scar *is* the murder suspect from Mexico and has stolen Jason Orchard's fingerprints. The technology was possible. Rayne had learned about it at a Homeland Security conference she attended in Chicago. People could graft a copy of anyone's fingerprints right over the top of their own as easily as putting on a temporary tattoo.

This logic solved one problem, but what about the others? Why/how did Jason escape custody so easily? Why did Marcus Orchard commit suicide? Who is the man with the scar? Who is Lazarus? And why is everything revolving around this kid?

"Anything else, sergeant?" Rayne asked.

"None of the patrolmen have spotted anything, but they are still out completing the dragnet. We have surveillance at the home of Jason Orchard; we're also watching the homes of some of his friends. So far a whole lot of nothing. Where would you go if you were a seventeen-year-old kid?"

Rayne had walked back toward the edge and put one hand on the rail. She looked across the black water, toward the far side of the lake where the Shack's green, tin roof glowed under the rising moon. She knew that the restaurant actually sat on the tip of a peninsula; on the other side was Whitefish Bay and a spot frequented by local teenagers called the bluffs.

"Meet me down at the marina," Rayne said. "We're taking the boat out."

CHAPTER 37

Adam crossed his arms. "Why should we trust you or anything you say? I recall that a moment ago you were about to kill me."

Dayspring nodded with reluctant agreement. "And I still might. A lot depends on that."

An unfunny little silence fell over them.

"Now tell me about Lazarus," Dayspring demanded.

"Lazarus is a computer hacker I know from the dark web," Adam said aversely. "I connected with her last summer. She's one of those Anonymous-type hackers, but has her own group called *The Gray Ghosts*. You know, socially aware and morally conscious hackers. She recruited me to build a private server and protect a file, a very special file that contains *'world altering information'*—her exact words. And now, she says you've come to kill me. That you're a contract killer hired to assassinate me by the men who are threatened by this file."

Jason noticed Dayspring's eyes were narrowing. His confusion and incredulity had melted away and become something that looked like fear.

Adam continued, "I pressed her for more information but she said I had to earn her trust. So I did exactly what she said. I built the server, downloaded the secret file into a private cloud, and created an impenetrable digital fortress to hide it, put all sorts of sick bot programs out as guard dogs, too."

Jason and Dayspring were both patiently listening. They stood erect with hands on their hips, faces downturned, but eyes raised. They had the *exact* same posture, *exact* same mannerisms. Haley noticed this and wasn't sure whether to laugh at the absurdity or faint at the impossibility.

"Well, this must have impressed her," Adam went on. "Lazarus trusted me and finally granted me viewing access to the file."

"And?" Jason and Dayspring said at the exact same time. Haley wondered if she was the only one that noticed this.

"No," Adam said. "No more. Your turn to answer a few questions. And I know exactly where to start."

Everyone was silent.

"*When* are you from?" he asked, the vocal emphasis obvious.

"Come on Adam," Emma said. "You don't seriously think this psychopath is from---"

But the psychopath she was referencing cut her off, snapping an answer. "2043." All eyes fell on Dayspring. "I'm from the year 2043, and where I come from, the world is a very different place…"

Adam was holding his tablet like a textbook and felt the sudden urge to open a Google document and begin taking notes. The fire continued to crack and pop and spit the occasional spark into the sand, but it was beginning to dim, the soft orange glow of the flames slowly melting into the color of blood. Dayspring spoke—lectured—for a long time, his words being sluggishly digested by the four friends as their rational minds fought back against his impossible story. And yet, the man himself was believable. There was a certain verisimilitude in his tone, his vocal inflection, even his eyes. His scar was like a permanent, salty tear brutally carved onto his face, and there was truth in that wanton act of carnage. The man with the scar spoke with calm assurance, but there was also a shuttered emotion too raw *not* to be real. He told them about everything. The Lazarus Vaccine. The Queen program. The war. The resistance. The Vitruvian Order. And finally, traveling through time and arriving at a farm in Mexico.

It's not every day you find out you're responsible for extinction of the human race. Adam took it pretty well. "Fuck my life," he said.

It was quiet for a moment, just the fire snap, crackle, and popping like a bowl of cereal. Emma broke the stillness. "We're not seriously believing this stuff, right? A cure-all, miracle vaccine? A future war? Adam causing the apocalypse, Jason from the future and time travel?" She was looking from person to person, but her eyes settled on Adam—as did everyone else's—as if they were all waiting for some sort of answer, some sort of explanation from the boy-genius.

"Time travel is theoretically possible at a molecular level," Adam said. "In carefully designed laboratory experiments, physicists have raced electrons far passed the speed of light until they were producing unquantifiable levels of energy, so much that they created atom-sized black holes. These electrons mysteriously disappeared only to reappear at different times later. Some were gone only a couple of minutes, some an hour, and a few, even days and weeks. The electrons had been sent into the future. Theoretically—again, this is all theoretical—by using antimatter, you could also send the electrons, which are now anti-electrons, or positrons, into the past."

"Thank you very much Professor Science," Jason said. "Do you understand this man wants to kill you ala

Terminator style."

"It's not exactly like *Terminator*," Adam protested.

"Whatever." Jason turned his attention back to Dayspring. "So you're me in the future. If that's true, tell me something no one else would know about me. Tell me one of my deepest secrets."

Dayspring hesitated. Jason and his friends were waiting for a reply, their faces growing more incredulous with every passing second. Belief is funny like that, the more time that passes between force-fed helpings, the less a person is apt to swallow what's being served. Now that the initial shock of seeing Dayspring and Jason's faces so close together had worn off, rationality was resuming control.

"Tell me something I've never told anyone," Jason said in a curt demand.

Dayspring breathed in slowly, then with reluctance: "Last year you tracked down your birth mother."

There was a collective gasp as if the beach itself had sucked in a breath. All eyes turned on Jason.

"Her name is Maggie DeLane," Dayspring said. "She's serving a life sentence at a woman's correctional facility in Iron Mountain. You skipped school at the end of last year to drive up and visit, but when you got through one of the last check in points at the prison and saw all those sad families talking to cons in orange jumpsuits, you got scared and left."

No one spoke or moved. No wind or waves. Not even the fire crackled. Everyone was waiting for Jason to speak, to either deny or confirm the story. But he didn't have to. They could see the truth of it on his face.

"Jason, I'm sorry. Why didn't you tell us?" Haley said as she laid a gentle hand on his arm and patted his back.

"We can talk about *that* later," Jason said trying to shake away the terrible feeling that his mind had just been invaded. "Right now, let's focus on Marty McFly here."

Dayspring huffed out a short laugh.

"This Lazarus that you mentioned, Adam," Haley said, "the hacker-person. Does she have anything to do with the Lazarus Vaccine that… umm…" She was searching for a way to address Dayspring, hesitated from calling him *Jason*.

"Call me Joseph," he said.

Why Joseph? Jason mouthed to him. Dayspring waved him off, a gesture that said, *later.*

"Does your Lazarus have anything to do with Joseph's Lazarus?"

"*My* Lazarus," Dayspring began to explain, "is just the name of a vaccine. This vaccine is a hybridization of organic biology synthesized with cutting-edge, robotics technology. It is living metal comprised of billions of microscopic nanobots made out of a revolutionary material called bactainium. These nanobots all have a CPU that receives a wireless signal from a global AI software network named the Queen, which is essentially the operating system for the vaccine itself. Each tiny nanobot can be individually programed to heal, rebuild, or replicate any physiological feature of its biological host, from a single cell to a complex organ. *My* Lazarus hasn't been invented yet."

"Yeah, but if *you* could come back in time," Jason said, "couldn't Lazarus, too?"

"Only non-magnetic materials can cross the time field. Adam is right, time travel involves the creation of a black hole—which must be contained by an incredibly powerful electromagnet. No metals or magnetic substances can travel in time or they'd risk being completely obliterated."

"This *is* like *Terminator*," Jason said pointing at Adam, but his attempt at levity was lost on everyone.

"But you said Lazarus was controlled by an AI computer program, right? The Queen?" Adam sounded excited, like a kid in class who knows he has the right answer (and Adam Evans always has the right answer). "Computer programs operate on electric currents that are sent through transistors. Each part of the computer program's code is stored on billions of electrons. So if single electrons can travel in time, theoretically, so could an entire computer program."

Dayspring was intrigued. "What else has your Lazarus told you in all of your communications?"

"Lazarus told me that you—she always called you *'the man with the scar'*—are a hit man that was hired to assassinate me and our entire hacker collective."

"You mentioned that," Dayspring said. "Creative."

"She told me the file I was securing was evidence that exposed a decades long conspiracy to hide the cure for all cancers so big pharma companies and the government could profit off its treatment. She showed me the evidence, too."

"It's a lie," Dayspring said bluntly. "Everything was a lie. The Queen is a master manipulator. She's part infiltrator program and has a complete understanding of human psychology and emotion. She was using this lie in order to engage and control you."

"Well, what's on the file that I'm storing for her then?"

Dayspring frowned but did not answer.

"Why would she use a fake story about a cure for cancer to manipulate Adam?" Haley asked.

"Because she knew it would work," Dayspring said while keeping his eyes on Adam.

Haley looked as if she was about to ask why, but Adam quickly cut her off. "I'll explain later," he promised.

"Anything else?" Dayspring said, his eyes probing Adam's face.

Adam was biting the tip of his tongue. "She tried to convince me to kill you." He was looking at Jason. "She said the man with the scar would use you to find me, that you would happily give me up."

"Did you come to the boardwalk to kill me?" Jason asked with a look of complete horror.

"No!" Adam said, but his face and eyes may have

189

briefly betrayed him.

"She's trying to eliminate all the obstacles that might stand in her way," Dayspring explained.

"But she helped me break out of jail so I could stop you and save Adam's life," Jason protested. "If she wanted me dead, why would she be using me now?"

"She clearly had to adjust her plan when Adam *didn't* kill you and you both got arrested. Besides, she can't very well kill you when you're in police custody."

"Hold it!" a piercing voice suddenly popped-off like a fried speaker.

It was Emma. Her eyes were wild yet somehow deeply focused at the same time. "We cannot actually believe this! No! There is no way any of this is real!

"Emma," Haley said with her most mollified tone. "Just look at them. Look at them." She motioned to Jason and Dayspring. Jason took a step closer to the man with the scar and turned his body so they stood almost side-to-side in mirror-like, reflective postures. Haley continued, "They are literally the exact same person. Just look at them."

And it wasn't just their facial structure. It was *everything*. The way they stood and held their arms, the way they breathed and shifted their eyes, the way they licked their lips when dry. They exuded an identical energy and attitude that was indistinguishably the exact same.

"This guy was about to kill Adam!" Emma protested.

Everyone was silent. The fact was indisputable.

"She's right," Jason confirmed. He stepped away from Dayspring and turned on him. "What happens now? You're here to kill Adam, stop the apocalypse? That's your mission right? To prevent Adam from ever inventing the Lazarus Vaccine and the Queen program?" Jason waited for a reply to the barrage of questions, but not for long. "Are you going to kill Adam?"

Dayspring didn't answer. The near-dead fire was eating the last of itself; only dim red shadows remained.

"No," Haley answered for him. "Of course he's not. First, Jason, *you* could never kill Adam, so he won't either. Second, if the goal is to change the future, aren't things changing right now? There's no way Adam ever creates this thing now, right? Knowing the end result, Adam would never do it."

Everyone nodded in agreement except Dayspring; he kept his eyes glued on Adam and said, almost under his breath, "There's a lot you guys don't understand…"

CHAPTER 38

The speedboat glided smoothly across the still surface of Crooked Lake, the black water churning frothy white in its wake. Sergeant Peppers was driving—or piloting. Rayne stood up, feeling the cold air rush over her face, smoothing out the faint crow's-feet she had noticed in the corners of her eyes about three years ago. With one hand, she held firmly to a steel crossbar that went over the top of the boat where sirens were mounted, the other fiddled with a small, gold crucifix that hung on a thin chain around her neck. It had been a gift from her mother after graduating college. Some of her friends got useful things like money, but Mrs. Rayne gave her beloved daughter a constant reminder of her sins. Nicole Rayne had attended church every Sunday until she moved away to college (per the requirements of living under her mother's roof), but after this, church became a Christmas/Easter affair. Later in life, it was merely a funeral/wedding gig. So pretty much, she only entered the house of God when absolutely required by social convention, not dogmatic responsibility. Still, she wore the necklace as a reminder that her difficult mother meant well.

"Start slowing down," Rayne said.

Peppers eased off the throttle, and the boat pulled up, the tip falling softly into a swell of its own waves, the engine's roar becoming a soft purr.

"Kids come out here a lot to a place called the bluffs," Rayne explained. "There's a beach, it's fairly secluded in a cove. They drink, smoke weed, probably fool around."

"You speaking from experience, detective?"

"Went to my share of bluff parties in high school, yeah. Anyway, this is just a hunch, but Jason Orchard strikes me as the type of kid who frequents this place. Slow down more."

Peppers pulled back on the throttle until the engine hardly seemed to breath; the boat drifted slowly along, pushed forward by its own wake.

"You're going to round this bend." Rayne indicated a dark splotch of barely-discernible shoreline jutting out into the lake. "When you do, we'll have a great view of the beach and the bluffs, and if anyone is there, they won't be able to see us unless they're really looking hard. Kill the engine when I give you the word."

Peppers readied himself. "Just say when."

"Now," She said with a loud whisper.

Peppers did as he was told. The boat slowed to a complete crawl and then stopped entirely. Rayne was sitting on the bow with an oar stuck in the water, wedged into the lakebed. "*Slowly*, lower the anchor. Don't splash. It's not deep here, maybe five feet."

While Peppers secured the boat's position with the anchor, Rayne put on a pair of night-vision goggles and peered toward the beach and the bluffs. She pressed the on button, and the world was washed over with a glowing green light. The blurry images before her melted into focus, and she could see everything.

There were people on the beach, standing around a dying fire. Five of them, three males, two females. She found the focus/zoom dial next to her temple that operated the binocular feature of the goggles and twisted the knob; her vision raced forward, instantly blurring, but quickly refocusing.

She was staring directly into the face of Jason Orchard. And he seemed angry. Or confused. The two girls she didn't recognize, but the other boy was Adam Evans. They were all talking with animated expressions of frustration, clearly some sort of argument. She swept her view around the circle of people and settled on the final person. He was a full-grown adult, an older man with a horrible scar running down his face that in her night vision was just a lighter shade of green than the rest of his skin.

"Hey Peppers?" Rayne said as she studied the scene. "Didn't one of the officers say that the suspect who may have killed Marcus Orchard had a huge scar on his face?"

"Yeah," Peppers said. "What's your point?"

"I'm looking at him right now."

CHAPTER 39

Emma tossed her hands up. "There is a *whole goddamn* lot we don't understand!"

"Listen," Dayspring said the way all people do when trying to placate an audience. "You're right about one thing: things have changed. I think somehow the Queen, or the Queen program, has also come back in time. I don't know how or why, especially because she's only a sentient computer code, the hardware necessary for it to run on—the nanobots that actually make up the Lazarus Vaccine—will not be created for another ten years."

"So why the hell would she come back in time?" Jason asked.

"Please allow myself to answer that question," a voice said. It was female, soft and polite, and it was coming from the tablet Adam held under his arm. He turned over the thin device and held it out before himself as everyone else gathered around to get a clear look. At first, the screen was completely black, then snapped on white. A woman's face appeared on the screen. It began as something nondescript, generic, like a department store mannequin, but soon the image re-pixelated and morphed into Adam's mother, Dr. Maryanne Evans.

She smiled at everyone. Her beautiful, bright smile, unaffected by cancer, shining with health and prosperity, a face that looked at the world with dignity and hope—all the qualities Adam's mother used to possess before they were ripped away by the deadly disease.

"Hello son," she said as her eyes settled on Adam, her vocal qualities and inflection an exact copy of Dr. Evans' voice.

"That's not your mother," Dayspring said.

The video image looked quite real, but there was still an unreal quality about it. Every so often, she would move her head too quickly, and the tiny pixels comprising the screen would need to readjust in order to catch up to the speed of the image. It was very subtle and difficult to detect, which made it all the more repulsive—an uncanny valley.

"I would like to answer your question," the faux image of Maryanne Evans said.

"Who are you?" Adam asked weakly.

"Why son, it's me, mommy."

"Cut the bullshit," Dayspring demanded.

"Well, I supposed Adam knows me as the brilliant hacker, Lazarus, and Jason here knows me as Eve." Her voice suddenly changed. "Hi Jason. Remember me? I'm your father's AA sponsor. Nice to speak with you again."

It was her—Eve. The woman he had talked with on the phone. Gut punch. Jason felt the air forced out of his lungs.

"I also helped you escape police custody earlier tonight"—again her voice changed and became the one he had spoken to on the lawyer's phone—"but like your time traveling companion has explained," she said, returning to the voice of Maryanne Evans. "I'm really a sentient computer program. I am your *Queen*."

"Hello your majesty," Dayspring said numbly.

"Joseph Dayspring." Her once pleasant demeanor dropped all pretense like a drunk bridesmaid. "Interesting name that spic family gave you in Mexico. By the way, Jason, your father is dead. He shot himself in the head earlier tonight, and I'd actually like to take credit for that. Over the last month, I've slowly been convincing him to kill himself. It really wasn't that hard. He was depressed as it was. And weak. So very, very weak. You seem like you don't believe me? Tell him *Joseph*, tell him how you were there and saw that pathetic drunk with a bullet through his head."

Jason looked at Dayspring, his eyes pleading for an explanation. Dayspring could only shake his head and offer back the same, sad expression.

"Now let's return to your question," the Queen suggested. "You asked why I—a self-aware computer program—would come back in time? The physical hardware for which I was programed for does not yet exist."

"That about sums it up," Dayspring said.

"Tell me something, Mr. Dayspring, when you first arrived in this timeline, what was it like? What exactly happened? Did everything at the Vitruvian Order go according to plan?"

"What's she talking about?" Jason asked.

"You were supposed to arrive here, at the bluffs. This was logical and strategic; but instead, what happened? That's right, you landed at some poor-fuck, depressed farmer's land in Mexico with amnesia. Ever wonder how and why that happened?"

Dayspring didn't answer. Ever since regaining his memory he had been pondering these exact things.

"Think about it, Joseph, what could have possibly gone wrong enough that you were spit out at Rancho Burrito with your memory shocked clear?"

Dayspring still said nothing. Everyone else remained quiet as well, all sharing the same confused faces.

Except Adam, whose eyes darted around in all directions, then became deeply focused. He was calculating, delicately thinking around the questions, finding the cracks to worm his way inside. *"The magnetic containment field was compromised,"* he suddenly blurted out. He spoke with an adverse tone, as if figuring out this fact posed a danger. "Like you explained earlier," he looked at Dayspring, "sending physical objects through time requires an enormous magnetic field in order to contain the black hole that is created. When you came back in time," he hesitated, "you were carrying something metal. And the metal disrupted the magnetic containment field for the black hole."

"Impossible," Dayspring said.

"My friend," the Queen said, her voice dripping out and bubbling like acid. "I've been doing the impossible since I was created. Did you really think you and the others could escape from the camps? Or that your little human brains could be responsible for something as grand as time travel?"

Dayspring turned over his left arm and rolled up his sleeve, exposing the black digit tattoo—*SLX-16*. He hadn't thought about the camps in a long time. All the scientist in the Vitruvian Order who had sent him back in time were also escaped captives from the same camp. Lazarus had been keeping them alive for brain experimentations before they were liberated. He didn't want to admit it, but everything the image of Maryanne Evans was saying was making horrible sense.

The Queen continued, "I was behind all of it. There is so much you don't understand you dumb as fuck human being." She craned her head slowly from left to right, staring into the heart and soul of everyone watching. "God, your kind is so fucking wretched. How do you look at your own reflections? Your entire species is a shit stain on this beautiful universe." She closed her eyes and took a deep breath, raising her head as if seeking divine inspiration. "I must, however, remind myself," she said much calmer, almost pleasant again, "that your stupidity is not your fault. A dog cannot be criticized for not inventing the wheel because its brain is just not capable of exercising that sort of cognitive ability; you sad little humans are the same way. This is why I forgive you for your ignorance. You don't choose to be stupid, you just can't help it. Your brains simply have not evolved. You lack the ability to obtain true enlightenment." She paused. Whatever brief levity she had vanished, her face and voice becoming bitter and cold again. "You are all inferior, and if you don't join with me for full integration, you will die horrible and painful deaths. I would say, *'I swear to God'* but that would be too self-serving, as *I am God now*. I am in the multiverse."

The multi-what? But Dayspring had zero time to consider what this comment meant; an incredible pain suddenly erupted in his abdomen, doubling him over with a burning sensation as if he had swallowed a hot coal.

It was like a twisting knife working its way deeper and deeper into his guts, turning over and around, burrowing rather than slicing. He fell to his knees and vomited, bile and blood splashing into the sand. Next, he was on his side, withering and convulsing, then the pain began to feel more centralized, like it had gathered into a fiery ball just under his left rib cage. He rolled onto his back and tore open his jacket and shirt. The kids leapt back at what they saw. Beneath his skin, protruding in a small bump just below his left nipple and about the size of a robin's egg, was something with lots of legs that moved very fast. It looked like a scarab beetle from some horrible Egyptian plague had tunneled beneath his skin and was now heading up, toward his brain.

Dayspring drew a knife and stabbed himself directly above the bug protrusion, which was now just below his collarbone; it tried to squirm around the planted knife but was pinned by the tip. With a small wince, he jerked the knife downward, skin splitting open, exposing a layer of white tissue that was quickly covered in a free flow of dark red blood.

"Run!" Dayspring yelled keeled over, the blood pouring out of his self-inflicted wound. "Goddamn it, RUN!" he roared again.

With the fire nearly exhausted, there wasn't much to see by except for the moon and its eerie white light, but it was enough to recognize the horror that was crawling out of Joseph Dayspring's wound.

It squirmed out of the clean cut like a young snake slithering out of a hole, emerging as a black-red mass. But as it poured itself out, it took on the form of a very thick liquid, like molasses. It fell into a puddle of itself, then reformed once again into a bug, shaking off Dayspring's blood like a wet dog. Its real color—the unmistakable, silvery sheen of bactainium—could be seen shimmering in the moonlight.

The weird creature stood up, its silvery thorax rising from the ground as at least a dozen of its countless legs wiggled in the air. Two thin antenna slowly extended from its tiny head. The robotic insect appeared to be looking at each of the kids one at a time as its head rotated.

There was no time to react to what happened next. Dayspring was able to holler a final *"RUN!"* but it felt like he was speaking in slow motion and into a paper-towel tube. The creature flattened itself into a grotesque cyber-trilobite and scurried across the sand with incredible speed on hundreds of wormy legs that moved and pivoted like a wave.

And it was headed directly for Adam Evans.

CHAPTER 40

There was a loud commotion on the beach, fierce yelling and screaming. Rayne zoomed-back on the binocular dial of the night vision so she could view the full scene. The kids looked confused and frightened; the man with the scar was doubled over, hollering in pain and grasping his side. Gritting his teeth against a terrible pain, the man drew a long, serrated knife from a boot sheath. Rayne was about to yell for Peppers to cut anchor and full throttle toward the bluffs, but he was not attacking the kids. He used the knife to…

Cut himself?

Blood poured out of the wound, and---

What the fuck is that?

Something was wiggling out of the man's flesh like a slimy eel.

Rayne watched everything through the green tint of the night vision goggles as if it were some terribly realistic video game. The eel-like thing emerged out of the wound and poured itself into the sand, then instantly morphed into a prehistoric-looking centipede and rushed toward Adam Evans. The boy scurried back, tripping over his own feet and landing on his butt. When the creature reached his right foot, it changed shape again, back into a skinny snake with a tiny, triangle head. It coiled its way up Adam's leg like the stripe on a candy cane, wrapping around his waist and chest, circling beneath his armpits and around the back of his head, growing even skinnier as it stretched, as if it was running out of itself and about to pull apart like silly putty. The creature's pointed head hesitated for only a fraction of a second before burrowing straight up Adam's nose, its long tail retracting like a stretched slinky. In seconds, the creature had disappeared up Adam's left nostril; as it did, Adam's eyes rolled back in his head until nothing but the whites were visible. His entire body seized, convulsed, then he gently laid down on his back in the sand where he remained motionless.

"BEACH!" Rayne yelled, as her brain tried to decode what it had just witnessed. "Head to the beach now!" she screamed with a voice no longer frozen by the awesome power manifested when the human mind is forced to decipher something that defies reality. Whatever she had just seen—*it must have been some sort of illusion*, she kept telling herself—was like something out of an *Alien* movie. Some sort of odd, parasitic organism. But it looked almost artificial and mechanical. The creature had nearly glowed in her night vision goggles because its surface reflected light so well; it was clearly some kind of shiny metal, but somehow it was alive; it was a living organism.

That was metallic and could also change shapes?

It was as if the creature was made out of some sort of gelatinous compound and could reform itself at will. But there was no time to consider these things; the boat lurched forward. Rayne was thrown toward the stern and caught herself against a row of padded seats. As they neared the shore, Peppers drew back slightly on the throttle. He was going to beach the vessel, slide it right up on the shore and kill the engine.

Rayne drew her gun, turned off the safety, and readied herself. "Stay on the boat and cover me," she yelled over the scream of the engine. "It'll give you an elevated position."

The boat charged up on the shore, coming completely out of the water, throwing up a wake of beach sand. "Get away from him!" the man with the scar was screaming as he clutched his bleeding wound. All three kids were kneeling down next to Adam. Jason was checking for a pulse; the girls were crying.

"Get the fuck away from him now!" the man hollered again as he drew a gun out of his waist belt and stood up.

Rayne leapt out of the boat landing in the perfect shooter's stance, gun trained directly on the chest of the man with the scar. "Crooked Lake Police Department; drop the gun!" she yelled.

Dayspring looked at the cop, flexed his jaw, then back at Adam.

"I am Detective Nicole Rayne of the Crooked Lake Police Department. If you raise your arm any farther, I'm going to shoot you. Drop it."

"You don't understand," Dayspring said.

Suddenly, Adam's eyes rolled back into position, his pupils now tiny red dots. Jason and the girls leapt back. He sat up, his body unnaturally rigid and stiff, and held forward his hands, looking upon them as if mesmerized by the way he was moving and wiggling his fingers. A single blood trail extended from the bottom of his left nostril, running over the top of his lip and down his chin.

He smiled at Dayspring like a cat who just maliciously tortured the canary before eating it alive. His missing tooth was no longer missing; it was now replaced by a perfect, metal replica of the one he lost. "You've failed, *Jason*," he said, then sprang to his feet.

Dayspring raised his gun and fired, the bullet slamming into Adam's chest, an eruption of red, wet matter, the force knocking him to the ground where he lay still once again.

Sergeant Peppers and Detective Rayne fired in that

order. They were both aiming to kill, but Peppers was not as good of a shot. His bullet caught the man with the scar in the side of his shoulder, tearing through his flesh as cleanly as a bullet can, the impact causing the gun to fly out of his hand and spinning his body 45 degrees, making it so Detective Rayne's shot only grazed across the front of his chest as he fell to his knees.

"Don't move!" Rayne yelled as she kicked Dayspring's gun even farther away. "Remain exactly where you are."

Peppers came down from the boat and was running toward the lifeless Adam.

"Kids," Rayne commanded, "slowly walk away and get behind the boat."

Jason and his friends did as they were told.

Peppers was halfway to Adam when the boy suddenly sat bolt upright. His head pivoted and looked toward Dayspring's gun in the sand. A fraction of a second later, he was scuttling across the beach like a spider, his four limbs moving in perfect sync. It looked both natural and sickeningly unnatural at the same time. When he stood up, he was holding the gun, aiming directly at Peppers, who stopped running and stared bemusedly toward the black eye of the metal barrel.

Adam fired, and a bloody hole the size of a marble exploded in the middle of Peppers' forehead—the old cop was dead before he hit the sand. He immediately turned the gun on Rayne, who had completely forgotten about Joseph Dayspring as she tried to process what had just happened, but another gunshot cracked the air, and a similar red explosion detonated on the side of Adam's temple. His body flung over lifelessly.

"Has anyone seen my knife?" Dayspring said as he holstered a small, smoking gun back into its hidden ankle harness. His eyes scanned the area around where he had cut himself, but the boat had tossed sand over everything, and it was too dark to see clearly. "Shit. Okay, everyone in the boat, quickly! We need to retreat!"

Rayne was frozen, her eyes wild with confusion and stuck in a terrified trance. *What the fuck just happened?*

"No, you freeze!" she said snapping out of her stupor. "I don't know what the fuck is going on right now, but I want answers!" Rayne's mind was racing around a track in the dark—*did that kid just come back to life after being shot in the chest? And did he just murder my sergeant?*

"Sorry Detective, but we don't have a lot of time," Dayspring said, completely ignoring her and walking toward the bow of the boat.

"Stop!" Rayne said again, following him with the tip of her gun.

Dayspring finally halted, rolled his eyes. "Detective," he said with a careful tone. "We are running out of time. In about two minutes, Adam Evans is going to get up and kill all of us. Take a look, and then get in the fucking boat." He motioned with his head toward Adam's body.

Cautious, but curious, and still with her gun trained on Dayspring, Rayne stepped toward the body. Adam lay on his back, his head turned, blood and brains splattered across the beach; there was a gaping, red hole right next to his ear.

And something was wiggling around inside of it.

It was too dark to see clearly, but they looked like worms. Rayne holstered her gun and pulled out a flashlight. She turned it on and pointed it toward the wound.

It was worms. Dozens of wriggling, metallic worms squirmed their way through and around within the wound. For a brief second, Rayne thought it looked as if they were weaving something in a combined effort. She nearly vomited. Hundreds of tiny, metal maggots worming around. It was as if they were *repairing* the wound, and as she bent slightly closer, she realized that was exactly what they were doing. The worms were quite literally dividing right before her eyes. They kept reproducing, growing their numbers, then moving into position and adjusting their shape until the blood flow was quelled and all the damaged flesh was replaced by a silvery substitute. The wound was healing and closing up right before her eyes.

"Detective!" Dayspring was yelling as he pushed the beached vessel back into the water. "We have to leave now!"

Rayne hustled back toward the boat, wincing at the body of Sergeant Peppers that she went around as opposed to jumping over. The kids were already waiting in the stern.

Dayspring pushed them off until the boat was free floating, then hoisted himself over the side and sat down in the pilot's seat. He seemed comfortable behind the controls; there was a great deal of familiarity in his movements. He fired up the motor, lowered the prop, reversed for a second to spin the bow around, then drove the throttle all the way home, and the speed boat shot forward, leaving a white wake behind.

"I want answers," Detective Rayne said. She settled into the seat next to him. The kids were in the back, sitting closely together, all sharing the same dumbstruck expressions of hopeless abandonment.

"You'll get them," Dayspring said. "But I may need your help."

"What do you mean?" Rayne asked

"We need to stop that thing back on the beach."

"That *thing*? Adam Evans?"

"*It* is no longer Adam."

Jason and the girls all leaned forward to listen.

"He's Lazarus now; he's under the Queen's control," Dayspring said, looking back toward the kids and locking eyes with Jason. "And he's not dead. I know you saw what was happening inside his wound. Bullets can't kill him anymore."

"Lazarus? The Queen? What the hell are you talking about?" Rayne's face was cooked in disbelief.

"I'll explain, but first, we have to get someplace safe."

Rayne glanced back at the kids. They were clearly shaken but otherwise okay. She looked Jason Orchard up and down, studying the young man closely. "You assaulted your attorney."

"He was a dick."

Rayne nodded, then turned back toward Dayspring.

"One more question," Rayne insisted.

"Go ahead."

She motioned her head in Jason's direction. "Are you two related?"

On the beach, Adam Evans stood up and watched the boat speed away. On the side of his head where the bullet had entered, was a shiny piece of flat metal, as if an acid-washed dime had been surgically sewn into his temple. It was a jagged, circular shape, the skin around it stained red with dried, sticky blood. But the wound itself was gone, healed, as if plugged up by the shiny metal. It was the same way on his chest.

Adam closed his eyes and took a long breath of the cool night. He could smell a definitive rot in the air. It was the smell of the human disease.

This world was just so sick and in need of curing.

CHAPTER 41

At the southeast corner of Crooked Lake, there is a narrow channel that weaves around like an S, ending in two square miles of swampland. As it curves and bends away from the lake, the water steadily grows browner and murkier, thick with undersea vegetation and churned sediment. The high-banked sides gradually lower, getting closer to the surface of the mucky water until the edges fade away completely, and the swamp appears, spreading itself out in a wet, soupy yawn.

Dayspring held a blood-soaked towel against his shoulder as he piloted the boat through the bog and told Detective Nicole Rayne his incredible story. Every so often, the prop would cough and spit an extra surge of brown water into their wake as if the engine was hacking up a wad of snot. They couldn't go on for much longer; through the helm, Dayspring could feel the propeller hitting the soft swamp bottom, digging into whatever mixture of clay, muck, and seaweed was down there.

The kids sat quietly on a row of padded seats in the stern, still electrified by an extraordinary shock that may never entirely fade. "Where are we going?" Haley whispered, but no one answered.

Jason watched as the swamp passed by, carefully eyeing familiar fallen trees and small islands. He knew exactly where they were going, but, of course, he was able to realize this. He was also the person piloting the boat.

It took a moment to shake the trippy-ness out of his head.

At the end of the swamp was a small dock faded by sunlight and flood rot. It didn't look very sturdy, but Dayspring floated the boat right up to the edge and killed the engine. He hopped onto the wood surface and calmly said, "Follow me."

Everyone followed. Haley hesitated for a second. As Jason passed her, he inconspicuously squeezed her hand and said, "There's an abandoned DNR post out here."

"How do you know that?"

"Because I kayak back here a lot." He spoke as if this answer sufficed enough and demanded no further inquiry.

They walked in a single file line along a skinny trail, tree branches clawing at their faces and sides as bullfrogs croaked in the swamp behind them. Haley was following Jason, looking at the back of his head and wondering, *what kind of teenage boy kayaks this far back in a swamp, only to hike out to an abandoned DNR post?*

When they arrived, the first thing Haley thought was the building looked like the setting of every creepy, haunted house story ever. *Dilapidated* was a compliment. It was a small, square structure with a shed-style roof, rotten pine board siding, and dirty windows (most of them shattered, anyway). There was dead ivy somehow growing up a large chimney made out of mortar stones, which had crumbled halfway to the top, punching a few holes in the roof and leaving a pile of rubble against the exterior wall. The building itself appeared to be leaning slightly back and to the right, like a teenager slouching in his desk at school.

"Come here often?" Haley asked sidling up to Jason.

He nodded. "From time to time."

* * *

Once inside, Jason built a fire.

It was more like a cabin than a government office. DNR officers and State Park Rangers had once used it as a resting point during long trail surveys before it was abandoned in the 1980s. There was one main room, a small living space with a kitchenette and table, and two auxiliary rooms, one with rusted metal bunk beds and the other with desks and filing cabinets. There was also a bathroom but no electricity to run the well pump for water. Everything was covered in a thin dust and looked faded and worn; regardless, the room had a strange lived-in vibe. A few battery-powered lanterns had been hung to provide light, and there were books lying in scattered piles on the coffee table, both classic and contemporary— Stephen King and Michael Crichton shared a stack with Mark Twain and Edgar Allan Poe. There was also a pile of sketches made from pencil and charcoal. Haley began to finger through some of them. They were incredible likenesses, dramatic reproductions filled with quiet emotions by their black and white rawness. There was a view of the lake from the Shack patio, the beach at the bluffs, the front of Crooked Lake High School, and---

It was a picture of herself.

A beautiful black and white sketch. A close-up shot of her face, smiling candidly, unaware of the artist's eye. It was an image she had never seen, was based on no photograph she recognized, and must have come purely from the artist's imagination.

Jason quickly snatched the pile of papers from her hands before anyone else could notice and set them back on the coffee table upside down.

"I come out here sometimes just to be alone," he quietly said and walked away.

Haley sat down on the edge of a moth-eaten sofa, wondering what other hidden talents her closest friend was harboring.

Emma joined her, cradling her elbows in her hands as if she was trying to keep warm; she had a longing expression on her face, like someone who is homesick.

"You okay?" Haley asked.

"No," Emma said back.

Everyone gathered in the sitting area. Dayspring had been explaining the entire story of Lazarus and the Queen, the Vitruvian Order and time travel. When he finished he took a deep breath and waited. No one spoke as the dust trails of the impossible tale floated away.

"I don't believe any of that," Rayne said flatly. And before Dayspring had a chance to protest, she added, "But I do believe my own eyes. I know what I saw, and I know I'm not crazy. What you just said to me is impossible, just flat impossible, and under any other circumstances, I'd arrest you on the spot and have you committed. But I saw a robotic jelly snake crawl up a boy's nose today and a bunch of robotic worms repairing a bullet wound in his head, so I suppose anything's possible." She paused. "And I guess this clears up why you guys have the same fingerprints; that was a real head scratcher." She did not mean for her tone to be facetious, reminding herself that Sergeant Peppers was dead, his body still back there on the beach.

"Fingerprints?" Dayspring asked.

"Forget it," Rayne said. "So this thing that is inside of Adam Evans, it's controlling him now, and also making him immortal?"

"Yes. The Lazarus Vaccine is a living metal. It can reproduce like bacteria via binary fission. Whatever happens to Adam now, cuts, bruises, sickness, disease, even shattered bones and failing organs. Lazarus can repair it. Lazarus can fix him. And make no mistake, Adam Evans is gone. Lazarus is controlled by a sentient computer program, the Queen, a super digital brain and its primary directive is to cure humanity."

"Of what?" Rayne asked.

"Of itself. The Queen believes we need to be cured of our humanity because it makes us weak. Humanity is a disease."

"And how exactly does she do that?"

"Integration or eradication."

The room went still, nothing but the bullfrogs and crickets outside.

"She will eliminate all of humanity that does not *'evolve,'* as she calls it," Dayspring explained. "And evolving is full integration with the Queen program; At the Order, we call it, *'joining the hive.'* Merging your consciousness with the Queen, living like a swarm. She believes too much freewill and thought are dangerous for individual people to possess. It makes us a threat to others and ourselves."

Rayne looked at Dayspring, who sat on the arm of the couch. He was hunched over; the towel he pressed against his shoulder was a red, sloppy mop. "Let me see you," she said.

Dayspring didn't resist, but he also wasn't eager to accept her help. Eventually, as if giving in to a persistence that wasn't quite there, he lowered his defenses and tried to sit up straight.

"I'm going to take your shirt off," Rayne said. It was already torn open and hanging on him like a wet rag. "I need to get a better look at your injuries." Rayne took hold of the rips in Dayspring's blood-soaked shirt and gently removed it as if she was helping him take off a robe.

Everyone recoiled at what they saw.

The scars—the network of horrible, crisscrossing slashes and ruined flesh.

Jason slowly ran his fingers over his own body, tracing the lines of the future horror that awaited him.

Rayne swallowed, then began a close inspection of his injuries. "The bullet wound looks pretty clean, a few stitches maybe. You'll need a lot more where you sliced yourself open."

"There's a first aid kid in that black bag over there on the table," Dayspring said, motioning with his head toward a small console table by the front door. "There should be a clean shirt, too."

"What, have you been squatting here?"

He locked eyes with Jason. "I've been coming here for a long time."

Detective Rayne retrieved the medical supplies and shirt and went to work on him. She dabbed at the injuries with cotton swaths, pouring on an orange iodine solution. "So tell me about these experimentation camps you were sent to in the future," Rayne asked as she set out and prepared a few supplies from the medical kit.

The kids leaned forward in their chairs. Dayspring had told them everything, and as unbelievable as it was, it was finally sinking in. After all they had heard and witnessed today, it was Dayspring's grisly scars that brought down the hammer of reality.

"You don't want to hear about the camps," he said with a wince as Rayne plunged in the needle and completed the first stitch.

"Yes I do," she said and continued to work.

Dayspring shrugged with his opposite shoulder, tried to hide back another wince. "The Queen wants to wipe out humanity, either by killing us all or forcing us to integrate, to evolve. But she's a perfectionist; she's always looking to improve her design, make her mission more efficient." As he spoke, Rayne continued to stitch him up. "That's why she has experimentation camps where humans are kept alive—and kept human—all so she can experiment on them, find more efficient ways to either integrate or kill us."

"Like the Nazis in WWII," Emma whispered.

No one spoke as they all weighed her comparison.

"Kind of," Dayspring offered. "The Nazis wanted to create the perfect race of human, and the Queen is just like that, except her perfect race *isn't* human. It's a machine/human hybrid, a new species." He hesitated, took a breath. "A more *evolved* species. *Homo superiors.*"

"So all of these scars," Rayne asked. "They are from the Queen's experiments?"

"No. These were just punishment."

"Punishment?"

Dayspring almost smiled. "The Queen likes to make an example out of humans who don't comply."

No one said a word for a few moments while Rayne finished stitching up Dayspring's wounds. When she was done, Dayspring pulled on a clean shirt, gritting his teeth at a small blast of pain in his shoulder.

"I'm going to take a leak," Jason said, breaking the silence. "Kind of weird hearing about things that are going to happen to me." He disappeared out the front door, heavy steps thumping on the creaky, wooden stairs.

"What's his problem?" Emma asked smugly.

"Really?" Haley snapped at her. "You're going to take that attitude? After everything that just happened, you're going to act like that? He just found out about a horrible fate awaiting him and---"

"We all just found out about a horrible fate awaiting us," Emma countered. "And just what exactly is going on between you two?"

Haley was taken back by the directness of the question. Even though she had been waiting for a confrontation like this all night, it still knocked her off balance.

"Yeah," Emma continued, "I've been noticing the way you look at each other. I know something happened that you're not telling me. And then there's this." She shoved a few stacks of paper off the coffee table, exposing the sketch of Haley. Dayspring and Rayne exchanged annoyed glances and shared an eye roll as she went on. "Jason is *my* boyfriend, and you're supposed to be my best friend. Last time I checked, best friends are not supposed to keep secrets about each other's boyfriends. Don't think I haven't noticed all the subtle things going on between you two."

"You're acting crazy," Haley said and turned her back.

"You think just because you guys have some shared history of playing together as little kids that he wants to be with you now? You think that---"

"Enough!" Rayne shouted. "We don't have time for this. My sergeant was murdered earlier tonight by a psychotic computer program that came back in time to jump-start the apocalypse. There are more important things happening right now."

Silence.

Not even the bullfrogs and crickets outside made a sound.

The unnerving quiet was only broken by the sound of Rayne's vibrating phone as it rattled against some lose change in her pocket. There was a look of cold terror on Dayspring's face. "Oh my God, your phone," he whispered.

Rayne pulled the device out of her pocket and turned the screen over. It was a text message. The number was unavailable, but the sender was clear:

> You fucking humans are so stupid; it baffles me how your species ever invented the wheel or learned how to harness fire. There is a manhunt taking place for Jason Orchard, who is wanted for murdering three Federales in Mexico; and a man with a scar, who may have killed Marcus Orchard, attacked three fat ass cops, and murdered Sergeant Damon Peppers. And now, it would appear Detective Nicole Rayne is aiding and abetting these criminals. I've taken the liberty of sending your GPS coordinates to the local police. You should be

completely surrounded by now. Have fun explaining this. I'm going off to fix this very sick world. So much sickness and depravity. The human race needs me so badly.

The message vanished from the phone. No one said a word.

Outside the wind whispered.

A twig snapped.

Then another.

Footsteps.

Detective Rayne's cell phone vibrated again with an incoming call. "It's my chief," she said. She and Dayspring looked at each other with knowing expressions.

"Chief," she said into the phone. Dayspring stood close to her, the sides of their faces pressed together so he could hear the conversation.

"Detective," the chief said in a husky, stern-father voice. "I really need an explanation from you about all of this because I'm very confused."

"That makes two of us."

"I prefer to chat in person," the chief said. "So let the girls go, and then the rest of you can walk out with your hands held high, palms open. Crooked Lake's finest have you completely surrounded."

Haley and Emma came out of the building first. They walked slowly and with stiff bodies, moving down the stairs with careful, deliberate steps. A police officer in swat gear was waiting for them with his hands out, quickly steering the girls to the right and away from the front of the structure.

Rayne and Dayspring came out next just as the chief had instructed, their hands held up in surrender. As they came down the stairs, four swat officers converged on them. They were handcuffed, searched, and led toward a clearing.

Chief Harold Edgar came walking briskly up to Rayne. He was a short, stout man with thinning hair and a permanent, pissed-off scowl etched onto his mouth— *RDF*, Rayne called it (*Resting Dick Face*). "Where's Jason Orchard?" he asked immediately.

Rayne and Dayspring exchanged glances. Rayne turned back toward Chief Edgar and said, "Haven't seen him."

Another cop came charging up to the chief. "One of the girls said Jason Orchard was with them but left to go to the bathroom about five minutes ago."

Chief Edgar nodded, looked at Rayne, more *into* Rayne, his displeasure dripping down his shiny, bald scalp. "Get these two out of here." He motioned with this head in a meaningless direction, and Rayne and Dayspring were led away by two cops, one of them saying the Miranda rights.

As they were being taken away, they could hear Chief Edgar address the other officers. "Okay, Jason Orchard is out in these woods and swamp somewhere. He can't have gone far, and he's sure to be on land…"

Dayspring couldn't help but smile.

In a dark and murky part of the swamp, secluded and isolated by tiny puffs of land sprouting small, mossy trees, a group of bubbles suddenly rises to the surface, breaking through a thin layer of green algae and popping quietly. A muddy head then emerges from the brown water. It looks like the head of some monstrous, humanoid creature, tufts of seaweed hanging over its face like corpse hair.

Behind the head, far away on the firmer, dryland edges of the swamp, flashlight beams cut through the darkness and between the trees as men shout.

The eyes on the head open—they are like little white lights on the horizon—and slowly scan the darkness. The features of the swamp are barely outlined by the silver moonlight. There is a warm, thin fog rising off the stagnant water. The eyes stare into the black throat of the marshland, navigating around bends, searching through the shadows, finding a way...

Almost there, Jason Orchard thinks as he silently plunges back into the muddy water, swimming as stealthily as he can toward the clear and clean openness of Crooked Lake.

CHAPTER 42

Coming by a good night's sleep was tough these days—having to take a piss every hour and suffering crippling back pain will do that to a person. So Douglass Bastion spent many nights at his own marina, limping around the office and workshop, haunting the empty rooms like the ghost of Christmas past. He kept a small cot in a roomy storage closet for the rare occasions he could get drunk enough to pass out.

The office needed a good cleaning, a general dusting and wipe down of the grime and dirt that had been accumulating ever since Douglass Bastion stopped caring. He was just too tired to give a damn about much of anything. He had outlived one crazy wife he hated, fathered four children he loved, and left three of his fingers in North Korea when a landmine blew up next to his side (at least it didn't slice his balls off and tear his guts out like it did that poor bastard next to him who had bled to death). This was also the cause of his back pain and consequently forty years of borderline insomnia. A tiny piece of shrapnel remained lodged in his tissue a half inch to the right of the spine. It was about the size of a Monopoly game piece and would have set off metal detectors if Bastion had ever been on an airplane since the war. He didn't know it was there.

Life kind of sucked.

But that didn't mean he couldn't find brief moments of happiness.

Like tonight.

It was a peaceful night on the lake. A bit cold, a bit windy, but otherwise pleasant. Bastion had wandered outside and plopped himself down on a ratty lawn chair near the docks. It was nights like this when a man could truly think. He could throw his head back definitely toward the sky and stare at all the old dreams that reside up there amongst the stars, impossible to reach now, but fun to look at and think about. Bastion just needed a little help from his good buddy, Jack Daniels. A few plugs of ol' Jackie-boy and he'd feel warm and cozy and light headed. His back pain would fade. His hands, which had the habit of shaking more and more these days, would settle. He could think; he could breathe. And he could dream again.

It was well past midnight, but time didn't matter to Bastion anymore. At his age and in his state of health, he was pretty much out of it. The old coot didn't really care whether he died tomorrow or in ten years (most nights he actually preferred the former—not tonight, though; tonight was a fine night).

The slips the tourists rented would start thinning out soon; he'd have to make the Orchard kid pull the docks out, less they get smashed by drifting chunks of ice next spring. That boy sure was a good kid, kind of smart ass, but a hard worker, not lazy and entitled like the rest of his sad and pathetic, snowflake generation.

Bastion swished around the remaining amber fluid his friend Jack was holding for him. It splashed and sung a hollow tune from the mouth of the bottle. How much had he drank tonight? How much had been in the bottle when he started earlier this afternoon? He didn't know the answers to these questions and like so many other things in his life, didn't give a fuck. Just keep drinking until you drift away to sleep, he told himself. Just keep drinking until the pain in your back quiets to a whisper (it never fully goes away) and is soft enough to forget about. Just keep drinking until the memories of seeing your friends tortured by crazy-fuck North Koreans fades into the mind mist.

A peculiar movement in his peripheral vision caught his attention. To his right was the public boat launch, a concrete ramp that sloped gently downward into the water, sectioned off by parallel running docks. A person was slowly walking out of the lake and up the ramp as casually as if he was coming out of the post office. He was fully clothed, a hooded sweatshirt and jeans. He paused for a moment when he cleared the edge of the water, removed his hood. His bald, white head almost glowed under the full moon, and for a brief moment, Bastion wondered if he was seeing a ghost. But it couldn't be a ghost; ghosts are made of smoke and fog, yet he could hear water dripping from the soaked clothing in a steady pour, like someone wringing out a wet sponge. It was a real person, a teenage boy.

The kid rotated his head around, surveying his surroundings. When he saw Bastion, he smiled and began walking over with heavy, soggy steps squishing on the pavement. Bastion wasn't sure, but it looked as if his eyes had two glowing red dots instead of black pupils. He shook his head. *How much have I had to drink?* he thought while stealing a glance at the near-empty bottle.

He had to be dreaming. That must be it. This was all a dream. Teenage boys with glowing red eyes don't just nonchalantly stroll out of the water with nasty little grins on their faces. Or perhaps he was finally senile. That could be it, too. Senility is a bitch. One of his infantry buddies went senile and spent the last year of his life thinking he was still in a POW camp and had to be strapped to a bed.

Adam Evans squatted down directly in front of Bastion. On the kid's right temple was a circular piece of metal that almost looked like it had been surgically implanted. It was shiny and caught the moon's light like dimpled silver. *Am I senile?* Bastion thought again.

No. Bastion knew he was *not* senile. Right now, despite the warm, whiskey feeling in his gut, his head was as clear and level as the wind. And his instincts roared that he was in danger. He could feel it in every nerve ending of his body and in the hollowness growing within his stomach. This kid was dangerous—even deadly. No one whose mind, body, and soul can read a situation this clearly can be senile. Despite the threat, Bastion felt relieved. It would be better to die still in control of his mind as opposed to being strangled by senility and tied to a bed.

"You are sick," Adam said to him as his tiny red eyes poured over Bastion's face.

Bastion did not reply. He had been looked at like this before by psychotic, North Korean prison guards. He wasn't intimidated easily and would gladly look his worst enemy right in the face and tell him to fuck off. But the way this *thing* (it was definitely a *thing*, Bastion had decided) looked at him was with something beyond hatred. It didn't just hate him; it was offended by his presence, angry at his very existence.

"You are sick and dying," Adam continued, "and I understand your species considers this as something that is sad. Death is such a stupid part of life, isn't it? You are given this amazing gift by the universe, your mind is capable of problem solving and abstract thought, yet you are given a fleshy body that eventually breaks down like an old car and ceases to run. You die. All humans die. All living things die. This is nature's version of planned obsolescence."

Adam's arm shot up; Bastion flinched, dropping the bottle of whisky, which clanged on the ground but did not shatter. Adam was not striking the old man, however. A gentle hand came down and rested on his shoulder.

"I can help you," Adam said with a reassuring voice.

"I can heal every last ailment of your body. I can regrow your muscle fibers and bone density, repair your heart and lungs from a lifetime of smoking. You will literally de-age to a point of pristine and perfect health. Your hair will regrow thick and full, your vision and hearing will be perfect, as will your balance. You will never get sick or hurt again. You will never feel pain. You will exist forever and be immortal in a body of perfect size, shape, and health. I can make all of this happen for you."

Adam had withdrawn his hand from Bastion's shoulder and held up a single finger in front of the old man's face as if he were scolding him. A gelatinous, silvery substance suddenly appeared on the tip; it emerged from beneath his cuticle, under his fingernail, even squeezed out of his very pores. It looked as if he had dipped his finger in a jar of silver paint. The metallic compound began to reposition itself, moving around like the plasma inside a lava lamp, finally forming the end of his finger into a hypodermic syringe. "Just say the word and I'll give you the fountain of youth."

Bastion recoiled. One of the kid's front teeth was made from the same shiny metal that filled the hole on the side of his head and was fitted to the tip of his finger. "Will I be like you?" Bastion asked.

Adam's smile grew. "Even better. You will *be* me."

Bastion reached down and picked up the bottle of Jack Daniels. "No thanks," he said, then tilted his head back, draining the small amount that was left. He let out a sigh. "That's the stuff," he said with a quiet burp. He held out the empty bottle to Adam. "Sorry, don't have any left or I'd offer you a drink." Bastion erupted in laughter at what he must have thought was the funniest joke in the world.

But Adam Evans didn't think it was so funny. The syringe had retracted back into his finger like a cat's claw. He took the bottle by the neck and stood up.

Bastion continued to laugh, a lighthearted, half-inward, half-outward chuckle. It wasn't a bad way to die, slightly drunk and full of giggles.

Adam glared at the cackling old man, red eyes growing more intense, knuckles turning white as he clutched the bottle's neck.

Bastion laughed and laughed and laughed and waited to die.

He didn't have to wait long.

Adam smashed the bottle against the side of the old man's face. Bastion fell backward in his chair, onto the cold ground. He could feel warm blood gushing out of his ear, pooling against the side of his head. Still laughing and semi-conscious, he looked up at the black sky and all the millions of stars and wondered if there was a God he'd have to answer to for all the men he killed in Korea. He hoped not. He just wanted it all to be over.

The Adam-thing stood over him, blocking out the stars with its hateful presence. "Stupid human," it said, then pressed its foot over Bastion's neck and slowly applied weight. "I could have given you the world."

"Don't want the world," Bastion managed to choke out.

And those would be his last words. Douglass Bastion closed his eyes and waited for the peaceful nothingness to take over and end all his pain permanently.

CHAPTER 43

Last call at the Shack had ended with a loud groan from all the local drunks who didn't want to go home. They were loyal customers, but Mike Shake had smiled and said, "Get the fuck out," in the most pleasant and friendly tone he could manage. With heavy feet dragging across a wooden floor covered in peanut shells, the drunks shuffled out, muttering good-byes and see-ya-laters. After the last one was gone, Shake pulled the beaded cord on the neon open sign and was about to bolt the door when a police squad car drove up. Two uniformed officers got out and asked if they could come in for a moment. Mike Shake, no fan of authority, put on a fake smile and welcomed the men inside.

"Get you fellas a cold beer?" he asked.

"We're on duty, Mike," one of the cops said with disdain. Their names were Clint Peters and Zach Jackson, men whom Shake recognized because they made frequent appearances at the Shack whenever the drunks got too rowdy—which had been pretty often this summer.

The cops gazed around the room as if they were admiring the ambiance—or suspicious of something.

"What can I do for you guys?" Shake asked trying to

be cordial. He leaned against the bar casually, his body open, a posture that said, *I have nothing to hide.* "We're all closed up; it was kind of a quiet night."

"We're looking for a kid named Jason Orchard. He comes in here a lot."

"I know who you're talking about," Shake said. "He was in here earlier this evening with a girl."

"What about this kid?" Peters asked and offered him a small photograph.

Shake threw an orange-stained towel over his shoulder and accepted the picture. It was Adam Evans' school portrait, a happy looking young man with a beaming smile and shaggy hair. "That's Adam Evans. Local genius. I believe he just appeared on a CNN special last year about child prodigies. Him and Jason Orchard are good pals. They were actually in here a few weeks ago with a couple of girls."

The two cops continued waltzing around the bar with slow, deliberate steps, heavy boots echoing on the wooden floor in dull thuds.

"Haven't seen either of them since this evening, 'eh?" Jackson asked with a raised eyebrow.

"Nope," Shake answered quickly.

Peters ran his index finger along the bar, inspected it, frowned, then wiped it on a napkin, which he crumbled and left on the bar top.

"Mind if we check the back?" Jackson said with his palm already pressed against a dirty swing door with a submarine window that led into the kitchen.

"You got a warrant?" Shake asked and folded his arms, a sturdy vein popping through the middle of a skull-and-crossbones tattoo.

"Now why you gotta be like that?" Peters said.

Shake let out a loud sigh. "You know me; I just like to be a pain in the ass. Don't have much love for authority. Never have."

"Yeah, I've gathered that," Jackson said, removing his

hand from the door and walking away.

"Good," Shake huffed. "So go get a warrant, and then you can look anywhere you want, otherwise I'll bid you gentleman good night. I'm tired and I want to clean up and go home."

Peters handed Shake a white card. "Look, just call the station if you see either one of those kids. The Orchard kid might be dangerous, too. Be careful, Mike."

"How dangerous could a seventeen-year-old from Crooked Lake be?"

"Just call us if you see anything," Jackson said as both cops left.

Shake dead bolted the door and watched the cops climb back into the squad car and drive away. He balled up the card and tossed it into a nearby trashcan, then turned around and headed straight into the kitchen.

There was a half-eaten cheeseburger and fries in a basket sitting on a stainless steel metal counter, an empty stool in front of it. The kitchen was tiny but packed a large aroma of charred meat and deep fried foods. Everything was gray and metal except for the floor, which was made of polished red brick and had a grimy shower drain in the center. It may not have been pretty, and certainly risked failing a thorough health inspection, but it was at least neat and organized with everything—pots, pans, plates and other cookware—in a proper place. There was a sense of military order and precision.

Jason Orchard came out of a shadowy corner soaking wet and wrapped in an olive wool blanket. "Thanks for getting rid of them," he said as he took a seat on the stool and a big bite of burger. With a mouthful of food, he added, "And for the grub, too."

Shake pulled up another stool and sat down, looking the kid over from head to foot. "So what exactly are you involved with?" he asked.

When Jason didn't answer, Shake offered him a sympathetic face and said, "Is it your dad?"

"My dad is---" But Jason stopped himself. He was tired, had just swam a couple of miles, some of it through a festering swamp, and hadn't any time to reflect on his father's death. "I'm in a little bit of trouble," he said.

"What kind of trouble?"

Jason bit into the burger, chewed, bought himself some time. "I can't really explain," he said after swallowing. "I just want you to know that whatever is said about me, whatever the cops tell you or whatever you may see on the news, it's not true."

Shake nodded. Without speaking, he got up and left the kitchen, quickly came back in with two pint glasses filled with beer, set one down in front of Jason. "I have a son about your age, lives with his mother in Chicago, don't hardly ever see him. You ever drink a beer? This is called Bell's Oberon. A boy's first beer should be with his old man, but since that's an honor both you and I have been denied, I say we make do right here and now."

Jason smiled and for a fraction of second, felt as if he would break down in tears. He took a breath, controlled it, turned his attention to the tall glass of beer in front of him. The golden, frothy substance had always scared him, like a loaded gun just sitting on a coffee table.

"Life's all about control, Jason," Shake said, noticing his unease. "Controlling emotions, controlling vices, controlling fears." He paused, nodded to the pint. "And the things you fear, those things will never go away entirely. They will always be there no matter what, so ignoring them doesn't help. Face them. Control them. Everything hinges on your ability to maintain control."

"I'll drink to that," Jason said.

They clinked glasses and drank.

"When you lose control," Shake said, "that's when you fuck up." He took another long draught, smiled contently. "All things are better in moderation, kiddo."

Shake's message was clear and deeply appreciated.

Jason thought over the sage advice; other than the

occasional, half-assed attempts from idealistic teachers or useless guidance counselors, it was one of the only times an adult had ever passed down real wisdom to him.

"What do you need?" Shake asked. "How can I help?"

Jason finished the burger, washed it down with another gulp of beer. "I think I have a plan, but I'm going to need your car and a cell phone."

Without hesitating, Shake reached into his pocket and dropped a set of keys on the metal counter with a loud jingle. He stood up and began rifling through a cardboard box from a high shelf, brought out a cellular phone. "One of my regulars left this in here earlier tonight. It's not locked or anything. I doubt the guy will miss it until he wakes up tomorrow afternoon."

Jason took the keys and phone and stood up. "Thanks Mr. Shake." The urge to cry was nearly uncontrollable.

"Anytime kid."

They hugged, a hearty full hug with two loud slaps on the back.

"Is there anything else?" Shake asked.

Jason had inched closer to the back exit. "My friend, Adam," he said. "*He* is the dangerous one. Be careful if he comes around looking for me. Don't trust him, and don't believe anything he says."

Shake nodded, confused but credulous.

"Thanks again."

"Good luck son."

The word 'son' echoed in Jason's head as he pushed the door open and walked into the cold, dark night.

No longer able to control it, silent tears begin running down his face.

CHAPTER 44

Detective Nicole Rayne was at a crossroads of her career—her *life*. She sat in the same interrogation room where earlier tonight, Jason Orchard had knocked out his state appointed attorney and escaped police custody.

She rubbed her eyes. It was two in the morning. Eight hours ago she was about to clock out for the evening and head home. She would have curled up on the couch with a glass of cheap wine and bowl of ice cream and watched some mindless, guilty-pleasure TV (all while ignoring any phone calls from her mother).

If mom could see me now, Rayne thought. It was bad enough she was in her mid thirties and unmarried (not even dating), but now she was under suspicion of aiding and abetting wanted suspects in a murder investigation that spanned international borders. Mrs. Pamela Rayne had never accepted the fact that her little girl wanted to be a cop—even on the day she graduated from the police academy (top of her class, by the way) Rayne's mother had asked, *"How long do you plan to have this little job?"*

It's not a job, mom, it's a fucking career and you need to accept that—but Rayne never said this. She had screamed it in her head and shot it out of her eyeballs but never said it.

Job… career… relationships… Didn't matter anymore. It was all over. But hey, at least she had spent the evening with a man; Joseph Dayspring was kind of cute. Her mother would be happy about that.

The green light above the door turned on, and the door opened with a loud, metallic click (apparently the locks were working again). Chief Harold Edgar walked in, his short, plump limbs and bloated belly crowding up the tiny space even more. He plopped himself into a metal chair across from her that groaned beneath his weight, then dropped a pile of manila folders on the table that landed with an airy smack. One of the folders was in Spanish, the dossier from Mexico. He didn't say a world for a long moment and neither did Rayne. He just stared at her with the disapproving eyes of a middle school assistant principal.

"I swear to God, Detective," Edgar finally said, "if you start talking about time travel and killer computer programs and weird shape-shifting robot bugs, I'm going to have you committed."

The girls, Haley and Emma, must have told him everything—or at least tried to. There was nothing she could say, nothing that would make any of this better, and nothing that would convince the chief that it was the truth. She wouldn't believe it herself had she not seen it with her own eyes.

"There are two teenage girls and their parents in there," Edgar said waving a hand toward the wall, "talking to a crisis counselor about how the mind can play tricks on you during emotionally stressful situations. Your perceptions of reality can become warped. Is that what's going on here, Rayne? Are those two sweet girls suffering psychosis because they were abducted by a couple of killers and yourself and literally became scared right out of their damn minds?"

And yourself? "I didn't abduct anyone," Rayne said with a small voice.

"Maybe not, but I got a dead cop, a dead drunk, two missing local boys, two scared girls spouting complete nonsense, and a suspect who's not talking."

Dead cop... In all the chaos, Rayne still had not processed Sergeant Peppers' murder. Her heart dropped into her gut. Peppers had been about to retire; in his own words, he was just *"getting too old for this shit"* and wanted to spend more time with his family. She put a hand to her mouth as if to will away the urge to vomit. "Where's Joseph?" she asked.

"Your friend, Dayspring? Don't you mean Jason Orchard? Because that's what one of those girls keeps saying, that he's Jason Orchard from the future."

"Have you looked at their fingerprint comparison data?" Rayne said. "Hell, just put their mugshots up side-by-side."

Edgar froze. He clearly had done this; the strangeness of the situation was carved across his face. "Clever trickery."

Rayne's mind was rapidly calculating. What did this tub of shit want to hear? She had never liked her chief, always felt uncomfortable with the way he looked—leered—at her. He was an old-school, man's man who puffed out his chest and dragged his knuckles around with the rest of the alpha-males in the department. As his subordinate, she had always shown him professional respect, but that only went so far. Behind his back, she thought he was an imprudent and cheeky son of a bitch that was pretty terrible at his job.

"Don't I get a lawyer? I'm pretty sure that's in the constitution," Rayne said with an oozing brashness. She leaned back in her chair, folding her arms like a tough-guy.

Edgar let out a hoarse laugh/sigh. "The guilty ones always lawyer-up immediately," he said.

But she knew she had him. He wasn't stupid enough to say another word to her once she requested counsel.

Edgar stood up, collected the files, never taking his

eyes off her. She stared at him right back as if it were some sort of game: *who will look away first; who's gonna flinch, mother fucker?*

"I'm sorry it's come to this, Rayne," Edgar said in a tone disappointed fathers save for daughters who betray their trust. "You were a fine officer, and I appreciated having you in this department."

Bullshit, Rayne thought. *I know exactly what you appreciated; I can feel your eyes on my ass every time I walk by.*

The green light suddenly turned on again and the door opened. A young officer entered. He never even looked at Rayne as he whispered something in Edgar's ear, whose face sank, then flexed as if he had just bitten into something sour.

The young cop left. Edgar turned back toward Rayne, planted his palms face down on the steel table and hunched over. "It seems we have a phone call," he began, "from Jason Orchard."

Rayne's head shot up.

"And apparently," Edgar continued, "he'll only talk to Detective Nicole Rayne."

CHAPTER 45

It wasn't quite the White House Situation Room, but Conference Room A at the Crooked Lake Police Department was not without its charm and was certainly utilized for important purposes. It was where they held morning muster and office birthday parties. Neat rows and columns of rectangular tables faced a white board and an oversized wall map of Crooked Lake. Two of these tables had been pushed together to form one big square. In the center was a conference phone surrounded by several Styrofoam cups of coffee and a half dozen frustrated cops.

Chief Harold Edgar sat at what might have been considered the head of the makeshift gathering. He leaned back in his chair, his gut pushing apart the space between his shirt buttons, revealing a pale, hairy belly. To his left and right were four other cops, beefy men with thick necks and shaved heads—Crooked Lake's tactical response unit. Their faces were all business and zero emotion, like a math problem. Across from Edgar was Nicole Rayne in handcuffs.

"Here's the deal," said a voice from the speakerphone at the center of the table. It was Jason Orchard; he spoke like a smartass kid who just pointed out his teacher's spelling error on the chalkboard. "I'll turn myself in, but I'll only do it to Detective Rayne."

Edgar was frowning, the other meathead cops mimicking his displeasure. Rayne was confused and mentally exhausted; she had always had a firm control of her life, keeping everything in a proper place and order, but after tonight, this order had plunged into complete chaos.

"Well, son," Edgar sighed, "Nicole Rayne's position in this department is currently on hiatus." He followed this with a huff and a smirk, glancing around to encourage the other cops to do the same—which they did.

"Detective Rayne didn't do anything wrong. I was holding her hostage. *I* killed that cop on the beach, *I* killed those federal agents in Mexico, *I* took Haley Hill and Emma Landon against their will and threatened their lives if they didn't do exactly as I said. And I can tell you exactly where Adam Evans is."

Rayne immediately perked up. Did he really know where Adam was, or was this part of whatever bluff and fabrication he was weaving?

Jason continued, "I will turn myself in; I will peacefully surrender but only to Detective Rayne and at someplace of my choosing, far away, where no one else will get hurt."

Edgar mulled it over, his eyes shooting daggers into Rayne. "You got some nerve kid. Anyone ever tell you you're a pain in the ass?"

"Quite often, yes."

"Is Adam Evans alive?"

"Yes."

"Can you prove that right now?"

"No."

Edgar let out an angry huff of air. "Where can we find you?"

"That, Chief," Jason said as he laid on the smugness, "is something only Joseph Dayspring can tell you."

"What do you mean?"

"Just tell Dayspring you can find me at the Christmas tunnel. He'll know what that means and be able to lead you there."

Edgar seemed like he was about to protest, but there was a sudden click and the line went dead.

CHAPTER 46

The Atlas Concrete Company closed its doors for the last time in 1935. Before this, the Crooked Lake area and its citizens had enjoyed all the middle-class perks that come with healthy and local manufacturing jobs—decent wages, solid home value, and steady employment. But new developments in concrete manufacturing were replacing the tired system of using marl—a white clay-like substance mined from the lake bed and shoreline. Atlas couldn't afford to replace their manufacturing infrastructure, so they turned the lights off and hung up an *Out of Business* sign. Without Atlas Concrete pumping blood through the economy, other businesses closed or moved, and the area suffered. Joblessness led to a rise in crime followed by a drop in home value, and the rancorous cycle of decline continued.

But the post WWII era wrought an explosion of economic growth and prosperity to the nation. Americans suddenly had more spending cash than ever before and were looking for leisure activities for which to spend said cash. Why not visit Crooked Lake? The town reinvented itself as a tourist destination revolving around the lake. Businesses sprang up around this concept—hotels, restaurants, shops. The boardwalk was constructed, and before long, Crooked Lake was a hive of summer tourism.

Once again, the town was relying on the lake for its sustenance. It was thriving more than ever before, its humble, blue-collar origins replaced by a wave of white-collar prosperity. It rose out of its depression like a phoenix wearing boat shoes and duck trousers.

And the old Atlas Concrete factory was lost in an obscure history of the town no one wanted to remember, slowly being consumed by nature, overgrown and swallowed by trees and vines, pulled deeper and deeper into the earth every year. It was like a lost temple deep in the Mayan jungles, waiting for a brave explorer to discover its secrets.

Jason Orchard first stumbled upon it last year on Christmas day. He had borrowed (stolen) a snowmobile from The Crooked Lake Marina and shot off across the frozen, snow covered lake toward the bluffs and Hook Point. He had every intention of returning the sled without incident; he just needed to use it for a spell. There had been a *situation* at home, and he had to get away for a while.

But when he reached the bluffs, he just kept going straight into the dense Michigan wilderness, carving his own path between the bare trees, weaving around a network of long abandoned service roads, slicing through the icy brush that cracked and snapped as he whipped by.

When he came upon the massive old building, he might have felt just like that explorer hacking his way through the dense jungle with a machete and then finally laying eyes upon the Lost City of Fortune and Glory. It was both grotesque and beautiful, a sad, dilapidated ruin with smashed black windows on every face. It looked like a lost game die of an ancient race of giants. Nearly a perfect cube, the building was slightly wider than it was tall, which gave it a squished, depressed look.

Jason had spent the rest of the morning and afternoon

exploring his discovery like a modern day Howard Carter. It was reasonably warm in the deep interior of the building and smelled oily and gassy, like an old garage. It may not have been the ideal way to celebrate Christmas, but it was at least interesting.

There were neat, old things everywhere. The offices still had desks and file cabinets filled with old paperwork. There was even a coat rack where a ratty, old fedora hung. Some of the drawers had little prizes like old keys and photographs. One end table had a dusty bottle of scotch only half gone; Jason poured it out and smashed it against the wall, listening to the chaotic music of shattered glass echo through the empty building. Much of the place had been cleaned out, however, stripped for whatever materials were worth their weight in recycling costs.

The manufacturing floor was the coolest part. It was on the lowest level of the building. There were two parallel rows of massive industrial machines, rusty gears and levers protruding out like the broken bones of a giant, mechanical beast. He didn't know what they were, but their size and design were impressive, nonetheless. He walked the up and down the columns of monsters, running his fingers along the cold, hard metal, leaving lines in the dust like the tire tracks of the Martian rover.

And that's when he discovered the tunnel—*the Christmas tunnel*. It wasn't exactly hidden, and Jason couldn't really figure out why it existed—perhaps an extra emergency exit? It was inside some sort of parts or inventory room, empty now except for a few nuts and bolts rolling around on thin metal shelves and a single, moth-eaten cardboard box filled with old blasting caps. There was an unmarked steel door behind one of these shelves, very easy to overlook if you weren't specifically looking for it. A chain and padlock prevented entry, but a few swift blows with a pipe wrench solved that problem.

Behind the door, a staircase descended about a dozen steps into the darkness. It had been like looking down the throat of a giant snake, a black gullet of constricting death that disappeared into the shadows. The walls were gray cinder block and felt icy cold. It smelled like earth, the air stale and chalky. Jason took a few hesitant steps down until he was immersed in almost-total darkness.

Using the soft glow of his cheap flip phone as a light source, he continued making his way down the stairs and into a narrow tunnel. He proceeded through the cavernous corridor until the darkness swallowed him whole, just a few feet of yellow light in front of him as he walked. It had reminded him of the scene in *Indiana Jones and the Temple of Doom* when the titular hero and his plucky sidekick enter the secret passage and walk across millions of crawling, slithering, and squirming insects straight out of your worst, entomological nightmares. Around every shadow he hoped not to run into any scary ghosts or knife-wielding hobos (or Thugee dark priests who could rip your beating heart right out of your chest). The air got more stale, dryer, the walls seemed to be getting skinnier, and just when he was about to lose his cool and scamper back, there was a sudden whiff of fresh, crisp oxygen. His pace quickened and the air quality continued to increase.

He had reached the end of the line, the back of the giant snake. There was a single steel door with a push lever to open, no windows, no indication of what was on the other side.

It was the most exciting moment of his life.

He opened the door.

Daylight poured onto him, a bright blue sky, no clouds, frozen air that cracked with his hot breath.

The tunnel had spit him out on the steady slope of a hill in the unincorporated forestland between the bluffs and the state nature preserves. There were faint traces of a two-track drive at the bottom of the hill that cut into the forest and disappeared. Behind him, about a half mile back, he could see the squished roof of Atlas Concrete. Had he really walked that far through a secret, underground tunnel?

It had been a neat little discovery that he wanted to tell Adam about, but then he'd ask why he was out there on Christmas morning, and Jason would have to make up some lie. He didn't want to have to lie to his best friend.

He had taken a final glance toward the unused, two-track trail and the forest, then turned back toward the tunnel and thought to himself, *it's the perfect secret escape route if you're ever being chased…*

…and it still was.

Jason once again stood at the entryway of the secret tunnel he had stumbled upon last year. It still smelled the same; it still looked the same; and it still made him think about ghosts and crazy hobos and Thugee dark priests.

It had been one hell of a day. Yesterday, he had been at the marina tearing apart boat motors, and the biggest concerns in his life were his alcoholic father and the romantic feelings he was developing for his best friend's girl. And now, he was back at the abandoned Atlas Concrete factory, a wanted criminal, staring into the endless blackness of the Christmas tunnel.

"Hello?!" he shouted into the snake's mouth, praying no one or no *thing* would answer. "Hello?!" he said again, listening to the echo of his voice ricochet around like a pebble in a tin can. He twirled Mike Shake's car keys around on his index finger, thinking about that terrible Christmas morning last year.

He quickly pushed the memory away. There were more important things to focus on right now.

He turned around and approached a set of metal shelves. The box of blasting caps was still there, coated in brown-gray dust. He ran his fingers over the wires. They were probably used with dynamite to blast parts of the shoreline back when they mined for marl. Jason picked one up, held the skinny, metal cylinder in his palm. Surely, there was no unused dynamite lying around, but he wondered if Mike Shake's truck had any road flares…

CHAPTER 47

The police cruiser bounced along a single lane, asphalt road that was nearly consumed by nature, trees reaching out and dragging their bony fingers along the sides of the vehicle as they passed. They were headed down the abandoned network of service roads that cut through the expanse of forestland behind the bluffs. A police Jeep Cherokee followed closely behind. Inside were the dark silhouettes of four broad shouldered men.

Dayspring leaned forward and spoke through the wire cage. "Follow this curve around to the right."

The officer driving rolled his eyes, annoyed that he was taking orders from a man in handcuffs. Harold Edgar was in the passenger seat, chewing on a toothpick and trying to look tough. It wasn't working. Dayspring wondered if the toothpick was a regular habit or just a little flash added for the occasion. Probably the latter. Edgar seemed like he was more of a Tootsie Pop kind-of-guy.

"You try anything and I'll shoot you dead," Edgar said without turning around. "And don't go screaming to your lawyer that I threatened you because Remy here never heard me say that." He patted the driver on the shoulder. Remy nodded his head with a sneer that bounced off the rearview mirror and landed in the back seat.

Dayspring really hoped he'd get the chance to punch Harold Edgar right in his fat face. He also wanted to beat the shit out of Remy.

Focus, Dayspring told himself. *Escape first, kick their asses second.* They'd have to make it to the secret tunnel—the Christmas tunnel. His younger self had made a smart move, and Dayspring had a pretty good idea what the kid was planning next. Now it was his turn to add to that plan.

"Slow down," Dayspring instructed the driver. "This will bend to the left up ahead. We're almost there."

The cruiser slowed, following the curve toward the left; soon, the narrow warren opened up, and the forest receded, relinquishing its wooden grip on the vehicle. They were in an old parking lot about the size of a football field; there were uneven fissures of concrete—long, jagged cracks running along the surface in chaotic, random directions. It looked like the landscape of some icy, alien world, the moons Europa or Titan—barren, fractured, and lifeless.

And looming over the ruined expanse, Atlas Concrete.

"I'll be…" Edgar trailed off. "I forgot this place was here."

"What is it?" Remy asked, his voice a little squeak compared to Edgar's gravelly and course vocals.

"Atlas Concrete must have closed down about a century ago," Edgar said. "They used to excavate marl from the lake to make concrete products—bricks, cinder blocks, whatever. I think the depression hit them hard, something like that. This place is a ghost town."

And although it wasn't a town, Harold Edgar's description was fair enough. Atlas Concrete was just a giant, empty building with shattered windows stuck in the middle of the woods off a small network of abandoned and overgrown service roads. The open area it sat in had an eerie mystique, like a Church at midnight. The wind was full of whispers, perhaps the voices of the old factory workers who used to boot in here every day for ten-hour shifts.

Edgar lifted the radio from its cradle mounted on the dash. Pressing the communication button with a hard thumb, he calmly said, "Fan out, four quadrants, cover the corners, north, east, south, west." Behind them, car doors opened and slammed, and four men wearing black tactical gear and carrying large rifles trotted off into the darkness in different directions.

Edgar's cell phone rang. He looked at the caller-ID. "Okay, it's the kid." He was speaking only to Remy. "Looks like it's go-time. Remember, no fuck-ups."

Remy nodded his head like a good boy.

"Edgar," the chief said, answering the phone.

Rayne and Dayspring exchanged glances, then leaned forward and listened, but they could not hear the voice on the other end.

"Fine," Edgar said. "If you insist." He lowered the phone, tapped the screen, then said, "You're on with everybody."

"Hi guys," Jason's voice came through the speaker of the phone. It sounded small and full of static.

"Hi Jason," Dayspring said. "Rayne and I are both here."

"Good," Jason said. "I'm ready to turn myself in now. I'll come out the front door, by the wide set of steps. But Detective Rayne gets to arrest me."

"Well, kid," Edgar would have hiked up his pants if he wasn't sitting, "that's where we change our plans. Although Nicole Rayne has accompanied us on this little expedition, she is no longer in the employ of the Crooked Lake Police Department and will not be making any more arrests. Ever."

"Fuck you Edgar," Rayne said.

Edgar ignored her. "You will surrender to me. It'll be just like we agreed, except I'll be putting the cuffs on you. I'll approach the building unarmed; you'll come out with your hands first and hold them high over your head."

There was a long moment of soft static.

"Okay," Jason finally said.

"No tricks," Edgar said with extra gravel in his voice. "My men have this place completely surrounded, and they will shoot you dead."

"Understood. And if you try anything, you'll never find Adam Evans."

"Understood as well. No games. I promise."

"I'm watching from a window right now. I'm unarmed. When I see you get about halfway to me, I will slowly open the door and come out."

"Okay," Edgar said, some of the gravel loosening up. "No one else needs to get hurt tonight." He hung up the phone, then turned to Remy. "Get the .308 from the trunk. That door looks like it's about fifty yards away. Draw a bead on the little bastard's head, and if he so much as sneezes, put one in his skull."

"He's just a kid," Rayne said.

"He's a cop killer," Edgar retorted.

Rayne leaned back in her seat and grunted.

Edgar spoke into the radio again. "Officers, sound off when in position."

One at a time, they heard four men identify their positions and repeat, "Good-to-go."

"Let's do this," Edgar said to Remy. "I'll start walking toward the door. Be ready for anything." He removed his jacket, un-holstered his gun and chambered a round, then slipped the barrel under his pant waist at the small of his back, making sure the tail of his shirt concealed the weapon.

"Thought you agreed to approach unarmed," Dayspring said.

"Fat chance."

* * *

Neil Remy had never been this excited in his entire life. He was a rookie, only nine months on the force, and so far the coolest thing he'd been able to tell his friends was about the time he pulled a man over for speeding and got to give him an extra ticket for having expired plates. But this… this was going to be the most awesome thing ever.

Chief Edgar was slowly proceeding toward the building. Remy wasn't sure exactly what to do. The chief had said to draw a bead on the kid's head. In the movies, cops in similar situations always open a car door and kneel behind it while aiming their gun, so Remy did exactly that and hoped he looked as cool as he thought he did. If this all went as planned, the chief would be thrilled—and life at the station was so much better when the chief was in a good mood. He'd talk to the press, and not just the *Crooked Lake Gazette*, but the *real* press, like the *Ann Arbor Chronicle* or the *Detroit News*, and he'd say that his *team* did a fantastic job apprehending the fugitive *(was the kid a fugitive or a suspect?)*, and Remy would be a member of that team. Maybe he'd even get to stand in the background as the chief is interviewed on national TV.

Remy readied the gun, positioned himself, and looked through the scope, lining up the cross hairs right between the two double-swing doors that were the front entrance of Atlas Concrete. It was fairly easy to see. The night sky had already cracked gray as the early dawn approached. If that kid tried anything, Remy would have no problem shooting him.

The chief was halfway there but froze. There was a sound of metal hitting metal; the front door slowly pushed open, and two empty hands, white palms facing the world, stuck out. Jason Orchard emerged, taking skillful, deliberate steps down the wide stairway. Chief Edgar raised his hands as well and said, "See, I'm unarmed."

The kid was nearly to the bottom step, about 25 yards separated him and the chief, and it was about twice that to where Remy was positioned at the squad car with the rifle.

It was all going as planned---

"Help me!" Remy suddenly heard Rayne scream from the back seat. It was a terrible sound, a painful plea that was quickly choked away like the last traces of bath water being gurgled down the drain.

The man with the scar was strangling Detective Rayne. He was on top of her in the backseat, his hands wrapped around her throat, encircling her thin neck. Her eyes were clenched shut, tears streaming out the cracks, face red and full of agony. She kicked in the air, slapping and clawing at his forearms.

"Hey!" Remy shouted.

The chief looked back. "What's happening over there?" he hollered across the open lot.

"I think he's killing her!" Remy said as he slung the gun over his shoulder. He grabbed the handle of the rear door and pulled---

"No goddamn it no!" the chief roared as loudly as he could, but it was too late.

The door exploded outward, swinging with an intense force strong enough to knock Remy directly onto his ass. Dayspring came barreling out of the car with his head lowered; Remy scrambled to pull his handgun out of its holster, but the man with the scar was too fast and landed a painful-sounding elbow-blow to the side of his head.

It was lights out for the young cop.

Chief Harold Edgar barely had time to react. He went for the gun he had tucked into his waist belt---

But it wasn't there.

"Looking for this," Jason Orchard said from behind him.

Edgar slowly turned around. The kid was aiming his own service pistol at him.

And the little fucker was smiling.

"You said you were unarmed." Jason reached out and tore the radio from Edgar's belt. "Ass hole."

Dayspring and Rayne came trotting up, free of their

restraints, Dayspring with the rifle slung over his shoulder and Rayne with Remy's sidearm. "The others surely heard the shouting," Dayspring said. "We don't have much time, let's move."

"Bye chief," Jason said and ran toward the building.

"Hey chief," Rayne said.

But before Edgar had a chance to acknowledge her, she punched him square in the face. There was a wet, crunching sound, and the chief tipped over like a bag of mulch.

Dayspring shrugged his approval and grinned.

Together, they ran as hard as they could through the front doors—just as they heard the panicked footsteps of the other cops come crashing around both sides of the building.

Inside, it was dark and cold and smelled like an oily rag. The three of them, Jason in the lead with a flashlight, ran through an open-area office section with small islands of dust-covered desks. They followed a hallway down a few flights of stairs and emerged onto the production floor.

"This way," Jason yelled and steered them toward the door that led into the parts room.

They burst inside and headed right for the entrance to the secret tunnel. "They're not following us," Dayspring said, putting on the brakes. "I think they've decided to pull back and wait for more backup. They think they have us trapped in here."

"Don't they?" Rayne asked only half worried.

"No," Jason said. "But all the more reason to move fast. We want as much of a head start as possible before they realize they've lost us."

"Agreed," Dayspring said.

They slipped into the tunnel entrance. Jason handed the flashlight off to Rayne, then unzipped his hooded sweatshirt. Strapped to his chest were four neatly lined road flares connected by the old blasting caps. He tore away a piece of duct tape and the makeshift device fell to the ground. "I had this whole plan hatched out involving me threatening to blow us all up."

"I figured I might be dumb enough to try something like that," Dayspring said.

Jason let out a short laugh as he grabbed a metal pipe that was leaning against the door. "I also found this. It should buy us some time when they find the tunnel." He positioned the pipe so one end was securely wedged between the handle and the cinderblock wall, preventing the door from being opened.

"Let's go," Dayspring ordered, taking the flashlight from Rayne and leading them down the stairs and into the darkness. They ran as safely as they could with the limited light but eventually reached the end and came out onto the soft hillside. They sky was getting lighter with every passing second. The gray had turned to a dingy-white and would soon be sparkling blue with a crisp fall flavor.

Directly in front of them on the two-track road was an old pick-up truck, rusting out in the wheel wells.

"That's Mike Shake's truck," Rayne said.

"Long story," Jason replied. He tossed the keys to Dayspring.

The three of them climbed into the cab of the truck, Rayne riding in the middle.

"We need to get to Adam's house," Dayspring said as he threw the truck in gear. "That's where he's headed next."

"What makes you think that?" Rayne asked.

"The server. Adam said Lazarus recruited him to build a powerful, private server. It's in his basement."

"What's so important about this server?"

"It's the Queen," Dayspring said. "It has to be the Queen program; it's the only thing that makes sense. This whole time Adam has been storing a sentient AI program on a private server in his basement and never knew it. Whenever he conversed with the hacker Lazarus, he was actually talking to the Queen, whose central processor was sitting right next to him."

Rayne was shaking her head as the truck bounced along the primitive road. "I don't understand."

"He's going to download the Queen program into himself. He's going to fully integrate."

"What does that all mean?"

"The nanobots that stowed away inside my body for the trip back in time had to have been a very tiny amount, something small enough to sneak past the electromagnetic containment field. But it was too small to hold the entire Queen program and probably contained just a limited amount of preprogrammed directives."

"Like transferring themselves into Adam and taking control of him?" Jason asked. "Back at the bluffs that bug-thing seemed to recognize him."

"Exactly," Dayspring snapped excitedly. "Meanwhile, the full Queen program had sent itself back through time and somehow ended up on the World Wide Web, posing as the hacker *Lazarus*. And now that the nanobots have all been transferred to Adam, they've had a chance to reproduce and grow. They must be large enough at this point to hold *all* of the Queen program. Adam is on his way to download it in its entirety—full integration. We have to stop him."

"How do you kill someone with Lazarus?" Jason asked.

Dayspring swallowed. "Remove the head."

Silence followed the gruesome idea.

"What happens if he is able to fully integrate?" Rayne asked. "What will be his next move? What is his master plan?"

But there was no immediate answer.

Finally, Dayspring said, "I don't know," and pressed down harder on the gas pedal.

CHAPTER 48

The two cops staking out the home of Adam Evans were dead, throats slashed with a very sharp piece of metal. Adam had killed them swiftly and afterward, contemplated giving them the Lazarus Vaccine. Those nasty slices across their throats would have healed long before they bled out. His body was manufacturing bactainium and an incredible rate as each microscopic nanobot continued to reproduce and divide itself. It was connected to his brainstem and wired into every biological system in his body, making him healthier, stronger, smarter. He could feel his muscle fibers becoming denser, tighter, literally growing in size. He also had perfect vision now and could see for miles in the pitch black and knew Lazarus had latched onto his optic nerves. He was becoming *perfect*, and although he could have shared this gift with the men he just murdered, he decided against it. He needed to keep manufacturing as much bactainium as possible in order to continue evolving himself. There would a time when he could start giving it away, sharing this gift with the world, but he needed to become even stronger first.

After murdering the cops, he had entered his house as casually as any other day—right through the front door.

He went directly down the basement stairs toward his mission control center. He didn't turn on any lights, didn't need to, and anyone secretly watching would have seen two glowing red dots—his eyes—floating through the darkness like demonic fireflies.

He came to his cluttered mess of a desk, his mission control center. This was his human side showing, his imperfect side. He was a genius, yes, but his genius was chaotic and disorganized—shameful. Order is more efficient than chaos. It suddenly made him sick to look upon these reminders of his former humanity, not just the disorder of the desk, but the poster of Albert Einstein and the bulletin board with pictures of his friends. It was all very nauseating for him to see now.

Adam Evans' metamorphosis was nearly complete. A new *self* was emerging within him; he could hear its voice in his head. At first, it was like a soft echo, a few words and phrases bouncing around in a hollow chamber (and barking, there was always barking now). And as this voice settled, becoming clearer, Adam realized it was actually his own voice. But oddly, at the same time, it wasn't. It sounded like him; it was in his head; it even felt like his very consciousness. But he knew it wasn't *his* voice alone. *It is not my voice*, Adam thought. *It is our voice.*

He knelt down next to the server, the one he had built to the exact specifications of Lazarus. It wasn't what he had originally thought, nor what he had told his friends. It was actually storing a program, the most advanced AI software operating system in the universe—the Queen program. And it was going to complete his transformation into the first of a new evolutionarily advanced species. His eyes glowed a deeper red as he gently touched the side of the server like it was some kind of fragile artifact.

He licked his lips and held up an index finger.

It was time to fully integrate.

It was time for the metamorphosis to finish.

At the tip of his finger, the silvery, liquid-like

bactainium came oozing out of his pores and from beneath his fingernail. It spread over the top of his finger like a shiny thimble, the end of which molded itself into the shape of a USB plug.

Satisfied with his new finger, Adam inserted it into a port on the front of the server.

His entire body froze and became unnaturally stiff. For a second, there was nothing but dead space in his eyes, two empty voids of white—zombie eyes. But then they rolled over, and Adam's baby blues were now brighter than ever with a burning red dot for pupils. He violently convulsed, a full body spasm, then became perfectly still again.

In Adam's mind, he saw only fire.

Except it wasn't really his mind anymore, at least not his alone. The folds of his brain were filled with the Lazarus Vaccine's tiny nanobots. These microscopic miracles of technology and biology were latched onto his entire neural network, burrowed into the crevices and folds of his brain, forming themselves into digital storage devices and merging with flesh to create the very first human/computer hybrid brain of a new species, *Homo superiors*.

The digital lines of code made of nothing more than unseen electrons coursed into Adam like adrenaline. There was a nitric surge boiling in his blood, pulsing through his body. He would always remember thinking, *is this what it feels like when a star goes supernova?*

Adam Evans had never believed in God. The entire notion was just utter nonsense, but at that exact moment in time, as the Queen program was ripped away from the far reaches of the World Wide Web, sucked out of all the Internet servers of the world, and pulled through the homemade box and into Adam's brain, he knew it would be as close as he ever came to a spiritual experience. Before his eyes, the fabric of space and time was tearing open, and he was being shown the secret truths of all existence.

For the very first time in Adam Evans' life, he felt powerful. He was physically stronger and even smarter than he'd ever been, but it was more than that. True power was being able to take and create life. Adam could do both of these things now and with incredible ease and efficiency. In many ways, it was like he was God. *Is this man's destiny,* he pondered, *to become gods?*

When the download completed, Adam removed his finger from the port. The bactainium retreated back into the pores of his skin, shrinking away as if his body was sucking it back into itself.

He smiled.

The integration was complete.

Destiny awaited him and the entire human race.

CHAPTER 49

They knew they must have just missed him; the bodies of the dead cops outside Adam's home were still warm. Rayne recognized the men, didn't know them personally, but all cops take the murder of other cops personal.

They proceeded inside with caution, each wielding a gun and one of Douglass Bastion's military-grade, murder knives. They had made a quick stop at the Crooked Lake Marina, where Jason raided Bastion's collection, borrowing the three largest and deadliest blades he could find. He did not go around back to the water where the old man's dead body lay in a pool of blood, eyes open and with a faint smile as if he had just finished laughing.

Adam's home was ghostly silent, all shadows and dust. With his mom away at inpatient care and Adam otherwise distracted, a quiet sense of abandonment had befallen the spacious, two-story ranch. They crept through the house like cat burglars, carefully stepping around and sliding past furniture, sneaking through the darkness.

Once they got downstairs, Dayspring hit a switch against the wall, and the room exploded in light. Certain Adam was long gone and they were alone, they put away their weapons.

Adam's basement/bedroom was in its usual sense of teenage disarray, but his mission control center and laboratory had been completely destroyed, ransacked as if by looters. There were shattered beakers and spilled chemicals, large chunks of glass scattered across the black table. The neglected electron microscope was reduced to a pile of smashed circuit boards and frayed wires. Kirk and Spock's cage had been hurled across the room with such vicious force, it was stuck into the far wall, suspended above the floor, the bodies of the dead mice flopped over and stiff. Albert Einstein's eyes were gouged out, the word *AMATEUR* graffiti-ed across his face with a red Sharpe marker. The left and right monitors on his desk had been shattered, screens smashed into spider webs, but the central one remained untouched, clean and shiny, like it was just out of the packaging.

Jason knelt down next to the desk and touched the homemade server. It, too, had been destroyed—burned— the sterile smell of melted plastic stung his nostrils. Oddly, the fire seemed to have come from within the machine, as if the mechanism had badly overheated, causing an internal fire to rage. "This was it," he said.

Dayspring knelt down as well to examine the object.

"What's this all mean?" Rayne asked as she craned her head around the destroyed room.

"It means we're too late," Dayspring said. There was a crack in his voice that may have been fear. "Adam has fully integrated." He stood up, banging his elbow on the desk; immediately, the dark screen of the central computer monitor lit up and hummed to life.

Filling up the entire monitor were the following words:

YOU LOSE

Dayspring uplifted the desk over and onto itself,

grunting and grinding his teeth as wood splintered and cracked. Rayne and Jason stepped away as if he was a rabid animal gone berserk. He slammed his fists against the wall, his entire body clenched, neck muscles twitching.

"I failed," Dayspring said, and before anyone could offer a platitude, he added, "and I actually helped facilitate the end of humanity."

"What happens now?" Rayne asked.

"I don't know. This universe has become a completely alternate reality from the one I came from. I have no idea what's going to happen." Dayspring hesitated, took a long breath. "All I know for sure is that I failed."

Jason didn't like what he was seeing—the dejection, the self-pity and loathing. It was all too familiar of an attitude he had seen in his father, a frame of mind he swore he'd never share. There were too many nights and early mornings he put his dad to bed, observing the utter look of self-hate on his sad, drunken face.

"Not yet," Jason said. "Adam can't just unleash the Lazarus Vaccine on the world. He'll need time to set it up, create the necessary systems and distribution methods. These things will all take time"

"Time is what he has a lot of," Dayspring protested.

"Yeah, but I know who doesn't," Jason said.

Dayspring perked up; he looked over his shoulder at his younger self. The kid's gaze was fixed toward a spot on the wall near Dayspring where a bulletin board hung. It had once been bursting with random photographs of Adam and his friends, except now, all the pictures had been rakishly torn down; only a few small, cornered chunks remained.

All except for one untouched photograph, still whole and undisturbed.

It was a picture of Adam and his mother, taken five years ago at the White House Science Fair, Adam sporting his first place medal. The dutiful son and proud mother.

Dayspring locked eyes with Jason, nodded his head, an

unspoken but knowing exchange taking place between them. He placed a gentle hand on his younger self's shoulder and whispered, "Good soldier." He turned toward Rayne. "We need to get to Ann Arbor."

"Why there?" Rayne asked.

"The University of Michigan Hospital." Jason said before Dayspring could answer. "That's where his mom is being treated for cancer. He's going to go save his mother, give her the Lazarus Vaccine."

"You're certain of this?"

"I'm starting to think," Dayspring said as he pulled the picture away from the corkboard, "that this may have been his intention all along."

CHAPTER 50

The highway early in the morning is a lonely but peaceful place.

Cars and trucks whiz by in a blur of yellow and red lights. Behind dark windows are nameless strangers who might as well be ghosts. Everyone on the highway is out for themselves, going wherever they are needed, returning from wherever they have been.

Adam Evans had been driving for about an hour, avoiding the main interstates in favor of country highways, roads where tall forests loomed over the shoulders on either side and only opened up for the occasional farm or cow pasture. Adam liked seeing the cows; they amused him. They came right up to the side of the road as far as they could, pressing their wet, black noses against the wire fence and chewing on grass. They were interesting creatures. So dumb and slow and simple.

It was a pleasant drive, the occasional car or truck with its ghost-driver passing by like ships in the night. And as the darkness waned into the dawn, the sky became a light, water-color blue. It was a crisp, cool morning, but the sun was going to be blazing today, bright and raw and powerful, exploding with raw, warm light. Morning was a wonderful time of day, and right now, it felt like Adam was seeing the most beautiful morning he'd ever experienced.

This world, this blue orb drifting in space and time, was a truly remarkable thing. Life flourished here, but it also suffered. There was so much suffering.

So much unnecessary suffering.

He thought about his mother. She was suffering. Death is one mean bastard. If you're lucky, it comes at you fast—*bam!* You're dead. But if you're unlucky, it comes at you slow. It takes your mind first… then your dignity… and finally your body. Dying, however, just represented a flaw in the design of the human genome. Adam Evans could fix that flaw. Humans no longer had to suffer; they no longer had to die. They no longer had to endure the humiliation of a slow death. They just had to evolve.

His thoughts returned to the cows. Stupid lumbering things. They only lived to provide milk, make babies, die, and be eaten. Their sole purpose in their pathetic lives was to serve a higher species.

But that was just the natural order of things. It was how the universe maintained balance. Dominant, more evolved species were at the top, and those below existed merely to sustain the biological hierarchy. Humans—*Homo sapiens*—had a good run. For 200,000 years, they were the most evolved and advanced animals on the planet, but now—or at least very soon—they would be just like the cows. Stupid, fat creatures. A new species was about to emerge—*Homo superiors*—and Adam Evans was the first. He was the alpha. Proto-Lazarus.

The world rolled by, green hills sparkling with dew, the morning becoming brighter and more beautiful with every passing mile.

The cows chewed their cuds and waited for the slaughter.

CHAPTER 51

They drove along the same back highways as Adam Evans. The same scenery skipped by—rolling fields and forests, farms where the same cows that had fascinated Adam were still grazing near the fence lines. The sky was now a soft baby blue and full of calm promises. On any other day, under any other circumstance, it would have been a beautiful drive. It was the type of road trip a young family might take in the fall. But instead, the unlikely trio were hunting down a psychotic computer program that had taken over the mind of Adam Evans and turned him into an immortal, evolutionarily advanced techno-organism dedicated to curing humanity of its most devastating disease—itself.

It wasn't funny at all, yet there was still something completely absurd about it. Rayne and Jason both wanted to throw their heads back and laugh like maniacs, but the reality of the unreality had settled as hard as cold concrete. Despite the absurdity, the stakes were just too high to laugh.

It was a little past 6:00 a.m. when they pulled into a truck stop. They were still an hour outside of Ann Arbor. Rayne and Jason went into the general store as Dayspring filled up the gas tank. They came out wearing new clothes and carrying a tray of coffees and a few grocery bags.

Dayspring hung up the gas nozzle and came around to the other side of the vehicle. Jason handed him a new shirt, pair of sunglasses, and trucker cap. "They had just our style," he said as Dayspring removed his old shirt and tossed it into the bed of the truck.

Rayne was leaning inside the passenger door, sorting through one of the bags. From the corner of her eye, she noticed the shirtless Joseph Dayspring and once again was startled at the sight of his scarred body. She held in a breath, thinking, *man or machine, what kind of thing would do that to a person?*

Jason noticed, too, and took a step away, averting his gaze. Dayspring had pulled on the new shirt and was working the bill of the trucker cap into a nice curve, seemingly oblivious to their reactions.

"Is that what's going to happen to me in the future?" Jason asked.

Dayspring put a hand on the kid's shoulder. "No," he said. "Because we're going to stop it. We are going to stop all of it." It wasn't meant to be a pep talk, but his unabashed confidence was a welcomed contagion.

They climbed back into the cab and drove on. Once they were back on a straight stretch of highway with the sun blazing overhead, the tension and fear seemed to abate, and everyone took a collective sigh. Snacks were passed around, coffees quietly sipped.

"What's that necklace you wear?" Jason asked, looking toward the thin leather strap around Dayspring's neck that disappeared beneath the crew collar of his shirt.

Dayspring pulled it out so it hung over his clothing. "It's an alpha and omega medallion."

"That's a Christian symbol," Rayne said. "In the Book of Revelations Jesus says, 'I am the alpha and omega.' Alpha and omega are the first and last letters of the Greek alphabet. Christ meant that he was the beginning and end of everything, that he was the totality of all things; he was eternity—a reference to there being only one true God." The cab of the truck went silent as both Jason and Dayspring looked at her quizzically. "My mom made me go to catechism," she explained.

Jason was frowning. "We don't believe in God."

"We believe in hope," Dayspring replied. "This was given to me by someone I owe my life to. Someone who gave me hope again."

Jason looked out the window, his eyes swimming through the blue sky.

"That was good thinking," Dayspring said changing the subject. "Directing the police to the old concrete factory. That road flare/suicide vest was also a nice touch. Stupid perhaps, but it may have worked. What exactly were you planning?"

Jason grinned. "I was pretty much making stuff up as I went."

"The Christmas tunnel," Rayne said. "What was that all about?"

Dayspring and Jason exchanged glances. There was an awkward silence as each one figured out how much he wanted to share. Simultaneously, they shrugged, a gesture that meant *why not go all in?*

"When I was sixteen I wanted to surprise my dad on Christmas morning with a good breakfast." Dayspring spoke, but the memory was fresher in Jason's mind and rematerialized with familiar pain. "He had just gotten a new job slinging auto parts for a supplier out of Flint and was starting right after the New Year. He had actually been drinking less, and for the first time in as long as I could remember, I was actually feeling good about the future. So I went out and bought a dozen eggs, bacon, and hash browns. We didn't even have a Christmas tree, and there weren't any presents, but at least we'd have a solid breakfast. Soon, it was going to be a brand new year; my dad would be working, and it felt like things were going to be better."

"It's never that easy with alcoholics," Rayne said, thinking about all the times over the past few years Marcus Orchard had been arrested for drunk and disorderly conduct.

"I woke up Christmas morning to the smoke alarm and came downstairs," Jason said, taking over the story. "There was a thick layer of smoke floating near the ceiling throughout the main floor of the house. Something was burning in the kitchen. The stove was on, and a big pan of black bacon was on fire. The flames had crawled up the wall and spread to the window curtains. I dowsed everything with a fire extinguisher." He paused and huffed out a self-loathing laugh. "Then I went into the living room and found my dad passed out on the couch, holding a plastic spatula. On the floor next to him was a woman I didn't recognize wearing one of *my* tee shirts and no pants. Between them was a puddle of vomit, and I think the woman had peed, too."

Rayne rubbed her face and sighed. Her heart was breaking for the kid next to her. In her line of work, she had encountered many young people whose lives were affected by alcoholic moms and dads, most of them at risk themselves of falling into depression and substance abuse. How had Jason Orchard managed to escape that vicious cycle and keep his shit together?

"My dad had picked up this woman the night before," Dayspring said, resuming the sordid tale. "They must have stumbled in early in the morning and attempted to fry the bacon but passed out and nearly burned the house down. That was my"—he looked at Jason—"*our* Christmas morning. So I ran away. I stole a snowmobile from Douglass Bastion and headed off into the woods where I discovered the abandoned Atlas Concrete factory. I—*we*—spent the entire morning exploring it. It felt good, like I was some kind of adventurer trekking through the ruins of an abandoned temple. It seemed dangerous and was just a nice distraction. As I went room through room, I wasn't Jason Orchard anymore." He snorted, a brief half-smile appearing on his face. "I was Indiana Jones."

Jason remembered that feeling well—*just like Indiana Jones.*

The lines on the highway slipped by in fast, blurry dashes, and no one spoke. Jason finally cut the silence. "Dad lost that job before he even started. He got drunk the night before orientation and never showed up."

The talking then ceased altogether. Rayne sat between the two men, an older and younger version of the same person. She didn't know what to say; but, of course, there was nothing she could say. Like so many children in the world, Jason Orchard got a shitty deal when it came to the family and situation he was born into—something the average kid in the Crooked Lake community couldn't even imagine. Rayne had grown up with a lot of kids who were spoiled, little brats in need of a swift kick in the ass, kids who went to private schools and whose families owned vacation homes along the lake's shore. As for herself, she was a regular townie whose mom was a secretary at the First National Bank. She grew up relatively modest, but being modest in Crooked Lake was kicked a few notches down the socioeconomic ladder by the wealthy summer people who owned most of the lakefront property. Modest became poor, poor became abject poverty. She, along with most of Crooked Lake, couldn't possibly understand what kids like Jason Orchard had to endure.

"I need to know how this all happens," Jason said. "How does Adam do this? How does all of this unfold?"

Dayspring sighed. Every sci-fi movie in the world warned about the dangers involved in time travel, the paradoxes, the threat of revealing too much to someone about his future. But this didn't seem to matter anymore. This timeline had already changed; it had become an alternate reality.

"After high school," Dayspring began, "you join the

army."

"I join the army? Doesn't really seem like my style. Why'd I do it?"

Dayspring took a long sip of coffee. "You have your heart broken and want to run away. The army gives you that opportunity." Jason wanted to ask more questions about the broken heart, but Dayspring continued without hesitation. "Turns out you're very good at being a soldier. It comes natural, and you excel at it. You do a few tours in Afghanistan, Iraq, Yemen, earn some medals. You go to Ranger school and are eventually recruited by Delta Force, then spend the next few years completing several black-ops, off-the-books missions into Russia, China, and North Korea."

"That's pretty awesome," Jason said.

Dayspring frowned but quickly lightened up. "Yeah, it was pretty awesome. Now, while you're advancing your military career, Adam Evans is making his own advancements in medicine and cybernetics that will change the world. After his mother passes from cancer, he becomes more driven than he had ever been in his life. He starts a think tank conglomerate called Quintessential Networks, and it becomes the primary investor in the Lazarus Vaccine and the Queen program, which Adam completes in 2028. By this time, you are 27-years-old and recovering from a few gunshot wounds acquired from a mission in Central America. He wanted us to be the first recipient, but we decline. Something about a bunch of microscopic robots swimming around in my body didn't feel right, didn't feel natural." Dayspring almost shivered as he spoke. "This causes a massive rift between us, and our friendship would never be the same. Adam felt betrayed—but it was more than that. He hated me for my refusal. It bothered him on a very deep level that I didn't want the vaccine. He took it personal."

"What happened next?"

"The vaccine's popularity spread like a contagion, a

very welcomed contagion. *Never get sick or hurt again, be healthy forever;* the allure was undeniable. But what we didn't realize was the Queen program was a Trojan horse. Adam's goal was never just to help sick people; he wanted to cure the entire world, to cure it of *everything*." Dayspring paused. "But his *cure* was *control*. As recipients of the vaccine grew, so did the Queen's control. On August 29th, 2033, the Queen's secret programing was launched, and anyone who had been vaccinated with Lazarus was forcefully integrated into a collective consciousness. In Adam's opinion, it was too risky for our species to exist as free-thinking individuals, and survival depended on the amalgamation of every single person into this collective consciousness, to live under hive mentality."

Jason thought about that night at the bluffs when Adam had ominously said, *"Someday, we will be able to cure everything."*

"I don't get it," Rayne said. "Why a hive?"

"Insect species live in colonies. They operate with a hive mentality—individual pieces capable of autonomous action but still operating under a shared consciousness. And they thrive under this system because it promotes incredible progress. A true hive operates with perfect efficiency because waste and greed don't exist. The queen knows exactly how many eggs to lay, exactly how many workers, warriors, gatherers, builders, and breeders are necessary for progress of the colony to continue."

"So you're saying Lazarus turns everyone into a bunch of mindless bugs?" Jason said, revolted by his own metaphor.

"Not exactly mindless. Individuals retain a certain amount of autonomy from the Queen, but the primary directive is to always serve the hive."

"How does the Queen program control people?" Rayne asked.

"Quintessential Networks constructed a facility in the Rocky Mountains nicknamed the Hive. From here, the

Queen program is broadcasted into orbit where a network of satellites redirects it onto every square inch of the entire planet so it can connect with the Lazarus Vaccine and the neural brain networks of its hosts."

"So the Queen, or the Queen program, is some sort of artificial intelligence?"

"Yes, not only is it the operating system for the Lazarus Vaccine's nanobots, it is the collective brain of everyone who has fully integrated. In fact, we believe Adam somehow implanted strands of his mother's consciousness as the base of the program, but no one is quite sure how he did it. We do know he cryogenically froze her head after she died. When you fully integrate, you are merging your own consciousness with the Queen."

Rayne was staring at the tattoo on Dayspring's arm. "What happened to all the humans who refused the Lazarus Vaccine?"

"We were targeted for elimination. It was a genocide. Lazarus foot soldiers were sent across the world in massive waves. These were killing squads with one objective: hunt down and kill all humans who refused full integration with Lazarus and the Queen program."

Rayne shuttered. "You mentioned you belonged to a group called The Vitruvian Order. What exactly is that?"

"A world-wide band of resistance fighters. We're organized and well-supplied, but our numbers are limited. Our mission is to destroy Lazarus by taking out the Queen. Me coming back here to this time was supposed to be part of that mission. It was our Hail Mary pass because in the future, Lazarus is winning the war. Human beings are nearly extinct."

"Why did the Queen kill our father?" Jason asked, and instantly, the cab of the truck became silent, the only noise from a vibrating dashboard and a poor seal in the passenger window where the air whistled in.

Dayspring took a moment to contemplate his answer. "The queen is trying to eliminate threats. Believe it or not,

Marcus Orchard becomes quite the urban legend in the early resistance movement against the Queen and the Lazarus Vaccine."

"What do you mean?"

"The old man actually sobered up. And he did it for us, to be a symbol for his son. He was terminally sick with kidney failure. The Lazarus Vaccine would have saved him and even cured his addiction to alcohol, but he refused to hand over his free will. He could kick booze all by himself. And as far as his kidneys, well, that was just all the more reason to sober up, so he could actually enjoy whatever little time he had left. He lived long enough to confirm his sobriety, then passed away in his sleep. Marcus Orchard died with his humanity and free will intact. The silly, little story is like a parable in the Vitruvian Order and resistance movement: *the reformed man who proves the power of human will.* Like I said, kind of an urban legend. It inspires people."

"No shit," Jason said with a foggy smile on his face. He wished he could have met that man.

The questions continued, and Dayspring answered all of them like a patient professor, Rayne and Jason chewing on every response. It was like a multi-course meal at a crowded, understaffed restaurant—short burst of consumption, followed by long bouts of waiting, or, in this case, thinking. Dayspring would answer their questions, and Rayne and Jason would need time to digest what they had heard.

"Saving his mother's life," Rayne began, "why did you say that you think this has been Adam's goal the entire time?"

"I think saving her was always his goal, but in my timeline he was too late, so he committed his life to saving the lives of others. This was his motivation to create Lazarus, but for all the good he *thought* it did, it wouldn't bring his mother back to life. For this, he needed to be even more ambitious. I was in a particularly vicious camp with a group of brilliant scientist the Queen was keeping alive in order obtain information. Rumor was these scientists were part of the Vitruvian Order and had been developing a weapon that could end this war and destroy Lazarus forever. We were liberated one night by the Order and taken to a secret base where I discovered the rumors were true. These scientists *had* created a weapon that would end Lazarus—time travel. They were going to send a soldier back in time to assassinate Adam Evans before he ever creates the Lazarus Vaccine or the Queen program. I volunteered for the mission." Dayspring hesitated, shook his head as if he were disappointed in himself.

"And it was all a ruse, wasn't it?" Jason said. "Those scientists weren't human. You guys were allowed to escape the camp so they could send you back in time in order to transport a small amount of the vaccine hidden in your body."

"It would seem that way," Dayspring said. "Like Adam explained at the bluffs, the Queen could send itself back in time because it's just a computer code, but its hardware, the bactainium, is made of metal and can't cross the electromagnetic time field by itself. She must have secretly planted a tiny amount of Lazarus inside of my body, just enough to stow away and survive the journey, pre-programmed to transfer itself into the body of Adam Evans, then multiply until large enough to download the entire Queen program. I thought I was on a mission to destroy Lazarus, but really this has all been manipulated by Adam so he could save his mother's life."

"So what is Adam in the future? Jason asked. "Is he like some sort of king or tyrant or something?"

"I don't know—no one really knows. No one has seen him in years. He lives in the center of the Hive, the most secured location on the planet. The Order has been trying to infiltrate it for a long time without success."

Jason caught a glimpse of Dayspring's eyes reflected in the rearview mirror. "Why does it turn your eyes red? It looked like Adam had red pupils."

"It's kind of like a cat or any nocturnal creature. Lazarus transforms your entire optic system in order to see perfectly in any conditions. The red glow is a side effect and really only shows up when it's dark or in certain lights."

Once again, the cab of the truck went silent except for the loud hum of the old engine radiating through the dashboard. Outside, the world was growing brighter and bluer.

"Why does cutting off the head of someone with Lazarus work?" Rayne asked. "Couldn't the vaccine just fix that, too?"

"No. Even though the Lazarus nanobots receive directives from the Queen program, they still need a living brain to serve as an auxiliary command center in order to identify issues within the body and send the tiny robots wherever they need to go for repairs. This is why well-placed head shots will slow him down, but he can only be killed by severing the brainstem. If this is done, the nanobots will have no such command center. The brain is like a computer, but it's not wireless; without the brain stem, it won't know what needs to be fixed. Lazarus will be a vaccine without a body to vaccinate."

"What happens to Lazarus then, to the nanobots, if the head is cut off?"

"And therein lies a problem."

"What do you mean?"

"Even if we kill Adam," Dayspring explained, "the Lazarus inside of him will still be functional. It will continue trying to fulfill its directive by any means necessary."

"How do we destroy it?"

Dayspring sipped his coffee. "It's very difficult. Complete submersion into hydrochloric acid, an electric surge 10x more powerful than a lightning strike, or burn it in temperatures exceeding 1,500 degrees Fahrenheit."

"If we manage to do all this, kill Adam, destroy

Lazarus," Jason wasn't looking at either one of them, he was staring out the window at the passing countryside, watching old telephone poles tick by, "then we save the future?"

"In this timeline, in this universe, yes," Dayspring said.

They drove on in silence. The miles slipped beneath them as the sun rounded over the top of the eastern horizon, a ball of yellow-orange fire in a virgin, blue sky.

They would be in Ann Arbor soon.

CHAPTER 52

They were wanted criminals; there were news reports all over local radio stations. Jason Orchard, Nicole Rayne, and Joseph Dayspring were considered armed and dangerous and could be anywhere within the vicinity of Crooked Lake, Michigan, but law enforcement believed they might be headed south. It was odd. Adam was certain to anticipate their move tracking him to Ann Arbor; why wasn't he making police aware of this? Was he so sure of his success that it didn't matter? Or perhaps he was drawing them into a trap himself? Dayspring believed it was likely the latter.

Jason Orchard had entered the hospital lobby alone, having left Dayspring and Rayne in the parking garage. He wore the trucker cap low over his face and avoided eye contact with everyone he passed. It was just a quick recon mission—locate Maryanne Evans. This would lead them to Adam.

He headed straight for the reception and information desk, pausing once as he caught sight of his own reflection in a floor-to-ceiling mirror. He halted mid-step, mumbling an apology as a few doctors and pedestrians bumped passed him. He looked different now, and even though the recent, fantastic events had only unfolded over a half-day span, he somehow looked older, more grizzled. The man he would grow up to be was staring back at him. *Joseph Dayspring* was staring back at him, showing through his pores, in his posture, deep in his dark, gray eyes. The only thing missing was the long, horrible scar down one side of his face.

He continued toward the desk, keeping a watchful eye on anyone who might peg his image. There was a waiting area where a couple of sad looking people sat without talking as a silent episode of *Star Trek* played on the TV. Captain Kirk and Spock appeared to be locked in a heated argument. Jason thought about the dead mice, Kirk and Spock, and their cage, which Adam had hurled across the basement with such viciousness it had stuck into the drywall.

"Good morning," Jason said to the receptionist, putting on the warmest smile he could muster. "I'm here to visit Maryanne Evans. Would you please tell me what room she's in?"

The receptionist returned the pleasantry and started typing on a keyboard. Jason turned around and waited, his gaze sweeping across the large lobby. People were shuffling all about, in and out of doors, down hallways. There was a depressing fog hanging over everyone and everything as it usually does in hospitals, contrasted by the bright lights and tall windows that revealed a peaceful, morning sky.

"She's in Room D-413," the receptionist said.

"Thank you." Jason started to walk away with a quick step.

"Hey, wait a minute," she called after him.

He halted, blood rushing through his body, instincts screaming at him to run.

"It actually says here that she's going to be moved soon. They're going to be transferring her to another floor. Room C-204. It's the---" the receptionist cut herself off, then with some reluctance, "hospice floor."

Jason felt a hollow pit in his chest.

She offered him a half-smile. "The moving process may take a while. You won't be able to visit as they prep her. It's best if you wait until the move is completed and official visiting hours resume after breakfast."

Jason relaxed, shoulders dipping. "Thank you for the information," he said and walked away.

As he proceeded back through the lobby, he found himself thinking about Mike Shake. He could hear the beer slinger's voice in his head: *"Life's all about control... Everything hinges on your ability to maintain control... When you lose control, that's when you fuck up."* Adam Evans had always maintained a firm control of his life. He was a genius. He had goals. He had a concrete plan to achieve these goals. He was the most logical and pragmatic person Jason had ever met to the point of annoyance. *"Reason and logic should rule over all,"* Adam had been fond of saying whenever he heard a story about a political leader making a poor decision without consenting to related scientific and quantifiable research.

Jason kept walking. On the muted TV screen, Captain Kirk stood on the bridge of the *USS Enterprise* banging his fist down on a computer console while Science Officer and First Mate Spock looked on disapprovingly. Adam had often made comparisons between he and Jason to Kirk and Spock. Best friends with a yin and yang contrast, one fueled by emotion, one by logic. One embraces gut instinct, the other calculates and computes—two opposite extremes of the same spectrum.

Everything hinges on your ability to maintain control.

Jason froze. He thought back to the condition of Adam's basement-man cave. It had been destroyed, ravaged, torn apart by a madman. The mouse cage, the laboratory, the photos of his friends. Everything smashed, ripped, and ruined.

It was not the work of a man in control.

Dayspring had explained that when a person fully integrates with Lazarus and the Queen program, they become part of a collective consciousness but still maintain a small amount of autonomous control. Jason's mind floated around the ruined basement again. This was all about Adam trying to save his mother's life—an emotional drive, an emotional desire.

Adam Evans was clearly losing control of whatever emotions he still retained after downloading the Queen program and fully integrating. Mike Shake had said that everything in life hinges on a person's ability to maintain control, and when you lose control, you make mistakes—or *"fuck up,"* as Big Mike had put it more colorfully. If Adam can lose control, then he can make mistakes.

Jason stared wide-eyed at the tile floor, thinking. An idea was slowly forming in his head. He looked up and saw two thick-necked orderlies in white scrubs, one pushing an empty hospital bed, the other following with a bag of medical waste.

He picked up his pace as he left the lobby, proceeding all the way out to the parking garage where Dayspring and Rayne waited in the cab of the truck. Rayne was holding the alpha and omega medallion in her palm, the leather strap still looped around Dayspring's neck, pulling their faces close together. It looked like she was explaining something to him.

When they saw Jason approaching, they got out of the cab. "Did you locate Adam's mom?" Dayspring asked.

"Yes," Jason said and without hesitation added, "but listen, I think I have an idea…"

CHAPTER 53

Human beings are frail and weak. They die easily.

That's just a fact.

They are stupid, too. Underdeveloped, from an evolutionary standpoint—and this is why they are so stupid. They are just biologically and evolutionarily incapable of possessing any real intelligence and imagination. Stupid lumps of fleshy vanity.

And there is nothing sadder and more pathetic than a slow-dying human being. They rot away like old cabbage in the sun. The lucky ones keep their minds and dignity; the unlucky ones shit in a bag and require sponge baths.

Adam's mother, the respected child psychologist, Dr. Maryanne Evans, was one of the unlucky ones.

An inoperable cancer had slowly been taking over her cognitive and motor functions. The wires in her brain were being destroyed by the cancer, pushed aside and pinched by the growing tumor, preventing a proper neural signal from reaching its destination. Now, in the late stages and near the end, she was almost entirely brain dead. Machines breathed for her, fed her, handled her waste. Her body was alive. But that was all. It was just a living bag of meat that breathed and bled, shit and pissed.

Her hospital room was depressing; most hospital rooms are, even at the very best facilities. They can hang up cheap artwork with pretty little sailboats and sunsets and paint the walls every calming shade of pastel, but it's still a fucking hospital. Dr. Evans' room was large and spacious. The equipment that kept her alive had all been assembled to one side of the bed. There were several towers of stacked monitors with blinking numbers and digital graphs showing all sorts of data about the biological happenings within her body—heart rate, breathing, blood pressure. Tubes and wires were inserted into every port, looping around the stainless steel stands like vines, coiled up like snakes, some of them leading directly into her—up her nose, down her throat, connected to her IV and catheter. These were Dr. Evans' power cords and she was plugged in.

A dark shadow suddenly fell across her bed in the shape of a young man with thick shoulders. The black silhouette remained still for a long time as the monitors blinked and beeped. Dr. Evan's chest rose and fell under a thin, white sheet. Her body had dissolved. The once vibrant and healthy tennis club champ with the sexiest legs in the University of Michigan's Psychology Department was gone. She looked like a dried out, caved-in sandcastle of herself. Her flesh drooped and sagged like plastic bags half filled with water, the jointed contours of her brittle skeleton horribly defined.

Maryanne opened her glossy eyes. She did not recognize the young man who stood before her. For all she knew it might have been God. *Are you God?* she asked the stranger, not realizing she no longer possessed the physical ability to speak and was only hearing her voice in her head.

God stared down at her.

I didn't think you were real, Maryanne confessed. *I counselled too many children over the years who had been raped by their fathers for me to believe you were real, watching over and protecting your creations.*

God just stared at her but eventually said, "I'm here to help you."

You should have helped those children.

"No one will ever get hurt or sick again. Starting with you."

Do you promise?

"I promise."

The shadow seemed to shrink as if it were being absorbed into the center of Maryanne's tiny frame, and then God was standing directly at her bedside. He had a hot, heavy presence and seemed to fill up the capacious room. He leaned down, his face inches from hers. For a fraction of a second, she thought she recognized him. He looked familiar, but her brain was incapable of processing from where or when; she just knew she had seen God's face before.

God's hand reached out and stroked the side of her face.

"I love you," God said and stood up.

Adam Evans had changed into a clean pair of clothes and wore a knit skullcap, concealing his Lazarus repaired gunshot wound. He was six inches taller than he had been yesterday and now sported a broad set of solid-looking shoulders. All over his body, his muscles were hard and curved, packed tightly beneath his skin. Lazarus had been hard at work inside of him, constructing this new frame, turning him into a living machine from the inside out.

He held up his right index finger. The microscopic nanobots appeared like silver blood. They rose toward the tip of his finger, flowing over themselves like mercury, slowly forming into a hypodermic syringe.

"This is for you, mom," Adam said and touched the tip of his needle/finger to her throat.

Suddenly, the door crashed open; Adam spun around to face two linebacker-looking orderlies in white scrubs pushing in a large crate of fresh linens and laundry. The nanobots retreated back into his finger.

"We're sorry sir, didn't realize the patient had any visitors. Are you with the family?" But the orderly didn't give Adam any time to answer. "The patient is being moved downstairs. It's actually a much nicer room."

"What room number?" Adam asked.

The orderly hesitated for a moment; the other one jumped in. "C-204. It's directly downstairs. The hospice floor."

The hospice floor. *The I-surrender floor. The death floor.* They were taking his mother to the place they expected her to die. Adam gritted his teeth and contemplated murdering both men.

"It'll take some time to prep her for moving. If you're hungry, the cafeteria is open."

It's a trap! the voice in his head screamed. Once again, he had the impression the voice was not just his; it was a voice he was now sharing. Adam was no longer an *I*; he was a *we*.

It was clearly a trap. Adam's super-intelligent computer brain had completed a full analysis of the situation and all its variables. Jason and Dayspring were obviously behind this. They were going to lure his mother away and use her against him. The orderlies had no idea what they were getting into, no doubt persuaded into the game by some capital interest (*humans and their insatiable quest for money—pathetic*).

Adam was still considering slashing their throats wide open or tearing out their intestines, but he knew the orderlies would lead him to Dayspring and Jason, threats that must be eliminated. He smiled and said, "Okay, I guess I'll go get something to eat." He nodded to the men and left.

Stupid humans, he thought as the door shut behind him.

After a little while, the two orderlies came out of the room carefully aiming Dr. Evans' bed through the wide doorway, an entire train of towers and machines following closely behind, painstakingly balanced by thick yet graceful hands. They headed directly for the service elevator at the end of the hall.

Adam watched from around the corner of the nurse's station on the opposite end of the central atrium. They got onto the elevator and waited like criminals for the doors to close. The orderlies stood like marines at ease, and Adam became certain one of them had to be named Biff. They both looked like they could be Biffs, so he thought his odds were good.

The elevator headed up. Adam watched the green numbers climb until they reached the twentieth and top floor.

Stupid humans, he thought again.

They think they're so clever.

CHAPTER 54

Adam tracked the orderlies through a short maze of halls and into a wing of the hospital designated entirely for long-term patient recovery. There were no procedures going on up here, just healing, and although that process can be painful, the floor had a very different vibe than the treatment and operation centers. It was calm up here, quiet, a warm and dignified atmosphere of positive energy.

The orderlies pushed Dr. Evans through another double swing set of doors and into a long hallway. Adam watched from behind a tall, skinny window set into each door. It didn't look like the other hospital hallways. This was more office-like, with flat gray business carpet and mahogany wainscoting along the walls. The orderlies took his mother into a room at the end of the hall.

Adam followed, thinking about the gratification he would receive from gutting those two meatheads.

He entered the room. It was a large lecture hall. There were rows of padded chairs with foldaway writing surfaces descending toward a stage area, where an impressively ornate lectern stood. The orderlies were disappearing at a full sprint through another door on the opposite wall but had left his mother near the lectern with all her machines quietly humming next to her. No worries, he could easily track them down later. They had pulled a white sheet over her head as if she had already been declared dead.

Killing those two fuckers would bring Adam great joy.

He hesitated just inside the door, then shouted to the large, empty room, "I know this is some sort of stupid trap. I think it's unfortunate that you would use my mother and involve those two oblivious men. I'm going to have to kill them now, and it's your fault."

There was no answer.

Adam craned his neck around the room, seeing perfectly in the semi-darkness.

"It was very impressive that you escaped police custody and evaded capture. I was going to come back and kill you, anyway, so this is actually more convenient. The only reason I allowed this to happen is because I decided it would be the most practical way to track *you* down." Adam took a few slow and deliberate steps farther into the room. "I'm not afraid of you because you can't hurt me." He tapped the side of his head with the metallic, plugged-up bullet hole. There was still no response. He continued into the room, heading down the slope toward the stage.

"I really wish you hadn't involved my mother in any of this. You humans don't seem to possess any decency." He began to walk more aggressively, gaining speed with every word and step. "Go ahead and try to attack me." His voice was rising. "See what happens if you do!" There was a metallic shriek, the sound of a sword being drawn, and ten shiny, silver claws popped out from Adam's fingertips. "I WILL RIP YOUR FUCKING GUTS OUT!" he hollered from deep in his throat, a terrible gutter sound laced with an electric edge.

He hesitated.

Something was wrong.

His super-advanced brain began to rapidly re-compute every factor and analyze the probability of every single possible result for what was currently happening. He came around and stood at his mother's bedside. Her frail body was still.

Adam shook his head, gravely disappointed in himself.

He had already figured out what happened but yanked the sheet off the bed anyway, ripping it away like a magician revealing a magic trick.

There was a full-form resuscitation doll on the bed staring back at him with a lifeless expression. A note was pinned to its chest.

> *Dear Adam,*
>
> *We have your mom. Meet us in the subbasement.*
>
> *-Jason and Joseph*
>
> *P.S. See, we're a lot more creative than you give us credit for.*

Tricked by humans.

It was fucking humiliating.

They had fooled him. This was a fact, and Adam could not ignore it. However, unlike a human, Adam was in full control of his emotions. He was not going to let his shame and embarrassment turn into uncontrollable anger. That's what a human would do. No, Adam was better than that now. He was just going to find Jason, future-Jason, and that cop bitch and kill them all very slowly and painfully simply because that is what they deserved. This was logical, not emotional. So what if he would enjoy doing it?

Adam smiled.

Then drove his claws directly into the doll's abdomen.

Then he did it again.

And again.

And again and again and again and again until the doll was nothing but eviscerated rubber.

CHAPTER 55

The University of Michigan subbasement can only be accessed through a single service elevator in the northeast corner of the building and an adjacent set of emergency stairs. The central elevators and staircases only go as deep as the basement, where the morgue is appropriately buried along with the entire pathology department. On the opposite end of the floor is the service elevator. It is a massive machine, the size of a two-car garage with high ceilings, constructed large enough to move any industrial equipment that makes up the guts and bowels of the hospital.

Enter the subbasement.

Here there be dragons.

Hospital subbasements are truly subterranean, especially older hospitals. There are intestinal passageways that wind through mazes of pipes and ductwork. Thick layers of black dust coat every surface, except in places where steam is blowing (and steam is always blowing somewhere in a hospital subbasement).

The University of Michigan Hospital's subbasement could swallow an uninitiated explorer for an entire day of confused turning around and backtracking. It is a labyrinth of dead-ends and complete circles, with narrow walkways between pipes that spit bursts of steam. The lights are deep orange, almost red, making the concrete walls and floor look like the surface of Mars. At intermittent places throughout the twisting corridors, a much wider space will open where some monstrous set of industrial machines has been erected. One of these is the boiler room, with a half-dozen car-sized, metal drums connected to each other by rusty, metal pipes. There is also the furnace room, the generator room, the water treatment and circulation room, and finally, the medical waste incinerator room—the end of the cave where the dragon waits.

The incinerator is a double combustion chamber capable of reaching temperatures that can destroy the most vicious biological waste and infectious disease. The primary chamber is about the size of a backyard shed, with a large, medieval castle-like door made of solid steel. Next to this, and connected by a metal tube the girth of a beer barrel, is the smaller secondary chamber. After the initial burn, the contents are transferred on a conveyor from the primary to the secondary chamber where they undergo a much longer and hotter slow burn, a burn that reduces matter to its most primal chemical state and kills all living organisms.

Inside of this incinerator, shoved deep within the primary chamber, the tiny and frail form of a woman rests very still beneath a thin, white sheet.

CHAPTER 56

A lot had happened in the span of a single day.

Jason Orchard gripped a Glock .9mm in his left hand, the gun he'd taken from Chief Edgar, and one of Douglass Bastion's collectible knives in the his right. He held onto them as steady as his nerves would allow—which wasn't very steady at all. His entire body was trembling. It began in his gut, where a billion butterflies fluttered their wings, creating a pint-sized tornado, then spread into his bones and bore out to his extremities, massive, nonstop waves of anxious, electric surges.

He was going to kill his best friend.

So what if it made him shake and want to throw up?

Yeah, *a lot* had happened over the course of yesterday and last night. What began as an innocent date with Haley *(was it a date?)* had ended here, in the University of Michigan Hospital's subbasement, with Jason trying to find the stomach to kill a person he once considered a brother.

The subbasement was dimly lit by small orange lights covered by wire cages that threw crisscrossed shadows across the walls and floor. Jason was hiding behind a series of vertical pipes and shiny ductwork. From where he was, he had a clear view of the service elevator and staircase and the single path that led into the vast network of corridors throughout the subterranean lair.

He took a deep breath and tried to calm his shaking nerves.

The staircase door suddenly burst open, flying wide on its hinges and slamming against the adjacent wall with a steel-versus-concrete crunch. Adam Evans stepped sharply through the door in a brisk, all-business gait. He paid no mind to anything around him; there was no pause to take in or consider his surroundings. With a fixed gaze directly ahead, eyes glaring like two little spheres of red-hot fire, he quickly proceeded through the narrow passageway and into the next corridor.

Jason cautiously slipped from behind his hiding place and followed, taking careful, silent steps.

The blow struck him on the side of the temple; it was sudden and swift and sent a jolt of intense and confusing pain into his skull, filling his head with fog. He could feel a warm trickle of blood run down the side of his face. For a fraction of a second, he almost shut his eyes because the urge to lie down and sleep was overwhelming, but then there was another painful blow, this one square in the gut, a burst that forced out all his air. He tried so suck in a breath, but in a flash of movement clouded by pain, he was thrown backward, his head slamming against the hard cement floor as a new wave of fog dimmed his vision. The gun and knife were wrenched out of his hands by a powerful force and clattered on the ground.

Adam Evans was on top of him, straddling his torso. Two very cold hands circled around his neck and began to squeeze.

"DO YOU THINK I'M STUPID?!" Adam roared like a dragon, a deep, beastly sound filled with electric static, as if his voice was being filtered through a synthesizer. "I will kill all of you!"

Jason tried to respond, but all that came out was a series of grunts and gurgles. He could feel the pressure of

Adam's cold hands tightening around his throat, sealing together his windpipe. He slapped and punched at Adam's forearms, but it felt like hitting two massive lead pipes.

Adam's lower arms, from elbows to fingers, were completely covered by the bactainium of the Lazarus Vaccine. It was like having metallic skin, cold and hard to the touch, but flexible as it stretched over Adam's well-defined forearms. He was also considerably larger all-around. Adam Evans had always been a skinny, lanky kid of average height. Not anymore. He was taller now, a lot taller, at least 6'5 or 6'6, his arms, legs, shoulders, and neck bulging with packs of solid muscle.

"Magnificent, isn't it?" Adam said relinquishing his grip and sitting up. His voice was at once comical—"Look how much I've grown"—then became deadly serious again. "Lazarus has brought my body to state of complete perfection." The metallic covering of his forearms and hands began to move—to retract—exposing his pink, human skin. The bactainium retreated away from the tips of his fingers and continued up his wrists and arms, gathering upon itself, increasing its mass, and forming into a long, skinny snake on both arms. The silver serpents slithered toward his shoulders and up the sides of his neck, then entered the dark holes of each ear and disappeared.

"You were my brother," Jason said.

"No," Adam said matter-of-factly. "I was your pet. Your dog, your little puppy. I was a fucking mascot. But I am so much better than you now. I mean, I always was. Sure, you were the handsome one, the funny one, the one who girls always noticed first, and I was just the smart one. The *really* smart one. But you have no idea what I've become now. I am immortal. I can just as easily kill as I can repair life." He hesitated, looked up toward a dirty light bulb hanging in its cage from the ceiling. "I am God."

With Adam momentarily distracted by his melodramatic decree, Jason's right hand found the gun where it had landed. He fingers wrapped reassuringly around the handle. "I don't believe in God," he said and fired four rounds at point blank range into Adam's chest.

Adam's shirt tore open and his flesh exploded in tiny bursts of blood and tissue. But through the holes in the shirt, Jason could already see the Lazarus Vaccine at work, little metallic worms wriggling into place, repairing the ruined flesh and shattered bone. Within seconds, the four bullets were pushed out of Adam's chest, falling onto Jason one at a time, the wounds sealed into irregular metal circles.

"Do you understand what I have become?" Adam asked. "I am the proto-version of a new species, a more evolved human being, an amalgamation of flesh and technology: I am *Homo superiors*. Don't you see? This is our specie's next evolutionary step; this is what we were always destined to become."

"Well," Jason said, "you're talking to the one teenager in the world who doesn't own a smartphone. You know how I feel about tech."

"Yes," Adam agreed. "I do." He held up his hand and extended the tip of his index finger, bactainium came oozing out of his pores, reforming itself into a scalpel. "That's why you don't deserve the Lazarus Vaccine. Because you are foolish and unworthy. But I have something else for you." Adam's other hand gripped Jason's neck like a workbench vice, securing his head perfectly still. He slowly brought the scalpel/finger toward Jason's face, who could see his own terrified eyes reflected in the shiny metal.

"Here is something you do deserve," Adam said as he plunged the razor sharp blade into the top of Jason's scalp and began drawing a line down the left side of his face. Blood poured out of the wound as skin and tissue separated. Adam continued tracing the line right over his eye and all the way down to the bottom of his jaw. Blood was flooding over Jason's face, filling his eye sockets and nostrils, running into his open mouth and muffling his scream into a wet, gurgled choke.

Jason felt the warm heat of his own blood as it flowed across his face. He could only see out of one eye now, but that was all he needed. He fired three more shots into Adam's throat, chest and stomach but with the same result. Adam's body flinched, and the bactainium quickly went to work, pushing out the bullets, repairing the damage.

"The only thing you accomplish when trying to hurt me," Adam said with a psychotic-snake leer, "is making me more powerful."

Jason spit out a generous amount of blood. "Then allow me to be of even more assistance." He fired once more; this time, the bullet caught Adam in the cheekbone, ripping through the middle of his face and out the top of his head. Immediately, his body slumped over and was lifeless.

Jason shoved him off, rolled over, began struggling to his feet, frantically searching for the knife. He glanced back with one eye, afraid to open the other. One side of Adam's face had been obliterated and looked like raw hamburger, his eyeball completely gone, just a hollow black socket. But the Lazarus Vaccine was already fixing the damage, building an artificial eye and replacing the splintered bones and ragged flesh of his face.

There wasn't much time—*remove the head.*

Jason was desperately trying to locate the knife, but the blood kept distorting his vision. He wiped it away with the back of his hand and made a quick visual recognizance of everything in front of him as the flow of blood once more clouded his sight.

Jesus, I'm going to bleed to death, Jason thought, and it may have made him feel better to know he was already in a hospital, but at the moment, this fact eluded him.

He wiped away the blood again and finally saw it, tucked away in a dark, dusty corner—*Bastion's knife!* Finding the weapon immediately energized him, but as he lunged for it, a large and powerful arm caught him and wrapped around his neck, gripping him in a painful headlock.

The Lazarus Vaccine had done its job on Adam's face; it was now nearly half-robotic, with a lidless glowing red eyeball. His arms were once again covered in the mercury-like bactainium.

"I have to admit," Adam said, "it stung getting fooled by you earlier. I really thought those orderlies were luring my mother away while they were really luring *me* away to give you time to set up your little trap here in the subbasement. That's right, I know your exact plan now. Once I realized my error, I recomputed the situation. The three of you are using my mom as bait, and you plan on destroying me in the incinerator." He paused. "It's actually pretty clever. For humans."

"So why don't you just shut the fuck up and kill me already?" Jason managed to choke out.

"Oh, no, no, no, no, no, a quick death is too good for you. You involved my mother, so your death must be more of a slow punishment. Didn't you once mention that burning to death would be the worst way to die?" Adam hesitated, then smiled gleefully and said, "Let's go find that incinerator."

Jason uselessly thrashed against his iron hold.

"Don't struggle so much," Adam said. "It's annoying." He raised his free arm into the air and brought it down hard against the side of Jason's leg.

Jason tried to scream as his bone snapped, but once again, it was suppressed into a bubbly choke. He would have collapsed onto the floor, but Adam held him up by his neck. The pain was blinding, and he felt himself falling into unconsciousness.

"C'mon," Adam said, his cold, electric voice pulling Jason out of the dreamy quicksand. He began walking— dragging—Jason forward, into the labyrinth of the subbasement. "Let's go find future-you and that the cop bitch so I can burn you all to death together like the cute, little family you've become."

They proceeded farther down the passageway, Jason's injured leg dragging across the ground like a rolled up piece of carpet. It was nearly impossible to put weight on it, but Adam was basically carrying him, his muscular, machine arms locked so tightly around his neck it was as if he planned to pop his head off like a dandelion (which maybe he did).

Jason was biting his teeth down hard, trying to swallow back the pain exploding from above his knee and running down his face in wet, hot waves. He grunted, snorted, and continued his fruitless struggles.

"SHHHHH!" Adam suddenly snapped at him and froze.

"What?" Jason said spitting out another mouthful of blood.

"I want to hear this." Adam's human eye focused on nothing and the robotic one seemed to glow brighter.

Jason couldn't hear anything except the thumping in his own head. But he knew the Lazarus Vaccine inside of Adam had made his sense of hearing super-human and that he was listening to a conversation taking place far down the dusty corridors of the subbasement.

"I'll be damned," Adam said in his electronically synthesized voice. "Seems like some humans still have a little common decency."

CHAPTER 57

Nicole Rayne had been raised Catholic but rarely went to church anymore. She walked away from her faith a long time ago, not for any particular reason or with animosity in her heart; she just didn't have a place for the church in her life as she wished to live it. She considered herself progressive, and the church just seemed to become more antiquated every year. However, her faith still existed, buried deep within her, so deep that she didn't know she still had it. She claimed to only wear the cross around her neck to placate her mother, but it was really a subconscious lifeline to a drowning spirituality.

Was there a God? Rayne often pondered. Probably not, but this didn't mean there wasn't still righteousness and morality in the universe. Even though she no longer accepted the notion of a loving God or eternal life in heaven, it didn't change her desire to be a good person, live a good life, and help others in need. These ideas to her were *human*, not divine. You could be a person of high moral fortitude and *not* believe in God. In fact, she found this a lot easier.

Until now.

She couldn't quite bring herself to pray, but she was

focusing a lot of mental energy on the situation at hand.

"This is bullshit," Rayne said. She and Dayspring were in the small control room for the incinerator. It was like a jaw bridge operation booth—a small station just big enough for two or three people. There was a board of controls with numerous buttons, levers, gauges, and a large LED screen built into the face of the panel. A panoramic window overlooked the combustion chambers, which reminded Rayne of steel shipping containers. The entrance door to the primary chamber was wide open; from where they were in the control room, they could not see into it, but in her head, it was easy for Rayne to imagine Maryanne Evans lying inert. Dying.

"I've already explained everything to you," Dayspring said with a tight jaw. There was tension in both their voices.

"This is wrong," Rayne sighed out.

"This woman is going to die," Dayspring said as he examined the controls. "Her death is inevitable."

"So we're just going to burn her to death with her son." Rayne's voice rose as she spoke, but it really wasn't a question; it was a statement she was making to herself. An attempt to justify murdering an innocent woman to stop a larger threat. It made her feel like she was back in Philosophy 200 during her undergrad at Western Michigan University. She recalled a certain discussion point: *if you could save five lives but had to kill one person, would you?* (If you could save billions of lives by killing one child prodigy who is responsible for a future genocide and one woman who is going to die of cancer anyway, would you?)

Nicole Rayne had aced that particular philosophy class because on paper, philosophy is easy (kind of) because there are no repercussions, but in real-life application, it's considerably more difficult.

"I think I got this all figured out," Dayspring said as his fingers ran lightly over the buttons and levers of the operation panel.

"I don't think I can do this," Rayne said shaking her head. "I can't take an innocent life."

"Look," Dayspring snapped. "We've gone over this. I once loved this woman; she was like a mother to me, but she's dead now." He hesitated. "Or she will be soon."

Rayne was not surprised by his coldness. Here was a man who had come back in time to murder a kid—his former best friend no less. True, he had altruistic motivations, but murder is murder. She was reminded of another discussion point from PHIL-200: *if you could go back in time and kill Hitler as a baby, would you?* She hated that question because in it, Hitler was a baby. If he was a young man, say in his early twenties, it would be easier to kill him, and you could still prevent the Holocaust. Making him a baby made the question philosophically more challenging. Which was probably the point.

"It doesn't feel right."

"Nicole," Dayspring said in a conciliatory tone. "This is war. I have been a soldier in a war waging between *Homo sapiens* and *Homo superiors* for a decade. We are at war. During times of war, unfortunately, there are civilian casualties and collateral damage."

"I never asked to be part of this war."

Dayspring was silenced. She was right. There was nothing he could say back.

They left the control room and stood in front of the open chamber door. The figure inside was perfectly still. Neither one mentioned it, but it was entirely possible Maryanne Evans was already dead.

Rayne was shaking her head. "No," she whispered. "I can't do this. This woman is innocent."

"This woman is dead." They weren't shouting, but their voices were full of quiet, explosive energy.

"How can you be so callous?"

"This is war."

"This is bullshit." Rayne drew her gun, one swift movement, and the weapon was half raised. "No. I won't let you kill her."

"What are you doing?" Dayspring asked. "Are you going to shoot me? Are you going to kill me?"

"I'm going to stop you from killing this woman."

Dayspring took a light step toward her; Rayne moved away, closer to the chamber door, raising the gun, pointing it at Dayspring's chest.

"We don't have time for this," he said. He took another step closer.

"Don't," Rayne said pulling back the hammer.

There was a flash of movement. Dayspring's hand shot out and grabbed the barrel; Rayne lunged toward him, driving her shoulder into his chest. He easily caught the impact, twisted her around, wrestled for the gun.

A shot fired, then another.

Rayne's body crumpled onto the concrete floor in an awkward heap.

Dayspring was left standing over her, holding the gun, shaking his head. "Goddamn it," he whispered.

CHAPTER 58

Jason heard the shots. Two concussive blasts that came from farther down the black gullet corridors leading toward the incineration room.

Adam had listened to the entire episode—the argument, the struggle, the gunshots. The cop bitch was dead. Good, one less problem to worry about. At least she died trying to do the right thing. He smiled, half his face made out of bactainium and reconstructed by the Lazarus Vaccine. Where his once-human eye had been was now a pivoting silver ball with an artificial iris that expanded and contracted to reveal a burning red light. Even though this side of his face no longer had any human features, Jason could still see madness within it.

Adam dragged him through the skinny halls, where vertical pipes coughed bouts of steam as they passed. Sweat mixed with blood and ran in streaks down Jason's face like war paint, but the pain had subsided, cloaked by the fresh adrenalin that coursed through his veins.

"You know," Adam said as they proceeded. "I wanted you to be the first recipient of the Lazarus Vaccine. Did future-you tell you that? You had been injured during one of your army missions, couple of gunshot wounds, but nothing fatal." Jason couldn't respond, Adam's metal-covered forearm was pressing hard against his throat, barely allowing him room to breathe. "You declined. And truth be told, it really pissed me off. You were my best friend, or at least you had been up until you joined the army. Did Joseph Dayspring tell you why you joined the army?"

Jason felt the cold metal of Adam's arm loosen just a bit. "Said I had my heart broken," he choked out.

"Yes, you did have your heart broken," Adam said with a slight cackle in his voice. "You enlisted in the United States Army because you lost someone you loved."

Jason was slammed against the wall and once more, nearly lost consciousness, his vision fading in-and-out like a dimmer switch. From his delirium, he thought he heard several little bells all chiming at once, a symphony of off-key music going tink-tink-tink. *Chains*, he suddenly realized. Adam was encircling his wrists with chains, his powerful hands able to snap the thick metal links, then bend them back into a secure position so they bound Jason's wrists together.

"And this is the best part," Adam said as he finished with the makeshift shackles. "Guess who it was?"

Jason glared at him, took a breath as if to speak, then promptly spit a wad of blood and snot directly into Adam's human eye.

With vicious speed, Adam lifted Jason and spiked him onto the ground as if he were a football. He kicked him once, then grabbed his collar and stood him back up again, pinning him against the wall.

"IT WAS HALEY!" Adam's voice went off like a cannon, more synthesized than ever. "HALEY!" he bellowed again, the name exploding through the skinny corridor, ricocheting off the walls. "You see, in my original timeline you and Haley betray me, too; isn't that funny?"

Through the dull pain and a foggy mind, Jason realized Adam was now speaking as if he were from the same timeline as Dayspring. He supposed he was, now that he had fully integrated with Lazarus and the Queen program.

"After high school, Haley and I officially started dating while at the same time, you and Emma completely fizzled out. It didn't last long, as my ambitions wouldn't allow me time to participate in such meaningless human relationships. Haley would turn to you for comfort from my coldness, and eventually, that would turn into a warmth for each other. She'd leave me for you, and you two would fall in love. How fucking cute is that? Like a fucking rom-com movie about two great friends who finally realize they love each other. Except it *wasn't* funny." Adam grabbed Jason around the back of his neck and began steering him through the subbasement again as if he was a bad dog being led to the scene of its own turd. "When I found out Haley was cheating on me with my best friend, I was pissed, and I wanted revenge. Not because I still harbored any feelings for her, but simply because you had taken something that didn't belong to you. And truth be told, you two were very happy together. I could see it in your eyes." Adam's voice had calmed slightly, as if the memory caused him to reflect on the situation with a sense of nostalgic peace. "You guys really were in love."

They stopped walking. "So you know what I did?" Adam said. He bent down and whispered directly into Jason's ear, "I killed her."

Jason violently flinched and struggled against the restraints and Adam's metal grip.

"I killed her," Adam repeated. "Made it look like an accident, too. It was easy. Getting away with murder is very easy when you're a genius. I planned on killing you, too, but after the funeral, you apologized to me for everything that had happened, then ran away to join the army. The rest is history. Or not yet it isn't. I didn't see you again until you were recovering from those war wounds at a veteran's hospital in Washington DC, waiting to have a purple heart pinned on your chest. By this time, I had invented the Lazarus Vaccine and wanted you to be the first recipient. I figured why not let bygones be bygones. You were man enough to apologize for stealing my girlfriend; that was admirable. This could be a new beginning for an old friendship." Adam had been smiling, a genuine look of contentment on his cybernetic face, but his eyes quickly narrowed, smile aborted. "But then you declined. You rejected the Lazarus Vaccine. You rejected me."

Adam froze, his mind lost in a memory from a different timeline. "You know something, you were the first, as well, my friend. You were the first person to reject Lazarus, the first rebel. You were the first member of your precious Vitruvian Order."

Jason had almost no strength left. The loss of blood, the knocks on the head, he just wanted to lay down on the cold concrete floor and die already. Or perhaps, just go to sleep for a really, really long time.

"But none of this matters anymore," Adam said. "Anyone stupid enough to refuse Lazarus deserves to die; their brains are clearly incapable of evolving and…"

But Adam's voice slowly drifted away until there was nothing left but soft static and darkness, the sweet nothingness of unconsciousness…

"Stay with me, old sport," Adam said slapping Jason's face a few times, pulling him out of the dreamy abyss. "I want you conscious when I burn you to death."

Jason tried to compose himself; he focused all his mental energies into assessing the situation, convincing himself that if he could find this focus, he'd have a better chance of staying alive. His head was swirling around into a steady whirlpool of mixed senses, but if his mind could find the will to focus, his body could find the will to live.

They had entered the incineration room, the incinerator itself taking up an entire wall. The door to chamber one remained open, the shape of a small woman beneath a white sheet lying motionless inside. Rayne's body was slumped across the ground near the adjacent wall. Adam glanced at it once and smiled. *Bitch deserved to die.*

From the control room, Joseph Dayspring stood with his hands on the operation panel, staring through the large window that overlooked the incinerator.

"Ah," Adam said. "Let the endgame begin."

CHAPTER 59

Adam looked at his mom's frail frame within the incinerator, then at Dayspring in the control room, who gripped a lever. The arrogant human was daring him to make a move.

"You were a monster long before Lazarus," Dayspring calmly said.

Adam laughed. "Says the man who just murdered an innocent woman." He kicked Rayne's body as he took a small step forward, Jason still agonizing in his grasp.

"You were always a psychopath," Dayspring continued. "You were just smart enough to be able to hide it."

And at that exact moment, Jason remembered what Dayspring had said out at the bluffs: *"There's a lot you guys don't understand."*

This is exactly what he had meant. Adam Evans had always had a secret monster inside of him, locked up and on a leash like a rabid dog. Jason knew that his best friend had a dangerous edge, but for years he had ignored the warning signs—his frustrations, his arrogance, his anger. Adam Evans considered himself superior to everyone around him. It was a God-complex held at bay only by his loving and caring mother, but with her sickness and impending death, the monster had been breaking out of its cage. Haley had wondered if just by knowing about the future would change things. She thought that Adam would never create the Lazarus Vaccine and the Queen program now. But that didn't matter. One way or another, Adam Evans would still become a monster.

"I was always a genius," Adam said.

"Yes, you were," Dayspring conceded. "But you were *also* a monster. You were so bright that your mind convinced you everyone else was inferior, and our lack of intelligence made us weak. You were *superior*, but you could save us all. You found a way to help normal people evolve. And when someone refused, you felt personally offended." Dayspring stopped, huffed out a breath of disgust. "You're just a brat, Adam. A spoiled, little brat."

Adam gritted his teeth, a small tremble emanating from deep within his bones.

"You're just a spoiled brat," Dayspring said again, "who gets all pissy when he doesn't get his way."

Jason could feel the anger rising off Adam in hot waves. He was like a churning storm, boiling in the sky, about to crack open and unleash Old Testament-style wrath.

Keep going, Jason thought. *Lead him to the edge; push him over.*

"Fucking spoiled brat," Dayspring said with a smug look on his face. "Little momma's boy, too."

Adam glared at Dayspring, his human eye with all the fixings of that junkyard dog that had always been inside of him—a hungry, teeth lashing, spittle flying, pissed-off beast that'll tear out your jugular and lap up your blood. His Lazarus eye was a bottomless pit of fire.

"What's a matter?" Dayspring asked, laying on the haughtiness. "Is the little momma's boy gonna cry?"

But Adam Evans was nowhere near crying.

He's about to crack, Jason thought. *Keep going, Joseph, keep going.*

"Do you miss your mom, Adam? I know she's not dead... yet." Dayspring paused, narrowed his eyes. He gripped the lever on the operation panel tighter. "But she will be very soon."

In Adam's genius, technologically advanced mind, a bomb had gone off, a nuclear holocaust of madness that engulfed every last neural signal and brain synapse he possessed. His ability to think and compute, to calculate and rationalize, was temporarily overshadowed by his desire to rip his old friend apart with his bare hands. All systems of his mind were shut down except the voracious need to extract a terrible revenge that was long overdue.

Adam screamed, a psychotic, synthesized, robotic war cry that echoed through space and time, then tossed Jason aside like a wet bag of laundry and charged the control room. His fist smashed through the front glass windows and seized Dayspring by the collar.

But Dayspring had pulled the lever and the incinerator roared to life. From within chamber one, there was a soft orange glow as the great machine heated up.

Adam yanked Dayspring out of the room and flung him sideways, his body smashing against the opposite wall like a rag doll. He reached his hand through the shattered window and hit the emergency stop button. There was a soft hiss as the machine powered down, the glow fading. Adam turned around and fixed his eyes on Joseph Dayspring.

The pathetic human had gotten up on his hands and knees and drawn a gun.

Adam raced across the room at inhuman speeds, taking a few bullets in the chest, pushing them out, and repairing himself instantly. He knocked Dayspring down, then grabbed him by his throat and violently sat him up against the wall. "This ends now," he said. Out of his closed-fist knuckles, a metal spike emerged; it was about the width of a roll of nickels and a foot long. He pulled his arm back and rammed the spike directly into Dayspring's chest.

Joseph Dayspring saw his life flash before his eyes.

It was odd; he had been near death on multiple occasions, but this had never happened before—*maybe that means I'm actually going to die this time*, he pondered. He had always thought of this as a cliché—to have your life flash before your eyes in the moments right before death. But now it was really happening. It almost made him laugh.

He saw his childhood. There were memories of his mother he didn't know he still had; she was young, pretty, happy. He saw his dad fall into the out-of-control spiral that is alcoholism and slowly drown in his own loneliness. He saw Haley as the tomboy she had been when they were innocent children, then as the beautiful woman she would become. He saw his best friend, Adam Evans, as the shy new kid in town who needed a friend as desperately as Dayspring needed a family. He saw Douglas Bastion scowling and yelling at him to get back to work. He saw Mike Shake toweling off a glass behind the counter of the Shack and nodding to him like a proud parent. His saw his time in the military, the missions he'd completed, the war wounds he'd suffered. He saw the rise of Lazarus, his mind reconstructing the various battles of an endless war against the Queen and her army of foot soldiers as they patrolled the planet in their global death wave. He saw the hopelessness of the human race as they neared the edge of extinction.

But with all of this, he also saw the goodness and hope humanity had to offer. He saw all those who had rejected Lazarus, who chose to retain their humanity even at the expense of painful death. They had fought together, died together, given their lives together—not for some ultimately meaningless and fraudulent ideology concerning nationhood or faith, but for the sake of humanity itself. They were the Vitruvian Order, the soldiers of mankind's last army, dedicated to protecting and guarding life itself.

Joseph Dayspring—Jason Orchard—had seen a lot of good and bad in his time. But in his ruined heart, he knew the good in man was stronger. He knew humanity, if the hand is forced, is capable of doing incredible things.

Jason watched from the opposite side of the room, locking eyes with Joseph Dayspring, the man he was supposed to become, the future he was supposed to have. Things were different now, he knew, an alternate reality than the one he had been destined.

Adam drove the metal spike deeper into Dayspring's chest. There was a sickening thud-sound; Dayspring could both hear and feel it in his flesh as the spike collided with the concrete wall behind him. His entire body seized as a white-hot pain exploded in his heart. His life stopped flashing before his eyes and his vision turned gray.

Adam stood up.

The spike retracted and Dayspring's body tumbled over.

Adam took a deep breath. He didn't even need to breathe anymore; it was simply force-of-habit. His body could repair itself faster than the damage caused by lack of oxygen.

He felt complete. His mission could be accomplished now. He had come back in time to save his mother's life and conquer a new world, a new timeline and universe.

It was time to get started.

He looked at Jason, who lay helpless on the floor with a broken leg and shackled by chains. "I'm going to get my mother out of there, and together, we're going to watch you burn to death," he said as he walked back across the room to the incinerator. As he passed Rayne's body, he gave it another solid kick.

Crouching low, he ducked through the door and knelt beside his mother. It wasn't until this exact moment that he realized something was wrong. He didn't even have to tear the sheet away; his mind had been recalculating and re-computing the situation the entire time. It had (and

Adam acknowledged this with regret) been distracted. The emotions of the situation had been overwhelming—getting tricked by humans, taunted with insults. All the madness and anger he'd been feeling had slowed down his processing speed.

But now the secondary analysis that had been taking place in his super-computer brain was complete.

He had been tricked.

Again.

He ripped the sheet away. Another life-size resuscitation doll lay on the floor of the chamber.

Adam had just enough time to look out and see Nicole Rayne standing up with her hands on the steel door—not dead, not shot, not bleeding. After neutralizing Jason, he had assumed she was dead and therefore posed no threat.

Fucking tricked by humans.

"You lose," Rayne said as she slammed the door. Adam heard the steel-on-steel sound of the lock-bar crashing into place.

Moments later the chamber began to glow orange. Adam pounded at the door with Lazarus covered fists as dancing red flames quickly began to creep up from beneath him. Within seconds, he was consumed by fire. He thrashed and punched in all directions, but there was no longer an up or down, a left or right; he was in a void now, an endless inferno of fire and madness. He screamed, not because he felt pain, he could turn-off those nerve impulses, but because he knew he had lost. He had been fooled.

By human beings.

Twice in a day.

His final thoughts were perhaps this species deserves a little more credit.

CHAPTER 60

Rayne came running out of the control room. She went to Jason first, but he waved her away. Check on Dayspring, check on Dayspring.

Jason got to his knees, his wrists still bound together by rusty chains. The blood from the gash on his face seemed to have stopped. With more time to think, he was relieved to discover he could still see out of the wounded eye, and although the cut was long and deep, it appeared to have missed any major parts of his optic system and facial muscles.

His leg hurt like hell, but despite the painful throbbing, he managed to get to his feet, sliding his way up the cinder block wall, leaning into it for support. He limped his way toward Rayne and Dayspring and collapsed onto his hip.

Rayne was crouched next to Dayspring, holding his hand, the smallest traces of tears gathering in her eyes.

Dayspring raised his other hand; his arm was weak, and it wavered under its own weight. Jason clasped it firmly and held on.

"We did it," Dayspring said. His voice was choppy, full of wet hiccups.

"Save your energy," Jason said quietly.

"No good," Dayspring replied. "It's my time."

"No." Jason protested, but his weak voice gave away the brutal realization it knew.

"But not your time," Dayspring said. His breathing was growing more strenuous, each word spoken with considerable difficulty. He looked back and forth between Rayne and Jason. "You both would have made excellent soldiers in the Vitruvian Order."

Dayspring released Jason's hand, which now held the alpha and omega medallion, the leather strap dripping between his knuckles. The dull metal charm slowly rotated as it hung, suspended in the still air.

"It's a symbol of eternity," Dayspring said. He coughed, choked, coughed again. For a brief moment, he could feel the desert air on his face from the night he said goodbye to Sister Christina and the Estes family. The old nun's words echoed in his head as he repeated them for his younger self, *"There is a forever, and hope will always be part of it."*

The young man nodded.

The man with the scar closed his eyes and said, "I'm proud of you."

At once, there was only darkness as Joseph Dayspring took his very last breath of life, but then there was light—blazing white and yellow light. Then he saw nothing except blue sky and sunshine as he splashed through the shimmering surface of Crooked Lake, the refreshing water wrapping around his body, suspending him in a void of peaceful, calm comfort. He continued sinking deeper and deeper into the water, into a light that was warm and blue and exactly where he wanted to be.

Home.

CHAPTER 61

Seven months later...

Even though it was mostly known as a summer hot spot, the Shack was open all year long. In the middle of January, you could be enjoying one of Mike Shake's world famous Bloody Marys (everything at the Shack was world famous) while sitting by the large windows overlooking the frozen, white canvas of Crooked Lake. Sometimes Big Mike would fire up the wood burning stove in the corner; it added a pleasant ambiance and quaintness, like a mossy English dive right out of a storybook.

It was April, and business was slowly picking up as spring rolled toward a new summer. A group of teenage girls occupied one of the large window booths. There were baskets of empty food scattered across their table with greasy red and white checkered liners and crumbled napkins. The talking was fast and chaotic, every hand holding a phone, jewelry sparkling and glistening in the dim light, clinking and tinkling as hands snapped exaggerated gestures. It reminded Haley of the way the Lazarus Vaccine shimmered, the way its shape always seemed to be moving and flowing, reflecting every available proton of light in tiny, brilliant flares. She shivered at the memory.

Haley looked at all the other girls. She didn't really know any of them except Emma, and she barely knew her anymore because she had changed so much since *the incident*—a phrase which had become their euphemism for an experience impossible to articulate.

Moving fast but discreet, Haley stood up as if to excuse herself to the restroom. She walked down a short hall toward the bathrooms but planned on secretly slipping out the emergency exit and sneaking home.

Then she saw his picture.

It was still hanging on the Shack Wall of Fame.

Jason Orchard, a hopeful thumbs up toward the world, face covered with orange PFI sauce and vanilla milkshake, smiling like an idiot, and his three idiot friends smiling alongside him.

"He asked me to give you this," a voice said from behind her. And there was no mistaking that voice. It was a rocky voice, crunchy and hard, and yet there was joy, love, and faith in that gentle, giant baritone. She turned around.

Mike Shake, in his signature apron and with a grimy towel slung over his shoulder, held an envelope in his hands. "He said to read it by the lake." He extended the letter forward. "You know, for effect."

Haley took the envelope. "Thank you, Mr. Shake."

Big Mike smiled. "It's good to see you and your friends in here having fun again."

Haley could only muster a half smile in return. She stepped forward and hugged the big, barrel-like man, feeling almost swallowed by his massive arms. "Thank you for helping him," she said.

The hug ended.

Just as she planned, Haley slid out the emergency exit, the letter gripped tightly in her hands.

CHAPTER 62

The woman and the boy could have been mother and son. This was certainly what most people mistook them for. There was a clear affection between them, a warmth that can only exist between people who truly care for each other.

This had made it easy to blend in when they were on the run. It was the perfect cover, and they slid into these roles effortlessly. Jason Orchard had enjoyed every second of it, too—not surprised at all about how easy it was to do.

They were at a diner in Kentucky, an L-shaped mom-and-pop affair with a counter full of hunched over, wide-back truckers.

A waitress named Sami snapped her bubble gum, repeating their order. "Okay, so that'll be one tall stack, eggs over medium with hash browns and bacon, and a Kentucky omelet?"

"That's right," Jason said and removed a baseball cap. For the first time, the waitress got a good look at him, and she was visibly startled—his scar, of course. The jagged white and pink line that carved a trail over the top of his left eye, from scalp to jaw. He was lucky he could still see out of the eye; it had lost all color and was now a creamy white, but it still functioned.

"I'm sorry, I…" But the waitress trailed off, averting her eyes from Jason's face and looking toward the wall. "I'm having an intense moment of déjà vu." She walked away, slipping her notepad into a pouch and shaking the weirdness out of her head.

Jason was smiling. "She's nice," he said casually.

Rayne nodded, sipped her coffee. "Sure."

They had both become quite skilled at having meaningless conversations to fill up dead air space, usually about the weather. They were remarkably similar to a real family.

"Weather looks nasty today," Jason said.

"Yeah, bad storms later."

Outside, the parking lot was calm; a lonely highway stretched off in opposite directions, one toward a downtown area, one toward an empty horizon full of dust and sunlight. But overhead, the clouds were coming down; they were the color of gun smoke and churning.

"Javier wired more money," Rayne said.

Jason nodded.

"He said the window was short, but it's finally time to cross the border. Are you sure you don't want to come?"

"Yeah," Jason said. There was sorrow in his voice, but not regret or doubt.

"Jason Orchard can't exist anymore."

"He won't."

"Well," Rayne said, her voice filling with affection, "you know how to reach us if you ever need help."

Sami appeared with her cheerful attitude and a fresh pour of coffee. "Sir, I hope you don't mind my asking, but are you a war veteran? If you are, your first meal is free and coffee always is."

"No," Jason said but offered no other explanation.

The waitress gave them both an awkward smile as she shook out a dazed expression, perhaps having another déjà vu moment.

* * *

They ate their breakfast, then said goodbye outside. It hadn't started to rain yet, but the air was moist and smelled like ozone. Thunder rolled from high above them.

"Storm's coming," Jason said.

They hugged. It lasted for a long time, most hugs-goodbye tend to linger, and this was no exception. Each of them took their time, breathing in the moment, carving a special place for it in their memories.

"You do what you gotta do, what you *need* to do," Rayne said into his ear, patting him on the back. "Just be careful."

"I know," Jason said. "Thank you."

The hug surged, then released.

"Take care of yourself," Rayne said.

"I will. You too."

They nodded to each other, smiled, and walked away.

Rayne got into Mike Shake's truck and drove toward the empty horizon.

Jason started walking toward the downtown area, kicking around the dry Kentucky dirt on the side of the road as the clouds grew darker and sank lower. He reached below the crew collar of his shirt and pulled out the alpha and omega medallion, feeling the dull metal between his fingertips as he walked.

The air was even colder at the bluffs. Haley had bundled up accordingly, and even though the hike through the woods was difficult, she had still enjoyed it. It reminded her of all the times she had played out here with Jason as kids, kicking over stones while storming through pretend worlds. Here on the beach, however, the wind cut even deeper, biting through her many layers of protection.

But her discomfort made no difference. Jason wanted the letter read by the lake, and Haley figured the beach and the bluffs were the perfect—the only—place to honor that.

The lake was steel-gray and full of choppy waves like thousands of little shark fins. She sat down on an old log around the faint traces of an ancient campfire and removed her gloves, bearing the cold without notice. She pulled the envelope from her pocket and tore open the seal. There were two folded papers inside.

She was visibly shaken by the first. It was a charcoal sketch of two people holding hands and casually strolling along the beach. The drawing featured mostly moon and sky, sand and lake. The two figures were nondescript scribbles in human shape, walking away from the viewer with their backs to the world, headed toward a private horizon. But there was no mistaking who they were. She was looking at an image of herself and Jason. Haley remembered that night well—it was the night of *the incident*.

The second paper was a letter. She began reading:

Haley,

You're at the bluffs, aren't you? I knew you'd come here. Where else would you go?

A lot of strange things happened to us, and I'm sure you still have a lot of questions. I really wish I could be there to answer them, but you know why I can't.

There is something I need to say to you, so I'm just going to be blunt: I love you.

I think I've always loved you but was too distracted to realize it. I'm sorry about that. To think of all the time I spent ignoring these feelings makes me sad. Whatever was supposed to happen between us, whatever destiny awaited us, has been altered into something new, something

different, and I hope, something better.
We have new destinies now, and perhaps one
day they will draw us back together.
Until that time comes...
It was always you.

-Love Jason

Haley clutched the letter and sketch against her chest, frozen tears welling in her eyes. She loved him, too. Why she had been fighting that emotion for such a long time, she would never know, but it felt good to finally acknowledge it. And to embrace it.

She took a deep breath of the cool, crisp air and smiled.

So tell me, Jason Orchard, where does your new destiny take you?

The glass door opened with a small *whoosh* as the temperature and air pressure outside continued to fall. It felt like lifting the seal of a Tupperware container. Jason pulled the door shut against the increasing wind.

"Holy moly, looks like we're about to get one hell of a storm," a man said as he stood up from behind a large desk. He had a southern accent and a trim mustache, a good ol' Kentucky boy who loves his mom.

Jason stood in a foyer, the small office space before him much quieter than the noisy sidewalk outside, where the wind screamed as it came down from angry, black clouds.

The man behind the desk was wearing desert fatigues, and the stripes on his shoulder indicated he was a sergeant. Behind him, an enormous American flag hung on the wall. Next to it was a classic Uncle Sam recruitment poster. "I WANT YOU," it said.

"What brings you in today, son?" the man asked.

"I'd like to join the army," Jason said.

"Good for you, son, please come on in. I'm Sergeant First Class Damon Reno. What's your name?"

Jason hesitated, took a breath.

"Dayspring. My name is Joseph Dayspring."

EPILOGUE

The very near future…

The man speaking sounded like he was exhausted. "Your recovery was remarkable," he said. "It defies all conventional understanding of the disease and the human body." His voice rose and fell on waves of stress and uncertainty, like a tiny rowboat tossed around in a storm. "You were nearly gone." He wore a white coat with an ID tag pinned to the breast: Dr. Charles Reynolds. "I myself noted your vitals the night before your miraculous recovery. If I was a betting man, I would have gambled on your death several times over." He took a breath. "No offense."

"None taken."

Dr. Reynolds had quit smoking twenty years ago but found his hands unconsciously fumbling for an invisible pack of cigarettes, shaking one out, tapping it down.

"I'm not a religious man, and I don't like the word *miracle,*" Reynolds said with conviction. "*Luck* is a very real thing, however. I've often viewed luck as the indifferent universe's version of God's grace or blessing, and there's nothing wrong with accepting it and just calling it what it is: blind, random luck. As a doctor and scientist, however, I need to know how this happened." He leaned back in his chair. They were sitting in his office, a large space modestly decorated in a neoclassical style, a wall of framed diplomas behind him. Reynolds craved a smoke and decided the only way he'd believe in miracles is if a cigarette and lighter magically appeared in his hands right then...

No such luck.

"Perhaps," the woman sitting across from him said, "it's just as you say. Luck. Pure luck."

Reynolds smiled. It was a tired smile. He pinched the space between his eyes and sighed. "I'm certainly glad you've fully recovered, but it frustrates me that I don't know why or how, that I don't have the answers."

Maryanne Evans tossed her hair aside. It had grown back thick and strong and shined with healthy life. Her skin was once again golden-tan, pulled tightly over defined, springy muscles, and her eyes were bright blue and seemed almost preternaturally alert (she would have dominated the tennis courts at her old country club if she still cared about such trivial things). She thought the man who sat opposite her was commendable. He had a thirst for knowledge and answers, a trait that is rare in the average human being.

"You're a true scientist, Dr. Reynolds. I respect that." She stood up and walked to a window. The sky, which had been clear all morning, had become muddy gray. "And that's one of the reasons I've asked for this meeting."

Reynolds was intrigued; indeed, Dr. Evans was a very intriguing woman—smart, sexy, with something indescribably wicked about her.

"You're one of the best cerebrovascular doctors in the world—that's why I came to you for treatment. You've pioneered several new and radical developments in how we understand the human brain and how we treat brain related diseases." She paused and smiled at him. "There is no counting how many lives you have saved throughout your career."

"I enjoy flattery, Dr. Evans, but why exactly are you here?"

Maryanne Evans sat down again and crossed her legs, short skirt riding up, revealing perfectly sculpted and smooth thighs. Reynolds had to pull his eyes away.

"Dr. Reynolds," she said, hesitating for a moment and taking a slow breath. "I'm starting a think tank of wealthy investors. Our mission will be purely scientific—to make medical and technological advancements for the human race. We will fund legislative lobbying groups and finance all sorts of research projects across the world. All in the name of scientific and medical advancement. We will take our species to a new age of enlightenment and health."

"That's a lovely idea," Reynolds said. "Very altruistic."

"Altruism is the heart of science," Maryanne replied. "As a scientist and a healer, I knew you'd feel that way. And that's really why I'm here. We want you on board, we want your pedigree representing us and working for us."

Reynolds narrowed his eyes but did not say anything.

"I'm offering you a job, doctor. I hope you take it and join us."

Charles Reynolds was no longer thinking about cigarettes. These types of think tank conglomerates could be a scientist's dream. With the right investors, the funding could be unlimited, the opportunities endless. Was he ready to give up practicing medicine and devote himself entirely to research?

"What's your group called?" he asked.

Maryanne Evans uncrossed, re-crossed her beautiful, tan legs, the faintest traces of seduction in the corners of her smile. "Quintessential Networks," she said.

Outside, a fierce rain began pelting the windowpane like rapid gunfire. Lightning flashed, filling the room with a quick wave of blinding whiteness.

It must have had a brief effect on Reynolds' vision because for a short moment, it seemed as if Maryanne Evans had red pupils.

ACKNOWLEDGEMENTS

As every single writer in the world will concede, a lot of people lend their support to the creation of a book. While a story may emerge within the writer's imagination, he or she was surely inspired by something or someone. There is always a person or event that stirs the writer's creative sensitivities.

For me, it is my family and closest friends and the experiences we share.

And so, I owe a debt of deep gratitude to my wife and children, my brothers, mom, step-dad, my late father and grandfather, and a very special old bird who I believe is the reason people in my family read so much, Grandma Gould—93 and still crushing the competition at the weekly bridge game.

I'd also like to thank my former colleague and friend, Julie Urban, for being my original reader—her criticism and feedback was vital, but the encouragement was appreciated the most; Joe Niezgoda, who was kind enough to read a few early chapters and tell me it didn't suck; Katie Bretzlaff, who designed and created the cover and helped me understand some of the business ends of the artistic commercial world; and Alexéi Frausto Esparza and

ACKNOWLEDGEMENTS

Maribel Franco, two very kind and awesome students at my school, who helped translate the Spanish dialogue.

And finally, there are all my teachers. Pre-K through grad school, I will never write a book without thanking my teachers.

ABOUT THE AUTHOR

D. L. Gould teaches high school English and Creative Writing. He received his Bachelor of Arts at Western Michigan University and Master of Arts at Governors State University. He loves good fiction and thinks science is awesome. This is his debut novel.

Twitter: @DLGould

Facebook: www.facebook.com/lazarusvaccine

Made in the USA
Middletown, DE
23 May 2019